7/14/2017

Jenny,

purple neglect
near the arbor
area. —
Wonderful
marriage!

Brenda

Cracked

CRACKED

A NOVEL BY

Brianna S. Clark

RED ECLIPSE PRESS
2016

ISBN-13: 978-1530502639
ISBN-10: 1530502632

Red Eclipse Press
An Imprint of Chester River Press
Chestertown, Maryland

ONE

February 1997, Yakima Washington

The women were all white and middle class except for Lulu, whose coppery presence brightened the room. Her skin color was not the only thing that separated her from the other women; Lulu physically angled her chair in such a way that she was slightly removed from the group. She did not even pretend to be paying attention, but stared listlessly out the windows of the overheated room, her weary brown eyes searching the black, snowcapped mountains as if they held a secret. Her thin arms folded so she appeared to be hugging herself. Her knobby knee bones were visible beneath the fabric of her cashmere slacks. A champagne-colored silk blouse hung on her withered frame. Her fingers played idly with a strand of pinkish pearls that cascaded to her breastbone. Occasionally, she touched the matching earrings dangling from her ears, which cast a pinkish glow on her thin, hollowed face. A brown alligator loafer balanced on her sockless foot, and threatened to fall off with each impatient swing of her foot. She was assessing the territory, analyzing and judging the women emotionally giving voice to their drug experiences. Every now and then, a titillating aspect of each speaker's story caught her attention, after which Lulu would return to the smug, safe space of her head.

She was startled when the mediator, whose name she had not heard when she had been introduced, addressed her. "Well, Counselor?" The woman, Anne, repeated her question. "What brings you here?"

Angered at being caught off-guard, Lulu was embarrassed and felt attacked. She wanted to respond, *none of your business, bitch!* Instead, she said, "not the court." Her ferocity startled the group. The women looked around nervously, fearing the verbal violence might turn physical.

The mediator's face flushed with momentary fright. Lulu was intimidating because of her education, anger, and flamboyant clothing, so out-of-place in a state-sponsored rehabilitation facility. Anne was in her early thirties, part Native American, and had grown up in the tiny mountain community of Yakima, Washington. Nine years prior, she had obtained her degree in counseling with a specialty in drug and alcohol counseling. After reading Lulu's medical profile, Anne knew that she had to break Lulu's façade, and had prepared to do so in a very formal way.

"So you are a lawyer, yes?" She was not expecting Lulu to respond, so, instead, addressed the other women in the group. "We have a new member in our group. Her name is Lilly. Today, we are on the First Step. This facility is run on a Twelve-Step Program of Alcoholics Anonymous. In the First Step of Recovery, we admit as alcoholics that we are powerless over alcohol and drugs. Each of you has a notebook."

Reaching over next to the chair in which she sat, Anne picked up a notebook.

"This is your notebook, Lilly. Each day I want two pages in your journal. Ideally, what you write should reflect your insights from what we have discussed in group. These are your personal pages, although from time to time I will ask to see your notebook. Also, from time to time I will schedule a one-on-one with each of you to discuss your progress in treatment.

As part of Alcoholics Anonymous, we admit our alcoholism—it's the first step to getting better. Each of the women in this group have been here for varying amounts of time and the group will change as people are released from treatment and new women enter treatment. Will you please introduce yourself?"

"My name is Lilly, and I guess I should say that I'm an alcoholic or something. It's my first day here."

"Is it?" Anne asked.

"Well, no, I mean it's my first time in group. I've been here for two days."

"Aren't you an alcoholic?" Anne asked.

"I don't know," Lulu answered truthfully.

"Drinking since you were ten, and you don't know if you are an alcoholic?"

"I know I have a problem, but I think it's cocaine, not alcohol."

"Let me read you a definition of addiction: when you start you don't know when you'll stop. So you think you can handle alcohol, but not cocaine, right?"

"Well, no, I think I have problems with alcohol."

"Did you take a survey this morning?"

"Yes."

"How many questions did you answer yes to?"

"A lot of them."

"So you answered yes to missing work because you drank too much the night before?"

"Yes," Lulu answered.

"You answered yes to lying about why you missed work?"

"Yes."

"Did you answer yes to having lost a job because of your drinking?"

"I didn't know how to answer that question. It could have been because of other things."

"Like what?"

"I don't know, lateness?"

"Late due to traffic?"

"No."

"Got up late because you were partying? Had a bad attitude because you had a hangover? Were inappropriate at an office picnic where you had one too many beers?"

"It could be," Lulu answered.

"Lilly, what do you for a living?"

"I'm a lawyer," Lulu answered.

"Could this little stint in rehab harm your law career?"

"I suppose so," Lulu answered.

"Ever yell at your children when you had a hangover, Lilly? Were you late to pick them up because you had to have another...what? A glass of Merlot? Chardonnay? What was your drink of choice?" Lulu did not answer. "Come on, Counselor, you must have had a drink of choice."

"I liked several things."

"Why don't you tell us what they were?"

"If you must know, I drank Vodka and grapefruit juice or white wine or sometimes red wine, and I liked champagne."

"Expensive champagne, Lilly?"

"Sometimes."

"How about your last couple of bottles of champagne? What kind were those?"

"I don't know. Korbel, I think."

"Will you tell us non-champagne drinkers what a bottle of Korbel costs?"

"I don't know, about ten dollars."

"How about eight dollars, Counselor?"

"Okay, so eight dollars."

"Write any bad checks for that champagne?"

"Yes," Lulu answered.

"Isn't that against the law, Counselor?"

"Yes, it is, so what? I wrote some bad checks."

Anne looked at her notes. "Seems to me you wrote a lot of bad checks. About seventy-thousand dollars in bad checks."

"Could be," Lulu said.

"*Could be,* Counselor? Remember, this isn't going anywhere but here. You don't have to take the Fifth here."

"I wasn't taking the Fifth," Lulu answered defensively. "I don't know the total amount of the bad checks I wrote."

"Well, let's see here. On this paper you filled out you wrote between fifty thousand and seventy-five thousand dollars in bad checks. Did you guess wrong this morning?"

"No," Lulu said.

"What's the penalty for writing that many bad checks?"

"I don't know."

"Take a guess."

"I don't know, five years, but I'd probably get probation. I've never committed a crime before and..."

"And what Counselor? You're a lawyer and you can get out of it?

Was that what you were going to say? Never mind, don't answer. We're almost out of time."

The room is thick with emotion.

"What do you want me to say?" Lulu cries. Her anger has wilted and she is near tears. "Look, I had a thousand-dollar-a-day crack cocaine habit. When my boyfriend's family cut him off, I wrote bad checks, tens of thousands of dollars' worth. When the banks caught on to the fact that the checks were bad, I thought of being a hooker. A good hooker in Seattle earns almost the same amount per hour as I did as a lawyer. And..." Lulu struggles to say the words that are stuck in her throat. "The boys, my children, I didn't want to die because I have two boys." Lulu breaks down and sobs into her hands.

"Thank you, Lilly. Welcome to the group." Anne continued, "I want to recap what we've heard this morning. We've heard minimization—that's making things smaller than they really are so that you can discount the cost of your addiction. We heard lying by omission, another form of minimization. We've also heard denial. 'I didn't do street drugs.' And we heard justification, a rationalization of why we do or did what we did. 'I had an injury.' These are all symptoms of your addiction. These are the mechanisms you use to stop yourself from really being in the presence of the cost of your addictions. It's also what keeps you using. When you get present to the real cost in terms of human relationships, jobs, money, and health you'll start to get better and maybe you might actually get sober. The more you deny, minimize, and lie, the more you can guarantee that you will keep using.

Success in the treatment center business means that only three-percent of the people who go through a program stay sober for more than a year. The numbers don't inspire hope, but there are three-percent who do stay sober for more than a year. A year is considered the critical cutoff mark for whether a person will maintain their sobriety." Anne looked around the room. The air had cleared.

"Let's close. Whose father?" Anne asked, and the group answered "Our father," and they began to say the Lord's Prayer.

Across the mountains in Seattle, the rain fell in gray sheets, reflecting David Hughes' bleak mood. He paced along the wall of glass that made up the doors and windows of his home. He could not seem to turn away from staring as gray drops fell into the choppy, foaming waves that lapped the lush, green lawn of his Lake Washington mansion. He adjusted his titanium glasses, his blue eyes piercing the sheets of rain. A tall man, he was lean and agile, despite his height. He ran his fingers through his thick, black hair, streaked with silver threads. Hughes was, once again, one of Seattle's most eligible bachelors since his divorce from Lulu five years ago. He winced as he recalled the damage to his reputation, his heart, and mostly his pride, which still stung. He wrung his hands. He tugged the sleeve of his gray cashmere sweater, and looked at his expensive, water-proof watch. Less than five minutes had elapsed. Where was she? Why, after all these years, could she enrage him and distract him to the point of immobility?

"Damn her!" Lilly Marie St. Blanc had never taken on his last name. She had said that 'Hughes' was a name that didn't work for television. To the outsider, she looked like she had everything it took to make it in this world, except for self-worth. Lacking the ability to see herself as others did, Lulu had chalked her success up to luck. Never mind that she was beautiful and smart. They had not let her into one of the country's most prestigious law schools because she was beautiful, or black, or multiracial. Beyond ironic, Lulu did not believe that she was either smart or beautiful.

More than a decade ago, David had first seen Lulu when she had been anchoring the morning cuts, which was when the national networks gave air time to local news stations. He had forgotten which upstate New York city he had been visiting, but he was so struck by her appearance that he almost choked on his espresso. Lilly—he learned her name when she signed off the air—exuded sexuality, but he could tell that she was intelligent, too, in a cunning, street-smart manner, and David wondered whether she was playing with the entire audience. When she asked the audience to tune in tomorrow, he nodded, and, like a brief fragrance, she was gone. David began to plot how he was going to meet her. How would he get to know her? Years later, he was still asking himself that same question. Today, he added a new question: "Where is she?"

At that very moment, a yellow Lotus Europa skidded across the bridge which connected the bedroom community of Bellevue to Seattle. The driver, Steven Flaherty, was headed to his crack dealer despite the heavy rain. Heavy metal music blared from the car's audio system. His hair was the color of dried blood, and his skin was wind-burned from skiing. He had the lanky air of a spoiled juvenile on a joy ride, even though he was almost forty. He, too, was thinking of Lily Marie St. Blanc. *Exceptional woman*, Flaherty thought. Crazy, beautiful, and damaged—that was just how he liked his women, until they became too crazy, or too boring. He was relieved that she was in rehab. He was glad that he was free from her overly-analytical personality. If only she were a little less proper. But now that she was at that broken-down rehab center on the Eastern side of the mountain, it was time to party.

TWO

It was more than ten degrees colder in Yakima than it was in Seattle. It was cold enough to snow high in the mountains. The sky was pewter, and the clouds were heavy and full. A weak sun struggled to appear above the clouds, and Deborah wondered how the woman she had to wake up and enroll into the facility would behave. Sometimes addicts could be violent, but she could handle most people regardless of their physical size. Deborah looked at the file in her hand: L. St. Blanc. She saw that "L. St. Blanc" was a private-pay patient. The center had to treat private-pays with a little more discretion, since, unlike patients ordered through the court system, private-pay patients had the option to leave and to take with them their private-pay dollars, which the center sorely needed. The facilitator had seen a whole lot worse than the woman sitting before her. While very thin and under-nourished, the worst aspect of this woman seemed to be her mental lethargy.

Often times, people brought to rehab were unconscious, or so drunk or so high that they did not realize where they were. Legally, unless court-ordered to the rehabilitation center, patients had to give their consent to remain at the treatment facility. It was the facilitator's job to formally admit patients when they were sober enough to legally admit themselves.

Deborah saw Lulu when she arrived at the center. She had been leaning heavily on the arm of a pasty-looking redheaded man, and she teetered on black stiletto pumps. She was not physically dirty, like many of the patients who arrived at the facility covered in their own vomit and feces, and was wearing a tightly-fitting black jacket with tight black trousers of the same material. Wobbly black eyeliner exaggerated her eyes. Pinkish brown lipstick smudged her teeth. Blow-dried and sprayed black hair curled around her face. Most memorable to Deborah was that Lulu had tried to walk straight and with dignity, as if she could fool anyone that she was not high on something. It was not a good sign. It was an indication that Ms. St. Blanc was still trying to pretend that she was something that she was not. Deborah opened the door to the room where L. St. Blanc lived, and saw a woman covered in a pile of blankets. This was the part of her job that she didn't like, but it was necessary.

"Ms. St. Blanc, wake up. This isn't a health club. You have been here for two days now. You got to get up!" Lulu's eyelids fluttered and fought to stay open. The light hurt her eyes.

The voice sounded far away, as if in a dream. During the times her eyelids fluttered open, Lulu thought she saw a heavy-set black woman wearing a dark blue hospital uniform.

"Yeah, I'm real. I'm really here. You, too, are really here. It is 6:45 in the morning and you have breakfast at seven and you must make up your bed before you leave your room."

"Who are you?" Lulu asked.

"I am the Women's Facilitator. My name is Deborah. You have to get up!"

"What day is today?"

"It's Thursday," Deborah replied.

"Okay," Lulu said, as if it meant anything to her. "I'm so tired. Can I have a glass of water?"

"This is not a restaurant or a hospital. If you want water, you got to get it from the cafeteria."

"I'm sorry. What do you want? I am not sure what you mean," Lulu slurred.

"I want you to get up! Can you understand that?" Deborah asked.

"Why?" Lulu croaked through cracked lips.

"For one thing, you've been here for two days. For another thing, you're supposed to be up. And I said so."

"Who are you?"

"Girl, I just told you who I was. Now get up or I will write you up."

Finally, the insistent voice registered. She had to get up. The room swam. She was light-headed, her vision blurry, her throat scratchy and dry. She steadied herself by holding on to the side of the mattress. She raised her upper torso and groaned. She looked to Deborah for help. Deborah stood where she was. Deborah was not going to help her out of bed.

Lulu lifted her torso to a seated position, slowly placing her legs on the floor. She tried to focus on what was in the room. The walls were pale blue. The lampshade was the same blue as the walls. The dresser next to her bed was a pine veneer. There was another double bed next to hers. It looked like a hospital. "I am in the hospital," Lulu said, trying not to cry.

"No, you are not in the hospital. You are at the Yakima Drug and Alcohol Rehabilitation Center. You were under the influence when you got here. Your friend walked you in. You signed yourself in. Your sister's been calling about you. You've been on medical watch for 36 hours. You've been here since 7 p.m. on Tuesday night. It's now Thursday. We think you'll be fine, and you need to get up. I'll be back in ten minutes." Deborah turned and left the room.

Although her sense of time was off, and each second seemed long, ten minutes was not enough time. *Ten minutes? Was the woman serious?* She could not get ready in that short amount of time. She touched her green silk pajamas, which were damp with sweat, and she smelled like acrid chemicals.

The seconds were long and defined. Bathe. Brush teeth. Each second, as Lulu became more conscious, the worse she felt. "Shower." "Teeth." She lowered her feet to the blue-carpeted floor. She reeled as she stood up. She balanced herself, and shuffled to the bathroom. It was clean. She was shaking so badly she held on to the bathroom sink, where someone had left a tiny bar of soap, a toothbrush, and a comb in a Dixie cup. Lulu reached for the cup. She tried to remove the toothbrush, but her hands were violently shaking, and she dropped the cup into the sink. She blinked, and the room turned black for a second. Her body swayed, and she held on to the sink with both hands. Her legs wobbled, and she slid down to the bathroom floor. The coldness of the white tile floor caused her to urinate. She tried to reach the toilet, but the urine spread in a dark yellow puddle around her.

She held on to the base of the sink, pulled herself up, and flopped onto the toilet. The urine was rapidly cooling, and it smelled bad. With thick fingers, she pulled off her silk pajama top and threw it on the floor, onto the spreading urine. Thin, trembling legs kicked off the urine-soaked pajama bottoms. She carefully lowered herself to the floor and mopped up the urine with her pajamas. Then she picked up the soaking silk, threw them into the sink, and turned on the water. She began to shake even harder, now that she was naked and cold. She reached for the shower door and yanked it open. While holding on to the shower stall door, she turned on the shower, and sulphur-smelling water gushed from the shower head. She reached for the towel on the towel bar and wrapped herself in it. Could she stand long enough to take a shower? How long had it been since she had taken a shower? Three days? Four days? The room went black again, and Lulu held on to the shower door handle with all the strength she could muster.

"Stay up. Stay up," she whispered to herself. She was alive. She would take a shower and then leave. Certainly, they could not keep her in the rehab center against her will. She was about to step into the blast of the sulfurous water when the figure of another heavy-set, brown-skinned woman wearing a blue velour jump suit filled the entrance of the bathroom door.

"Oh, shit!" Lulu screamed. "Who the fuck are you?"

"Hey, didn't mean to startle you. I'm Pam. I'm your roommate."

"Oh, hi," Lulu stammered. "You did startle me. I just woke up."

"Girl, you been out of it for two days now. You must really have a jones for whatever you were using."

Lulu looked blankly at the woman who looked like a black geisha. Heavy makeup carefully applied to her face, with a ponytail swept up and to the side of her head and lips painted bright fuchsia. Instead of a kimono, the woman was wearing navy-blue velour sweat pants with a matching zippered hoodie. The woman leaned over with the bulk of her frame so that Lulu's exit from the bathroom was blocked. "You SODA?" she asked with a smile and crinkled black eyes.

"I don't know what that means," Lulu answered, and, for a moment, she was afraid.

"Seen on Designated Area Arrest."

"No, I've never heard of that."

"You not court ordered?"

"No, my sister sent me."

The woman laughed. "Your sister sent you? Who's your sister?"

"She's a doctor."

"Oh, so sis got you admitted."

"No, I called her, she called me, and I called her back. She's paying for it."

"So, the county didn't send you?"

"No."

"Oh, I see, you are one of the private-pays. Why didn't your sister send you somewhere nice? You know, California, or New Mexico? This place is a dump. When I was living in California, we had some nice places. This place, shit, I been at better motels on 99 than this."

"You've been to rehab before?" Lulu asked, suddenly more awake than the moment before.

The woman laughed. "You think this shit works? I'm here because I have to be here. I was on SODA. I'm in the business. My man, his name is Blackie. He's doing seventy-two months for possession, but I'm going to wait for him. It was an illegal arrest anyway. They brought a battering ram, broke down the door. They didn't have an arrest warrant or anything. I was there, and I'm not supposed to be anywhere in the vicinity of 85th and 130th on the 99, but hell, that's where I work."

"What do you do?" Lulu asked.

"Girl, you for real?"

"What do you mean?" Lulu asked. She wanted the woman to go away. To give her privacy in this most embarrassing and compromising situation.

"What do you do?" the woman shot back.

"I'm a lawyer," Lulu said as she looked at the woman before her.

"For real? You're really a lawyer?"

"Yes," Lulu said, struggling to keep her balance. Her teeth were chattering and she wanted to vomit, but her stomach was empty. "I got to get into the shower," Lulu said.

"Yeah, I know," Pam said, without moving. "I hear you got some nice clothes."

"I don't remember what I brought," Lulu said as her stomach rolled and she thought she would vomit.

"You see them silk pajamas you threw in the sink? There are people in here that would cut you for them."

Lulu was scared. "Really?"

"Where do you think you are? Half of the people in here are here because the court sent them as an alternative to jail. The other half is chronic alcoholics and drug users, and they were tired of putting them in jail, so they send them here. Most of the people here have records of some kind, and not only for drugs. They are people here who have done some serious shit. Yes, they will take your pajamas and anything else that they can. You better put everything you got in that drawer with a lock, and don't be surprised if your shit gets taken anyway."

There was a knock on the door, and Deborah walked into the room. "I see Pamela has been welcoming you."

The facilitator's voice grated on her ears, but Lulu was glad she was not alone with her roommate. She needed to return to bed. With glazed over eyes, Lulu looked at the woman in the blue work uniform. Perhaps she could beg one to go and the other to let her go back to bed.

"Why don't you step into that shower before the hot water runs out," Deborah said.

Without speaking, Lulu moved her frail body and entered the shower.

"Pamela, will you excuse us? Ms. St. Blanc is not finished dressing, and I believe it's time for breakfast. The two of you can continue to get acquainted during your free time."

Pamela snorted and without acknowledging, Deborah turned to Lulu and asked "What was your name again?"

"Lulu." Lulu looked over at Deborah, who was frowning.

"Bye, Lulu," Pamela said, and Lulu could hear her chuckling as she walked away.

"After you shower, get dressed," Deborah said, without acknowledging the departing roommate. As soon as Pamela was out of the room, Deborah continued with her formal introduction.

"You are aware this is a co-ed facility," the facilitator said without acknowledging the fact that Lulu was naked and shivering in the shower stall. "The men are on one side and the women on the other, but we join for meals and for meetings. Your counselor's name is Anne. She has the right to ask you to change clothes or shoes."

"You mean they can tell me what to wear?" Lulu asked.

"Yes, they can, if you choose to stay here."

"What do you mean, if I choose to stay here?" Deborah ignored Lulu's question.

"There are no open-toed shoes allowed, so only tennis shoes or closed-toed, closed-heeled shoes can be worn. I'm going to escort you to breakfast so that we can formally admit you. I want to go over the rules of this facility, and then I will escort you to your group. You have group sessions from 10:30 to 12:00 every day, and then you have an afternoon session. So, let's get going. Don't forget your shoes. I think you have a pair under your bed, but I suggest tennis shoes."

Lulu was still holding herself up by leaning against the shower stall door. She turned off the water, and stepped back into the bathroom. Lulu saw Deborah's look of pity and disgust. "I'm sorry," Lulu began.

"No apologies needed," Deborah interrupted. "Continue dressing, while I explain how this facility functions."

Lulu stared blankly, but Deborah was used to those kinds of stares. Deborah remembered that the man who had brought Ms. St. Blanc to the treatment center had identified himself as "a friend." He had given the intake specialist a Bellevue address for Ms. St. Blanc. The facility rarely admitted patients from that well-to-do community. Drug addicts or alcoholics from Bellevue or the Eastside could afford upscale treatment centers like Betty Ford in Southern California, or Hazelton in Minnesota. It was the average Joe who came to Yakima, and the average Joe was usually lower-middle class and white. Their drug of choice was meth. The older people were usually alcoholics, and were of all races. Since the Eastern part of Washington State was farm country and ranches, there was a large Hispanic and Native American population who were disproportionately represented at the facility. Very few black people actually entered treatment programs. Either they were helped by family, inducted into the military, or sent to jail.

Deborah had watched the intake team search Ms. St. Blanc's luggage for drugs, prescription or otherwise. The team found the suitcase packed with designer jeans, cashmere sweaters and silk blouses. A female member escorted Lulu to her room and helped her undress and put on the green silk pajamas that were now lying in the bathroom sink. Deborah averted her eyes, and although she knew the answers to everything that she was going to ask Lulu, she had to ask her anyway. Those were the rules. "Ms. St. Blanc, what does the L in your name stand for?" the facilitator asked.

"It's Lilly, but everybody calls me Lulu."

"There are no nicknames here, Lilly. My name is Deborah. I work with the women in rehab. There is a blue laundry bag by the side of your bed. Laundry is washed every Tuesday and Friday. Whatever you want washed, including your towels, linens, and personal items, must be outside your door by seven-o-clock on Tuesday or Friday mornings. Your laundry will be returned to you by 7 p.m. that evening."

"Breakfast is at seven. You must line up outside the cafeteria. All meals are on a first-come, first-served basis. Lunch is at twelve, same thing, first-come, first-served. Dinner is at seven. There is fruit and juice in the cafeteria all day. You will be given a schedule, and everything I have told you should be in your welcome package. You should keep anything of value in that drawer. Right now, your purse is in that drawer. I will open the drawer for you. While I am here, we will check to see if everything you brought with you is still there.

We have checked your luggage and your purse for drugs, prescription or street drugs. Anything that has been considered contraband has been removed. You can have any of these items returned when you leave here. So, here's the key. Let's open the drawer."

With shaking hands, Lulu took the key and turned the lock.

"Is this your purse?"

"Yes," Lulu whispered.

"Why don't you look through it and see if everything you brought is still there?"

Lulu reached for the bag. Her makeup was still there, as were her comb and her brushes. Her watch and rings were in a little sandwich bag with her name on it. Her wallet was there. There was no money inside, but there was her driver's license and a telephone calling card.

"Everything is here," Lulu said, and held the purse to her toweled chest.

"Okay, you have the key. Put the purse back into the drawer and lock it." Lulu put the purse into the drawer and shut it. She fumbled with the key, but finally she managed to turn the lock and extract the key. "Keep that key around your wrist at all times," Deborah said. "I'm going to leave you again, and I will be back in ten minutes. Please be dressed."

And so Lulu's day had begun, high in the mountains of Eastern Washington.

THREE

When Deborah returned, she found Lulu dressed as if she were invited to tea at a club. Lulu nodded, and Deborah continued with her introduction as they walked down a long hallway.

"The laundry area is to your left. Down this hall is the infirmary. Along this corridor are the group session rooms. The lobby is over here. On the other side of the lobby is the men's ward. For no reason must you be found over there. If you are found on the men's side of the facility, for any reason, you will be immediately asked to leave the facility. Is that understood?"

"Yes," Lulu said, becoming more sullen by the minute.

"Down the hall from the lobby is the cafeteria. You see this long line? It starts at about six thirty. There is only so much eggs and bacon and fresh fruit. After that, it's cereal, hot or cold, oftentimes cold."

"I don't like eggs anyway," Lulu said, but the woman ignored the comment as she led Lulu to the front of the line.

"Hey, Charles, we have a new patient. We need to admit her, so I brought her to the front of the line."

"Hello, miss. What will you have?"

"Bacon?"

"Yes," the man said, heaping bacon on Lulu's plate.

"Toast?"

"Wheat, white, raisin, or sourdough?"

"Raisin," Lulu said. "Oatmeal?"

"I've got plenty of oatmeal, miss."

"It's Lilly," she said, the name sounding odd on her tongue.

"You will address the chefs by their names, and they will address you as 'miss' or 'sir'."

"I was only being friendly," Lulu snapped.

"There is no fraternization between the staff and the patients."

"Good grief, that's a bunch of shit," Lulu spat.

"Profanity is forbidden in this facility. You can be written up for what you just said, but since you did not know the rules, I'll let that one pass."

"So what happens if you write me up? You throw me out? Big deal. What's with you people anyway? Your damn rules. The staff and the patients are not allowed to fraternize."

"Will you have oatmeal, miss?"

"Thank you, sir, I will," Lulu rudely replied. The man hid his smile, and served Lulu a bowl of oatmeal. Deborah turned without speaking to Lulu to exit the cafeteria.

"This is the Director's office," Deborah said, briskly knocking on the door, then sticking her head through the partially-opened door. "I have Lilly St. Blanc, who is a new admit. She's been here since Tuesday, but has not been formally admitted."

"Come in," a tired voice answered from within the office. Deborah opened the door and ushered Lulu into the room.

"Sit down. I'm Doctor Patricia Carmichael." Lulu put the tray on the corner of the woman's desk and sat in a chair.

"Thanks," Dr. Carmichael said, acknowledging Deborah. "And I will walk her to group, so you don't have to stop whatever you are doing to do that."

"Okay." Deborah nodded, and left Lulu with Dr. Carmichael.

"Am I to be escorted everywhere?" Lulu asked belligerently.

"No, but I don't imagine you know where your group room is, do you?"

"Touché," Lulu retorted.

The auburn-haired woman took off her glasses.

"Lilly, this is not a contest. You are here to get well. We believe we have a program and a system that will help you get well, if you want to. This program only works if a person wants to get better and to heal themselves. I saw you when you came in here. I put you on medical watch, because your heart arrhythmia was so pronounced. You are how old? Early thirties? You look as if you are in your mid-forties. You are a late-stage alcoholic. You will die, or go to jail, or become a streetwalker, like your roommate Pamela, if you continue using and drinking. Now, let's start over. My name is Doctor Patricia Carmichael. I am a psychiatrist, I run this program. I'm glad you're here."

Lulu was quiet, and then she said, "Thank you. I'm glad to be here. My sister is paying for me to be here. She's a doctor, too."

"I know. I talked to your sister yesterday. She's very worried about you."

"Oh, I know that she is. Maybe I can call her later today?"

"You can call her in a few days. There are no phone privileges for the first five days that you are here. She knows that. If she calls, I'll let her know that you are awake and doing well."

Dr. Carmichael smiled. "We have lots of forms for you to fill out, and I will let you eat your breakfast while I ask you a few questions. Then I will leave you for a while, and you can fill out the information forms by yourself."

"Okay," Lulu said.

"Your full name is Lilly Marie St. Blanc."

"That's correct."

"Children?"

"Two." Lulu's lips quivered.

"Males or females?"

"Both boys," Lulu answered.

"Ages?"

"Six and eight." Lulu took a sip of her coffee and her hands shook.

Dr. Carmichael noticed the tremor in her hands and said, "There's a technical name for the tremors in your hands. The fact that they are shaking is a sign of advanced alcoholism and withdrawal. The shaking may take up to eighteen months to go away, as long as you stay sober. They may go away sooner."

"Why does everybody keep calling me an alcoholic? I'm here because of cocaine."

"It's all addiction. Whether it's cocaine, alcohol, or prescription medication. We are all addicts. However, if you choose to call yourself a cocaine addict, that's fine with us."

"What do you mean, we're all addicts? Are you an alcoholic too?"

"I'm an alcoholic in recovery. I've been in recovery for ten years."

"What do you mean, recovery?"

"It means that I've been clean and sober for ten years. It doesn't only mean that I haven't had a drink or used in ten years. That's different from being clean and sober, but you'll find out about that while you're here."

"You can't tell me now?" Lulu insisted.

"You wouldn't understand it now," Dr. Carmichael smiled.

"How do you know? Try me," Lulu insisted.

"Lilly, how old were you when you first started using alcohol?"

"I was ten. You're not going to answer my question, are you?"

"Lilly, I've already answered your question. I said that you would not understand the difference between not drinking and being sober. I'd appreciate it if you stop trying to prove whatever you are trying to prove. We know that you're smart. We know that you are a lawyer. But here, you are an alcoholic or drug addict first. No one cares that you are a lawyer, or that you're smart or pretty. You've used all those things to get away from whatever causes you to drink and use. So, here you're Lilly, alcoholic/addict. That's what we care about. The sooner you give up the pretense that you have created to hide yourself away, the sooner you're going to get better."

Lulu looked at Dr. Carmichael, and took another sip of her coffee.

"What's your drug of choice?" Dr. Carmichael asked.

"Cocaine," Lulu answered.

"What other drugs have you used?"

"Is alcohol considered a drug?" Lulu asked.

"Yes," Dr. Carmichael answered.

"Alcohol, downers, diet pills, cocaine, crack, LSD, heroin. I think that's it," Lulu said.

"Have you ever used drugs intravenously?" Dr. Carmichael asked.

"No," Lulu answered. Her face registered disgust. Doctor Carmichael wrote the information into Lulu's medical file, and wondered how the woman before her had held on for as long as she had.

FOUR

At some point during that first day awake at the rehab facility, a ripple of anxiety ticked at Lulu's fogged brain. Where was Steven? Would he disappear as he had appeared at her front door three months ago, when he had come unannounced to her apartment one Friday evening? He had been wearing jeans and fawn-colored cowboy boots.

She had been home alone. The boys were spending the weekend with their father, David Hughes. She was working in her home office, and was heading towards the kitchen to get a cup of coffee when the doorbell rang.

It was rare for her doorbell to chime. She had few friends, and the apartment complex was hidden on a private road. Her apartment was on a section of the road that took a sharp incline, and visitors had to climb a steep flight of stairs. She had never put a peep hole in the front door, so there was no peeking through the peep hole. It was probably girls selling Girl Scout cookies. But it was seven in the evening, and Girl Scouts should be home doing homework. In her deepest voice she yelled, "Who is it?"

Lulu could only distinctly hear the name, "Catherine Connors."

While Lulu pretended to be contemptuous of the wealthy blonde "bad girl," Lulu envied her money, her big house, and her apparent life of ease. Lulu's children played soccer with Catherine's children. On hearing the woman's name, Lulu opened the door, and was positive that a bolt of white lightening flashed between the man standing behind the glass screen door and herself. She didn't notice the cowboy boots for a couple of seconds, because she was trying to figure out the color of his eyes, which appeared to be violet blue. Curly, blondish-red hair, cut to make the curls behave, and a smug white smile. He reminded her of a portrait she had seen of young Henry VIII of England. He was only missing a coat of arms on his navy blue cashmere blazer, but he was wearing a silk ascot peeking from a shirt of such finely-woven cotton that it looked like it was made of silk. And, of course, those jeans and those boots.

By the time her gaze had lowered to his boots, she realized she was staring, and that she must look like a frumpy school teacher in her gray sweater and old jeans that were not fashionably distressed, but were worn with age. Her hair had tumbled down to the nape of her neck. Her makeup had rubbed off in places, and wisps of hair fell from her tumbling chignon.

"Yes?" was all that she could say.

"Didn't Catherine tell you that I was coming?" His voice had a lilt to it.

"No," Lulu replied. Catherine had told Lulu a lot of things about the wealthy Steven Flaherty of Canada and the Pacific Northwest.

"It is a little late," she continued. "I'm sorry that there has been some misunderstanding."

"Am I interrupting? I drove through traffic. Catherine said you worked until six. I would shake your hand, but the screen door is in the way."

She almost smiled. He was charming. She liked that. Besides, what did she have to do but work? "All right," she said as she unlocked the screen door and opened it for Steven Flaherty. He brushed close by her, and Lulu could smell cigar smoke layered with something musky, and something else she didn't recognize. "I wasn't expecting you." She pointed to her shoeless feet.

"I like the look. Steven Flaherty," he said, reaching out to shake her hand.

Their hands touched, and they both took a hard look at each other. "Lulu St. Blanc. I was just about to make coffee, would you like some?"

The sound of the rehab's chimes announcing lunch had interrupted her reverie. She looked at the clock. She had forty eight hours before she could call him.

FIVE

Something was wrong. He had not seen this type of behavior from Lulu in many years. Years ago, he had wanted to impress her. He knew then, as he knew now, money alone was not enough. Neither was the condo on the lake, or the Porsche. She had reentered his life on a cold January evening on his 36th birthday.

He had recently purchased a condo on Lake Union, a trendy, up-and-coming area in Seattle. He had remodeled it himself, filling it with state-of-the-art audio equipment. The entire time he was constructing the condo, he wondered whether Lulu would approve. In his imagination, as he painted and sanded, he envisioned Lulu. His friends had teased him about doing the rennovation on his own, knowing that he could well afford a construction company. But David liked the fact that he could build things. The physical labor was a good release for all of his pent-up energy. Because he always thought that he and Lulu would live together in the condo, he called the condo, "the love shack."

One of his friends was told the reason behind the condo's name, and he dared David to invite Lulu to see the home that was prepared with her in mind. He had sent Lulu an invitation to a combined house-warming and birthday party. He had never expected her to respond, much less attend. However, when he answered the door for a late-arriving guest, his heart had skipped a beat. There she was, with a glamorous girlfriend, a makeup artist named Sydney.

They had driven three hours in the pouring rain from Portland to Seattle. The private drive leading to David's house was lined with the cars of the rest of the guests, and Lulu and her friend had walked in the rain to his front door. Both were soaking wet, and were holding gifts that were once elegantly wrapped, but now made sodden by the rain. Her friend Sydney had brought wine, and Lulu had given him a box of heavy, cream-colored stationery. "So you can write," she said sweetly. The real surprise was yet to come when Lulu took off her long red coat. She was very pregnant.

He couldn't remember whether he had cursed and put his hand to his mouth, or exactly what had happened. He was literally speechless. He felt as if he were seeing himself fall in slow motion, and his heart had constricted. He thought that she had gotten married. It was too late. He looked into her eyes and for a second he was everywhere and nowhere. He had lost his chance with Lilly St. Blanc.

"I guess I should say 'surprise,' or something," Lulu said, looking David in the eye. "Or, should I say, second surprise? Since me being here is the first surprise?"

Still, he could say nothing. He saw that she was tired, that the happy face hid sad eyes and a heavy heart. Something was wrong. "I guess congratulations are in order. Motherhood looks good on you. Let me get you some tea or juice...or?"

"A bathroom," Lulu said.

"Sure," he said, and he took her elbow and led her to a pearl gray powder room. "I'm going to wait out here for you," he said, as Lulu eased into the powder room.

"Sure," she said, and closed the door. He stood outside the bathroom door for what seemed like an eternity before Lulu stepped out and into the hallway.

"Everything okay?" he asked.

"Sure. No emergency births tonight, although that would be cool," Lulu laughed.

"No. No. While it would be cool, let's not," David said.

"I need alcohol," Sydney said, as she turned to find them in the hallway. "You two just disappeared."

"Bathroom," Lulu and David said together.

"Should have known," Sydney laughed. "But I would love something to drink."

"Sure, we have a full bar," David said, as he led Lulu and Sydney down a long carpeted hall where the walls were lined in contemporary art. They came to a sunken living room where one wall was all glass, and the room was filled with good-looking young people of every race. A disc jockey was spinning music, and there were washtubs filled with beer and white wine. On the dining room table there was an exotic tropical arrangement of fragrant flowers which competed with trays of Chinese food in black and red porcelain dishes with crystal glasses twinkling next to silver utensils wrapped in black and red napkins.

The sumptuousness of the table of food, the flowers—everything in the room was calculated to generate an exact reaction, which was to stop, as Lulu and Sydney had stopped at the top of the stairs leading to the living room. Lulu looked at David, and he could see her calculating the cost of his party in her head. "Help yourself." David gestured to the table and the tubs of beer. He turned to Lulu. "Come into the kitchen with me, where we can find you something more suitable."

After she was seated at the kitchen table and drinking chamomile tea, David asked, "Do you want to talk about it?"

"No, maybe later. It's a party," Lulu answered.

"All right," he said.

Lulu was the elephant in the room. None of David's friends or colleagues at the party had asked Lulu about her pregnancy. Most of his friends had never seen her, and wondered what a very pregnant woman was doing at a party heading towards the wee hours of the morning. Some of David's closest friends knew that Lulu and David had dated briefly, before she had left for a bigger television market. However, those same friends found Lulu to be self-centered and self-interested. They tolerated her because David liked her, and she was very pretty, and had insider information on "the next thing." Otherwise, they thought David could do a lot better than Lilly, or Lulu, or whatever she called herself. There were whispered questions about whether Lulu had gotten married, and about who the baby's father might be. None of them had ever expected Lulu to get pregnant accidentally. A child was not in her plans. She was headed to one of the three national television networks.

During the evening, the more uncomfortable Lulu became, the more she talked. David had purposefully kept his distance from her. He wanted just to look at her. She was beautiful. Even pregnant, she looked like a movie star. He knew that Lulu hated to be in any group larger than six. She hated small talk. She forgot people's names because she found them boring, and she never wanted to talk about herself, but more of what she did or had done. She was ever the journalist. She wanted to know who you were and was not afraid to ask the most personal questions of anyone—another reason she was so good at her job. Because he knew all of this, David was more touched than ever that Lulu had come to his party. He sipped his espresso-flavored vodka and watched Lulu verbally skewer a young programmer.

As the party was winding down, only David's best friends remained. It was clear that Lulu was growing weary. Urged by David, his friends agreed to host a baby shower for Lulu. Lulu had wept. "Thank you," she had whispered, genuinely touched that David and his friends were celebrating her baby. She was happy, but she could barely stand on her swollen feet. "David," Lulu yawned, "do you mind if Syd and I crash here for the night? It's just too damn late and too far to drive home."

"Not a problem. I was hoping that you would stay here tonight. Can I get either of you anything else? More tea?" David asked.

"No, I'm swimming in tea." Lulu yawned again.

"Anything for you, Sydney?"

"A pillow," Sydney replied. "And a bed."

"My guest quarters are somewhat incomplete," he said, as he led the women in to a room painted the color of winter sunshine.

"Unfinished, like in a magazine," Sydney said. "It's beautiful in here. All you need is a wife," Sydney said, and smiled provocatively. When David turned his back to Lulu to ask Sydney if he had heard correctly, Lulu mouthed to Sydney, "What?"

"Was that an offer?" David asked Sydney.

"Uh, no. I just meant your house looks so well thought out. You know, like you should be sharing it with someone." David chuckled, and turned to Lulu, who had just finished flashing her middle finger at Sydney.

"No comment," Lulu said, then added, "no one will have him. He's a nerd."

"He is not a nerd," Sydney came to David's defense. "If he was really a nerd, there would only be a computer in here and a case of beer."

"I love this! A catfight. Two beautiful women arguing over my merits, albeit nerd merits. I just want you to know that I also make a terrific Banquet TV dinner. Banquet, as in the *brand*. I am high-end all over," David laughed.

"I can attest to that," Lulu laughed wearily. "His refrigerator is stocked with gourmet TV dinners. It's quite impressive."

"I also have several kinds of fine espresso beans in my larder as well."

"Ok, enough!" Sydney said, "See these bags under my eyes? They are going to fill this room, if I don't hit a pillow. And Ms. Lulu," Sydney turned, addressing Lulu, "just where are you sleeping, my darling, since I got the yellow room?"

"She's sleeping with me," David answered.

"I am not!" Lulu said. "I am too big to sleep with anyone, and I..." she couldn't say the last part out loud, which was, "and I have not slept with anyone since I got pregnant."

"You are safe with me," David said. He saw that Lulu did not have the energy left to keep up her brave act. "I have a big bed. I am thin, even though you are not. Neither of us is sleeping on my white Haitian cotton sofa. So, to the big room." He winked at Sydney. Then he touched Lulu's shoulders. He looked into Lulu's eyes. "Your virtue is safe with me." He was not jesting.

Lulu turned to Sydney, and when David was not looking, she stuck out her tongue at Sydney. Sydney laughed out loud and covered her mouth when David looked over his shoulder to see what was so funny. Lulu gently pushed David out of the cozy yellow bedroom and followed him to the quiet space of his mauve-gray bedroom. Lulu stopped. Turning to David, she said, "I'm embarrassed. I never thought, I could not give it up, I'd already...oh, it just hurts..."

David reached over and pulled Lulu's head to the middle of his chest and held her while her body shook with sobs. When Lulu had cried herself out, she slumped onto the big bed. "David?" Lulu softly asked. He did not know what she might say, and he braced himself.

"I'm sorry, do you have pajamas? Can I change in the bathroom?"

"Sure. Look, I know I made a big fuss about not sleeping on the sofa, but I am happy to."

"No," Lulu said, and her voice cracked. "I have been so alone. I've been longing for someone to hold me." He moved towards her, but she held up her hand to stop him. "I'll be ok, please."

"Alright," David said, backing off. "I'll bring the pajamas. Maybe just the tops. The pants would come up to your neck."

"Thank you," Lulu replied. "You have always been so nice to me."

"Why is that so surprising, Lulu?" David asked.

"Because I attract every loser on the planet."

"You mean the baby's father?"

"Yes, and no. Just in general."

He looked away. "Let me get the pajamas. There are extra toothbrushes in the medicine cabinet. I'll put the pajamas in the guest bathroom. When you are ready, pick your side of the bed."

"Okay," she said.

When he returned, Lulu had fallen asleep on the bed with her clothes on.

SIX

As the luncheon bell chimed again, Lulu looked at her choice of shoes and clothes. The silk blouse was simply wrong. So were the pearls, but she didn't have time to change. She washed her face and bravely headed to the lunchroom. As she walked she fantasized about an espresso and a chocolate croissant, which took her back to that evening when Steven had arrived.

"I was just about to make coffee," she had said to him. "I think coffee at midnight is the perfect drink." She smiled, then stopped herself. She was flirting with this stranger. Why? She knew why; he was rich. She was tired after three years of poverty and law school. Even if he became a well-paying client, that would be just as good. She wanted him to like her. Steven Flaherty was like all the wealthy white boys she had gone to high school with. They all wanted to have sex with her, but nobody wanted to take her to the prom. But maybe this man would change the score on a number of levels.

"No, thanks," Flaherty replied as he looked at Lulu. She was not at all what he was told that she would be like. She was sweet, but had been hurt a lot. He could tell that she once lived some place other than where she currently lived. Everything in the apartment was expensive, including the original art on the walls. Perhaps both he and Catherine Connors had underestimated Lulu St. Blanc.

"Something else? Water? A glass of wine?" Lulu asked, wanting him to accept something from her.

"No, I'm fine," he said, as he looked around the foyer of her apartment. "Nice," he said, as he surveyed the living room and dining area, where black tweed furniture and smoked, bevel-edged glass starkly contrasted with red Chinese porcelain tubs. Fishtailed palms soared towards a sloped ceiling, and abstract art in bold reds and blacks hung from the walls.

A square-cut crystal vase filled with pink tulips sat on a smokey gray glass dining table. The fresh flowers mimicked the pink in a rich oriental carpet that covered a honey-colored, basket-weave wood floor.

Lulu had watched him as he walked towards the white marble fireplace where gold-framed photographs of Lulu's children and family sat on the mantle. He peeked out of the floor-to-ceiling windows in the dining area onto a small patio garden. Tall potted evergreens buffered the street noise, and flower boxes of late blooming blossoms spilled down the walls of the patio. Outside, autumn rain threatened the evening sky.

Lulu wanted him to like the apartment, to like her. "I think we should meet out here," she said pointing to the dining room table. "My office floor is covered with exhibits. I am in the middle of a case. Have a seat. Are you sure that I can't get you anything?"

"Nope," Steven answered with a finality that assured Lulu that she would not make another offer of anything to drink. But Steven did not take the seat he was offered, and walked over to take another look at the framed photographs.

"I'm going to get that coffee," Lulu said and turned into the kitchen. Steven did not appear to hear her.

When she re-entered the dining area from the kitchen, he was still standing in the middle of the living room. He turned to face her as she entered, and there was that current again. She wondered if he was feeling what she was. He stood still, and seemed to be staring at the cup in her hand.

"Did you change your mind?" she asked, as she set the cup and saucer on the dining room table.

"No, that is very fine china. Catherine told me that you were broke." And when she thought of the word "broke," she realized that she felt really broken now.

SEVEN

Pamela elbowed Lulu. "Hey," she said, when Lulu turned an angry face towards her. "You were somewhere else."

"Oh," Lulu replied.

"This is Michie. We've known each other for years." Lulu turned to look at the light-skinned little woman who looked like an aged child.

The woman named Michie smiled, and appraised Lulu's outfit.

"She's from Bellevue," Pamela said to Michie.

"Is your name really Michie?" Lulu asked.

"Yes." The woman smiled back.

"Are you…?" She was going to ask Michie if she too were a prostitute, but Pamela answered her unasked question.

"Naw, Michie ain't in the life. We met in County when she was arrested for boosting."

Lulu's face registered a blank. "I'm sorry, I don't understand." Both women laughed.

"Boosting is what you would call shoplifting," Pamela snickered.

"Oh," Lulu said. Pamela elbowed Michie. "She really don't know. She ain't pretending."

"Oh." It was now the Latina's turn to reply.

"Eat with us. Tell us about your man. We want to hear about him and everything about Bellevue."

After weeks of not eating, Lulu's body craved food. In between forkfulls of potatoes and meatloaf, she told the women about how she met Steven Flaherty. How he had come to her apartment attempting to get her to legally dissolve the trust which held his inheritance. Both women listened intently after Lulu said the words "trust fund."

Lulu was at the part of the story where she was telling Steven that she did not think she could help him. "Look, I'm sorry. This has not been going well. Let me return your check, or Ms. Conner's check. I have work to do."

"I'm sorry, too. Can I buy you a drink? I feel bad."

"No, it's okay."

"Do you mind if I indulge?" Steven had asked.

"In what?"

"Actually, I have something that could take the edge off. I'm sure whatever you consume is of high quality."

Lulu laughed. "Well, it cost more than three dollars a gallon, if that's what you mean. So, what are you going to do, pull out a joint and shock the Bellevue lawyer? Try again."

"So the reports are true?"

"Was that a question or a statement?" Lulu asked.

"Both."

"Perhaps you should tell me what you mean, Mr. Flaherty."

"Don't get defensive. I've heard that you've had a past drug and alcohol history."

"Well, isn't this the pot calling the kettle black?"

"Such indiscretion everywhere. See what I mean? One must be careful with whom you share your indulgences and your secrets."

"Are we at a tie yet?" Lulu asked.

"Truce, Counselor, truce. I have in my pocket several magic rocks of pure cocaine."

"Oh my God," Lulu said, as Steven pulled out a baggie full of cocaine.

"The elixir of the gods," Steven said.

"So, you are using again?" Lulu asked.

"Again?" Steven laughed. "I've never stopped."

"But what about...?"

"Idle, uninformed chatter. Now, how about a hit?"

"I've never tried crack."

"Crack, Ms. St. Blanc, is what poor people smoke. This is pure cocaine."

"So what's the difference?" Lulu asked.

"Quality, my dear. Quality."

"What about the reports I hear about people getting hooked and selling everything they have?"

"Do I look as if I've sold everything I have?"

"No, but you're rich."

Steven's laugh filled the room, and his blue eyes twinkled. "Ms. St. Blanc, here is my magic wand. It is your escape from the drudgery of the law, and your life as the suburban lawyer." Steven pulled a glass pipe from his pocket and took a yellow rock the size of a large pea from a baggie. From inside his breast pocket, he pulled out a gold cigarette lighter, and held the pipe for Lulu. With his thumb, he flicked the gold lighter, and a tiny flame shot from the lighter. For a moment Lulu looked at the fire, and then at Steven Flaherty.

Her heart was pounding. The pipe was a dare and an invitation to a world she could not even imagine. It was in her past to be reckless. She always told everyone that she would try anything once. Now was her moment. She took the glass pipe from Steven and put it to her lips. Steven moved the flame to the edge of the pipe, and the rock sizzled as it melted.

"Inhale gently," Steven said.

Lulu closed her eyes and inhaled the yellow acrid smoke. Within seconds her head began to throb and she felt as if she were having an orgasm. "Oh my God," she said. "Oh my God." She put her hand to her heart as her head fell backwards.

Steven smiled and said, "you ladies always call me God; my name is Steven."

Lulu had been caught up in her tale, but the women had lost interest. They had heard a lot of crack stories and done it themselves. Lulu was embarrassed. "Pamela, Michie, I'm so tired. I'm going to wash my face and see if that will help."

"No, tell us about how y'all got together," Michie pleaded.

Lulu looked at the woman and said, "I'll tell you another time." She had already said too much.

"Just one question?" Michie pleaded.

"Nope," Lulu said. "I am so tired I could fall asleep standing. I promise I will tell you anything you want to know about Steven...later."

"Well, I guess we are done here." Pamela said. They rose in tandem.

"We'll walk you back to the room."

"Sure," Lulu said, feeling uncertain.

The two woman chattered as Lulu walked ahead. When they reached their room, Lulu turned and went to the bathroom, where she pulled out a bar of black soap from an open cosmetics bag.

"What's that?" both women asked.

"It's face soap, Erno Lazlo."

"Erno who?" Pamela asked.

"Erno Lazlo."

"How much does that cost?" Michie asked.

"Twenty seven dollars for the bar of soap…and the rest…I don't know. I've used it since I was twenty."

"Alright, then," Michie said. "I'm going to my room and wash my face with the soap they got here." She and Pamela left Lulu in the bathroom.

After leaving Lulu in her room, Michie and Pamela went to get their coats and went outside to smoke. They sat side-by-side, silently smoking. They had known each other for a very long time. Their mothers had moved into the same Section 8 housing development before Michie and Pamela had started kindergarten. They had seen each other in the play area where their mothers sat and watched them play.

They immediately liked each other. Pamela was big for her age, and Michie was tiny. Pamela dressed like a tomboy, and Michie's mother always dressed her in frilly dresses. It was the beginning of a life-long friendship where the women over the years had been the only support and comfort for each other.

Over the years, as the lives of their mothers disintegrated, they began to steal food from wherever they could to feed each other. They stole cigarettes, and by the time they were eleven years old, they were dressing each other's hair and putting on makeup. They slept at each other's homes when their mothers were missing, or had been jailed for prostitution or selling drugs, or any number of things that their mothers were arrested for.

When Michie was twelve, her mother found a boyfriend who was really her pimp. The man was violent and cruel. His first attempt at controlling Michie was by prohibiting her from going to Pamela's house. The plan did not work, and the boyfriend began beating Michie. By this time, Pamela's mother was deep into her bottle of cheap vodka, and Pamela was left to do whatever she wanted. Pamela had grown to her adult height, and had learned to fight to protect herself from men who tried to hustle her as well as girls who tried to fight her, because it was what girls in her part of town did to other girls, and she had to avoid the gangs that roamed her housing development and stay clear of trouble as much as she could.

Pamela had dreams and plans, and, despite her erratic home life, she had done well in school. Her teachers liked her. She was helpful and wanted to help others with their math problems and science projects. Her teacher had once asked her whether she wanted to be a teacher when she grew up, and Pamela had said no, to the teacher's surprise. When further questioned, Pamela had finally disclosed that she wanted to be an engineer, and work at Boeing designing airplanes. The teacher had smiled, and wondered where her student had heard about aircraft design.

At the same time, Michie was not doing well in any area of her life. Red marks from whips and belts were visible on her legs and arms and back. The marks enraged Pamela, who, after seeing fresh welts, would run over to Michie's apartment to protect her. Pamela would knock on Michie's mother's door, and scream that she was going to call the police on them for mistreating Michie, but no one bothered to answer the door or respond. After weeks of trying to comfort Michie, who looked like she was eight, Michie banged on the door, pleading for Pamela to open it for her. Michie was bleeding from her mouth, and the boyfriend was running after her. Pamela had had enough. When she had turned twelve, she had started carrying a switch blade to protect herself from getting robbed and molested. The knife was in her pocket. As Michie ran to the door, Pamela let her into the apartment, and, as the boyfriend tried to push Pamela out of the way, she reached into her pocket and plunged the blade into the man's inner thigh. She had just wanted to stop him, not hurt him. But the knife had hit a major artery, and the man fell as blood spurted from his leg. As he grabbed his thigh and tried to stop himself from falling, he managed to punch Pamela in her face. In Pamela's case it was a lucky punch, because when she was tried for the murder of the boyfriend, her defense attorney said it was in self-defense. Pamela got five years. When she got out of juvenile prison, Pamela sought out and found Michie, who by then had become a prostitute. They were still together, and still the best of friends.

Pamela broke their comfortable silence and asked Michie, "what do you think of her?"

"About what? Do I think she is phony? I don't know. She speaks well. She's smart, but not really. The way she talks about men, she sounds stupid."

"What's her real story? There's something not right about her. She's weak."

"I know what you mean," Michie said.

"Michie." Pamela grew quiet. "What did you want to do when you were a little girl?"

"What do you mean?" Michie said, looking at Pamela.

"You told me that you wanted to be a fashion designer."

"Me, a fashion designer?" Michie laughed bitterly, and then turned to Pamela. "I know it was silly, wasn't it?"

"No, Michie, it wasn't silly. You could have done it." The women lapsed into silence.

"I love you, Michie." Pamela said.

"I know you do, Pamela. You have been the only person in my life who has always been there for me."

Pamela brushed away tears. "We aren't that old. We can still do something with our lives."

Michie tossed her cigarette away and looked into her friend's eyes.

"You been crying a lot lately."

"I know."

"You are not my Mama, Pam. I'm going to be all right."

"Do you think that lawyer woman can help us?"

"Who? Ms. St. Blanc?" Michie laughed a bitter laugh. "She can't even help herself. That's a weak-ass bitch. If she's a lawyer, at all. We are going to be all right. Really, Pam. It's cold. Let's go back inside. I don't think it ever gets this cold in Seattle, but it looks like it's going to snow."

"How do you know?" Pamela said, as she rose from the picnic table and headed back to the warmth of the rehab facility.

EIGHT

Soon it would be evening. The rain had stopped, and the air was fresh. David looked at his watch again. Why had things gone so wrong from that morning after his birthday? He had watched her as she woke up. She had looked so innocent and childlike. When she was fully awake, he had asked her out to breakfast because there was nothing in his refrigerator that a pregnant woman should eat.

"Great, but no truck stops where they cook the eggs in bacon grease."

"I would never take you to any place like that. What do you think I am?" he had countered.

"A guy who is sometimes amused by my discomfort."

"Was that why you stayed away from me?" David asked.

"Yes and no. I am terrible at relationships. I didn't know what to think of you or how to deal with you. You can be brutally sarcastic. I did not want to get involved with anyone. I didn't think I would be here for very long. You were way too nice of a guy. I knew you liked me, and I didn't want to hurt you. I don't know how to deal with nice men. It's part of my dysfunctional past. What I really wish was that the bad guys would simply wear black hats, like in the Westerns. Unfortunately, none of my many therapists has given me a checklist of things to avoid. I have trust issues. I have issues. I'm not good relationship material."

"I don't wear hats," David said.

"Please don't," Lulu murmured.

"Please don't what?"

"Feel sorry for me. I hate that."

"I don't feel sorry for you. I'm sorry that you are not happy and that this is not the happiest moment in your life. I'm sorry for that. I'm sorry that the baby's father is an asshole."

Lulu touched his lips with her fingers. "Please don't. No one is sorrier than me. But I am going to have this baby." With that, she got up. "Thank God, I still have my clothes on." She winked at him and adjusted her clothes. "I'm going to check in on Sydney." She returned and said, "dead to the world."

"Well, good thing, for now. Thank goodness Sydney is tiny, because if she was awake, she would have to curl up in the jump seat. The Porsche only has two seats," he said, as he walked her through to the garage where he housed his silver-gray Porsche Cabriolet.

"I don't know if I'll fit in that damn thing!" Lulu joked as she got into the low slung car. "Where are we going?" Lulu finally asked. They were both pensive. Both taking in the black trees against the white snow as the car wound through the roads banked with heavy snow.

"Don't know," David answered. "I don't know."

"I never thought that I would be a mother. Now here I am, eight months pregnant."

"Do you have everything you need?" David asked

"Yeah, everything but a father for the baby," Lulu said.

David looked at Lulu and took her hand into his. "I'll be the baby's father."

"David, David, no. For starters, we live in different cities. Number two, and this is not insignificant, we are virtually strangers. And why do you want to have the responsibility for a child?"

"Is that how you see it, Lulu?"

"Yes. I won't be the first woman to have a child without being married."

"I've always been taken by you, Lulu, from the very moment I laid eyes on you." Lulu remained silent and stared at the stark landscape denuded by winter. "Please say something."

"I really need some food. I'm not avoiding you. Right now I cannot think."

"Please think about what I have said." David said.

"Sure," Lulu answered in a dismissive way.

"You are always safe with me." David turned to Lulu, and then he kissed her on her forehead.

NINE

By mid-afternoon of the first day at the rehab center, Lulu felt lost and did not know what to do. She saw the journal sitting on her nightstand and sat down on her bed and began to write.

"The day I got my first period was Good Friday. I had no idea what was happening, but I was sure that I was bleeding to death. No one had warned me or prepared me for it. I was scared that something was wrong with me. At first, I stopped the flow with toilet paper and paper towels. I realized that I was having what my science teacher had called my menstrual cycle. But nobody told me how long it would last: hours, days, or minutes. When the paper towels proved not to be enough, I used washcloths and face-towels. On the third day, which was Easter Sunday, I thought that I had the situation under control. I didn't. The towels were bulky and I guess not positioned correctly and I bled through to my dress. My father saw the blood. I don't remember what he said to me, but I knew that something in our relationship had changed."

Lulu paused and read what she had written. Then she wrote, "My parents were never home. I read whatever I wanted to, ate whatever I wanted to; wore my hair and clothes any way I chose. I started shaving my legs when I was nine. By the time I was eleven I was wearing a garter belt and stockings—back then that's all there was. There was no pantyhose. I wore makeup and straightened my hair and nobody noticed, cared, or said anything. At the time, I didn't care," Lulu wrote in her journal. "As I look back on my life, my parent's disinterest was equal to their actual abuse. Now I know that I would have chosen that they continue to ignore me." Lulu looked at the journal and tucked it in the drawer of her nightstand. It was time to go to her individual therapy session. She walked through the hallways, ignoring everyone that looked at her. She finally found the room, knocked, and entered.

"How are you today? I'm Terry Berkquist. I'm a psychologist, which is different from a medical doctor. Here we say that drugs are the symptoms of underlying problems. We don't do long term therapy here. We can't. We don't have the time. So, how are you today?"

Lulu started to tell the therapist about her day and then simply answered, "sad."

"What are you sad about?" Terry asked.

"Everything." Lulu fought back tears.

"Is there anything in particular that you want to talk about?" Terry asked gently.

"No."

"Maybe we can talk about your first experience with crack cocaine?" Terry offered.

"What do you want to know?"

"Why?"

"I don't know why." Lulu looked down at her hands as tears slid down her face. Terry offered her a box of tissues. Lulu cried for a few more minutes, and then Terry asked, "so you smoked crack with him, and then what?"

"No, we didn't have sex, if that's what you are asking."

"No, I wasn't asking that. I want you to tell me how you felt after smoking the crack. How you felt about Steven."

"I don't know how to explain this, except to say that he was the most exciting thing that had happened to me in years. He had sexual energy and he was funny. He brought color and excitement when he walked into my apartment. Do you have any idea what it's like to go to law school as a single mother of two young children?"

Terry shook her head. "No, I don't know, but I can imagine it was difficult."

Lulu responded with a bitter laugh. "When the door closed behind Steven Flaherty it was as if he had sucked the air from the room with him. After smoking the crack—for that was what it really was, despite Steven's statements otherwise—I was sexually aroused. My underwear was wet, and it took every bit of my will power not to have sex with him."

"So why not?" Terry asked.

"He wasn't interested." Lulu looked down at her broken nails.

"But you were sexually interested in him?"

"Yes, it was Steven's Flaherty's apparent lack of interest that prevented me from carrying out the sexual images racing through my head. *What would that mustache feel like running across my inner thigh? How would I feel as those blue eyes pierced me as he entered me?* Every moment I spent with him was a struggle against my raging desire and my diminishing common sense. When Steven told me that he had to go, it was only my pride that prevented me from pleading with him not to go. When he left, I groaned out loud. 'Shit, fuck, and damn! What was that?' My heart was still pounding, and I wanted that man inside me."

"Then what did you do?" the therapist asked.

"I was frustrated and disappointed and ashamed of myself." Lulu saw the therapist's unspoken question. "I wanted to be desired. I remember, as I stood leaning against the door to the apartment, my thoughts turned to my grandmother, who was a devout Catholic. I guess I felt guilty. I felt cheap. Dirty."

"Why would sexual fantasies make you think about your grandmother?" the therapist asked.

"I just recalled the kind of woman she was. I wondered what she would make of me lusting after Steven Flaherty."

"And…?" Terry said, urging Lulu to continue talking about her grandmother.

"She was a beautiful woman. She seemed to float through the air, and I loved her so much." And Lulu told Terry about her grandmother, Celestine St. Blanc.

The island off the Sea of Cortez had little industry or commerce, and teamed with people who had little to do but to think about ways to find their next meal, or how to earn a little bit of money to buy food. During the height of the American slave trade, the island had been a dumping ground for sick or pregnant slaves, indentured white people, people of all races, Indians, and Chinese, who, for one reason or another, could not be put to work on the vast plantations of the American South and the West Indies. The dominant features of the place were the Catholic Church and the rum shops that ringed the island, and it was these two elements that fought for the soul of Celestine Payne.

She was born at the turn of the century in 1902, as the daughter of two Indian orphans who had been abandoned on the streets of Bombay, India to die. The Portuguese sisters of St. Andrews Church had found Celestine's parents at separate times, and both had been raised in a Catholic orphanage in Bombay. The Sisters had given them English names, as Bombay had been English for more than four hundred years after it had been granted to the English in the 15th century, as a part of a dowry from the King of Portugal when his daughter married Charles the II of England. At the turn of the 19th century, many of the orphans were given the opportunity to leave Bombay. They had to get married, and promise to work for the Catholic Church for a period of time. The two orphans who became Celestine's parents had chosen to get married, and two years later, Celestine was born.

While still under the control of the Church, Celestine's parents behaved within the strict confines of the Catholic Church. When they had completed their time with the Church, they reverted to their Hindu culture. Part of the reason for this switch was that after they had left the Church, the Church took back their housing, and the small income on which they lived. While they knew how to read, write, and speak English, they had no skills, especially to live in a place where people committed desperate acts to survive simply. Celestine's parents knew that they could not really care for their daughter, and when Celestine turned thirteen, she was offered as a bride to a much older man. It was a life that no thirteen-year-old should have to endure, and Celestine turned to God and the Bible to survive the life of wife and mother when she was a teenager. Her husband wasn't unkind or cruel; he was simply very old, and could have been her grandfather instead of her husband. Six years later, when her husband died, Celestine was to undergo another traumatizing event, in addition to the sudden death of her husband. On the morning of her husband's death, Celestine, then nineteen, was awoken by her mother and her mother-in-law, and she underwent the ritual of widowhood, which included shaving her head and wearing the white sari of a widow. If Celestine had been living in India, she would have been sent to an ashram for widows, where Celestine would have survived by begging or by prostitution. There was no ashram on the island, and Celestine and her young daughter had to return to live with her parents, who were already struggling to feed their other two children. There was no place for Celestine to live, and, for two years, Celestine and her daughter lived in the kitchen next to the stove, and ate whatever scraps the family didn't want. Her family treated her like a servant, forcing her to wash their clothes as well as clothes they took in. By the time her father found a man who was willing to marry her, Celestine was malnourished and worn, but her beautiful face and eyes could not be diminished by poverty and grueling physical labor.

In the therapist's office, Lulu blushed when she thought of her grandmother, who had died when Lulu had been in her early thirties. "My grandmother was widowed again when she was fifty, and I was five. I see those last twenty five years of her life as the only time she was free. She finally could live the way she wanted, which was to live a life of devotion to God. She had wanted to be a nun before she was forced to marry. I think it was her opportunity to live in the lifestyle of a nun. And she wanted me to be a nun as well."

"How did that sit with you?" the therapist asked.

"Which part? Her being widowed at fifty? Or that she wanted me to become a nun?"

"The latter," Terry said.

Lulu smiled. "I wanted to be a nun. I think I would have enjoyed being a nun."

Terry looked up at her beautiful client, sitting in a beige high back chair. The last thing that Terry could have imagined for this woman was that she should become a nun. "Well, we will have to discuss that at our next session."

"Thank you," Lulu said, and got up and left the therapist's office. "I need to talk to my children. They haven't seen me in weeks. I've got to make that right," Lulu said, as she walked towards a row of pay phones. They were all busy, and Lulu burst into tears and ran outside. She was wearing only her silk blouse and slacks. It didn't matter though, she had to get out of the building. "Fuck the rules. Fuck rehab. Fuck it all." She felt so old. She looked so old.

Outside, on the grounds of the rehab facility, Lulu tried to stop crying. She could not. It was as if someone had opened the dam of her heart and her tears were a river set free. As she fought to control her emotions, Lulu's attention was diverted to the entrance of the rehab center.

"No," a young black woman in a hospital gown screamed. "No, you cannot take my baby!"

A young man had gotten out of the car, and had gone to the side of the woman holding an infant. The young man reached for the child, and the woman ran a few awkward steps. An older man got out of the car. He was red-faced, and seemed angry. Words were exchanged between the two men. The young woman wailed and clung to the child. The younger man tried to take the child from the woman's arms. The young woman backed away and screamed. From the rehab center, two facilitators joined the group. A blonde-haired counselor moved towards the woman holding the baby. The woman backed away from the group of people, but the blonde woman moved in tandem with her. Then the child began to cry, and its whimpers were like that of a small hurt animal. Lulu averted her eyes. The young man and the rehab facilitator surrounded the woman. The young woman wailed again and the blonde woman put her hands on the baby. The young man said something, and the young girl reluctantly gave the baby to the blonde woman. The blonde woman gave the baby to the older man with the red face. The young man comforted the weeping woman for a few minutes, and then the blonde woman ushered the young girl through the doors of the rehab. The older man handed the baby to the young man. Together, the men got into the car and drove away.

Lulu tried to figure out what had happened at the entrance of the facility. Another woman, another child. The world of drugs had ugly tentacles, and the children were its worst victims. "Holy Mary, Mother of God, prayer for us sinners, now and at the hour of our deaths," Lulu silently mouthed to herself, as she hurried back to the rehab center.

TEN

When Lulu gave birth to her son, Teddy, the baby's biological father was absent, and David was at the hospital for the birth of Lulu's baby. When David looked in the baby's eyes, there was love, and from that moment on, David treated Teddy as his natural child. In August, when Teddy was only six months old, Lulu's contract with the television station expired. It was clear from the negative publicity about her pregnancy that management was not going to offer her a new contract. No other television station had offered her work. When her last day of work came, David had offered his home to Lulu and the baby until she got on her feet. Lulu reluctantly packed her things, and baby Teddy, and moved in with David. After a few months of living together like a family, it just seemed to be in the natural course of things that Lulu and David should get married. So they did.

After the marriage, things began to be strained between Lulu and David. It was mostly because Lulu felt that she had made a mistake in marrying David. Lulu would forever think that she was with the wrong man. She was not sure if liking David Hughes was enough. She had always wanted to be "in love" with the man she had married. She was not in love with David Hughes.

Lulu's anxiety about her decision to marry David began to show itself in odd ways. The first thing that they disagreed upon was David's wish for a formally-set table at each meal. David had come from a long line of Irish Scottish gentry, whose initial fortune came from land handed over to them for betraying the Irish to the English. David's branch of the family had immigrated to the wilds of Canada. There, the family began their history as land barons in western Canada.

David's father, Bradford Hughes, had been one of the few Hughes to actually work for someone else. Bradford Hughes had made his fortune at the age of forty two. When that happened, he retired to the Caribbean with his wife and sons. Growing up in the Caribbean, David learned to love the water and the happy-go-lucky islanders. At the same time, as much as he admired the natives, David was taught to be superior. David's family was part of the ruling white class for whom many of the islanders owed their livelihood. As David grew older, he retained his love of the cheerful islanders, but he had learned how to be a snob. As an adult, and now living in New York State, he wanted his dinners to be formal, with wine glasses and the proper cutlery to accompany each course.

Had Lulu the maturity or even the awareness to ask David why he wanted formal dinners, David could have explained that he thought that dinner should be a meal where the entire family ate together. Family was important to David. He would have shared with her the disintegration of his family and the loss of his hero, his father.

When David was fourteen, the dream of his family living on an island imploded. No little boy loved his father more than David Hughes loved his father. Bradford Hughes was an easy man to worship. Bradford was tall, ruggedly good-looking, an avid sportsman, a self-made millionaire, and a lady's man. Bradford had married Louise Cooperman-Hughes, a blue-eyed, dark-haired woman, whose beauty could rival any movie star, but Louise Cooperman was not interested in fame. She was only interested in fun. For a while, a woman who could play a hand of gin rummy like a pro, who could dance like a Rockette, loved to drink, smoke, and have sex, was a fantasy for any red-blooded male. She had gone to college, but had failed planning her wedding to Bradford Hughes. It wasn't that she wasn't smart; she was very smart, but she had very limited interests, and those interests were clothes, jewelry, and shopping. She had a housekeeper and a cook, a requirement, because she couldn't boil an egg, and didn't care that she couldn't. She was a woman meant to be married to a wealthy man, and what she didn't count on was that she would age, and what was exciting for a man like

Bradford Hughes when he was twenty was completely inappropriate for him at forty. Bradford wanted someone to share the pursuit of his next fortune, to guide him through the dinners where private deals were made. He needed a friend, a partner, a wife, and a mother to his three sons.

Louise never dreamed that Bradford Hughes would divorce her. People just didn't get divorced in those days. She ignored Bradford's request for a more sedate lifestyle. She continued to spend her days on the beach, drinking until it was time to get dressed for dinner, where she drank some more. As the relationship became more strained, Bradford began leaving the house before his wife woke up to lay in the sun. The children were left to the care of the servants, but Bradford always returned home for dinner.

Dinner was always a formal affair: Bradford wore a tie to dinner; Louise wore a cocktail gown. The boys were bathed and dressed in shirts and long pants, and were expected to maneuver around the water glasses and the silver. During dinner, Bradford would tell stories of the world of the stock exchange, the price of gold that day, and how he, Bradford Hughes, had made another fortune by outwitting another business person who had not gone the extra distance. If he could take notes, David Hughes would have done so while eating dinner. David wanted to be just like his father. He, too, wanted to outwit the smartest of the smart. David wanted to be the next Wall Street multimillionaire. Then came that fatal summer when he was fourteen. It was the summer that his father stopped coming to dinner, because his mother was too drunk on the beach. It was the summer that ended David's family.

Within a year, David's father had moved away from the island and gone to Europe, where he managed his fortune. David's mother remained in the house, but without his father's income, one by one the servants left. The land surrounding the house became overgrown with weeds, appliances broke and were not repaired. Bills went unpaid, and the children were left to fend for themselves without the concerned eyes of the elderly Puerto Rican woman who had cooked for the family. Then, the worst happened. His mother could no longer afford the house on the island. She packed up what was left of the house furnishings, and moved herself and the children to a suburban community outside of New Jersey.

David's life quickly spiraled downward. Louise had never really taken care of herself, or the children for that matter. She had no practical skills to speak of, and when she was forced to work, she could only work as a saleswoman in a boutique. The money she earned was used to buy clothes, so that she could continue to look the part of a suburban wife with an executive husband. In the meantime, the children lived on peanut butter and jelly sandwiches and cans of soup. The dinners that he had grown up with were gone, and so was the life that he thought he would have forever.

When the time came for David to go to college, no one had planned anything. His father did not attend his graduation because his mother did not tell him the date. The moment David was old enough, and when he had enough money, David crossed the border into New York State and he never looked back.

Now, years later, David Hughes was reflecting upon the fact that, in some ways, his mother and Lulu were very similar. To Lulu's credit, she had managed to pull her life together. She entered law school a few months after the divorce was finalized. Her schedule had been grueling. After going to bed at midnight, Lulu woke at 4:30 in the morning and studied until 6:00. At 6:00, she prepared a hot breakfast for the children, and then woke them. While they ate, she made their lunches. The children were dressed and out of the house no later than 7:15 every morning.

Lulu would drive Christopher to daycare at a nearby community center. After that, Lulu and Teddy would drive to the last exit before crossing the bridge which separated the east of Lake Washington from the west side. Lulu would drop Teddy off at his kindergarten class. Then Lulu would rush across the bridge to her 8:30 law class. Her classes were usually over by 3:20 in the afternoon. Lulu would make the reverse trip across the bridge; pick up Teddy and then Christopher. She would make dinner, put the children to bed, and then study.

It was remarkable. In her second year of law school, Lulu managed to spend half the morning at each of the boys' classes every week before she went to her 11:00 class. Lulu had made it through three difficult years at a top-ranked law school. She had received no honors, no Order of the Coif or Magna Cum Laude or Law Review, but she had graduated within three years, and that had been enough for Lulu. She had passed the Washington State bar on the first try, and for the past few months, Lulu was trying to make a go of a fledgling law practice. But on this

Friday evening, when there was no suitcase for the children, David's gut clenched. Lulu had come far, sacrificed much, and had worked hard. David had hoped that nothing or no one had led Lulu off track. He hoped that the events of the past few weeks did not signal a change for the worse.

He sighed. He heard the car pulling into the driveway. He opened the back door to let his live-in girlfriend, Verna, in. In doing so, he silently vowed to himself that if things were going bad with Lulu, he had to take the children from her. There was no telling, if she fell again, how far she would fall, or how long she would stay down. He could not let the children suffer. He would take the children. It might hurt the children in the interim, but they would thank him in the long run. Had he really been so in love with her years ago? David wondered as Verna got out of the car to enter the house.

ELEVEN

It was midnight. None of the women could sleep. Pamela and Michie sat on one bed with Lulu. The women had been listening to Lulu talk about what it had been like to be on television. There was a moment when the conversation had stopped. Lulu was not sure what had happened. In the absence of conversation—and during the conversation—she had noticed that her roommate had perfect white teeth, and she felt that she should remark about them. "You have really beautiful teeth," Lulu said, as she looked at Pamela.

Pamela rolled her eyes and stared at Lulu. "Don't be expecting any compliments back. Everybody here already been talking about you. They think you Phillipina." Pamela chuckled. "I said to them, why can't she be just Black? They say, 'she mixed with something.'"

"You really pretty." Michie chimed in. "I could believe you were on television."

"What?" Lulu asked and it dawned on her that Michie and Pamela didn't believe that she had been on television. "You don't believe I was on television?" She looked at Pamela and Michie's faces.

"I mean, there's no way we could prove you were on television. It's not like we can call a television station, can we? "Pamela asked.

"No." Lulu stopped.

Michie looked at Lulu, who was sitting in her freshly-washed green silk pajamas, and said, "listen, you look like you could have been on television, but you got to understand people in here tell a lot of lies. This place ain't nothing but lies. Lies you tell yourself, lies you tell your man, lies you tell to get over or out of something." Lulu was silent.

"I was on television for years. I left because I couldn't stand the trauma that I saw everyday. And by trauma, I mean people who were shot, or murdered, or children who died in fires. Then, I got pregnant with my first son, and the whole world knew I was pregnant and unmarried."

Pamela and Michie exchanged looks. They could see that Lulu was emotionally raw, and talking about real issues overwhelmed her. Michie, who was always the peacemaker, turned the topic of the conversation. "Tell us about your second date with your man. And we want details."

Lulu realized that they were giving her a pass, and began to tell them about the night Stephen Flaherty called back after their first meeting.

"When I answered the phone, about four days after I first met him, he didn't say hello or ask, 'how was your weekend?' Instead, he said, 'I will be at your house at seven.'"

"What time was it when he called?" Pamela asked.

"It was five in the afternoon."

"Kind of late, for a seven o'clock date, don't you think?" Pamela asked.

"I didn't care. My heart was pounding when I heard his voice. Four days had gone by, and I had not heard from him since that Friday when I first met him. Then he told me to wear a dress. I was surprised."

"What?"

"'Wear a dress, for me,' he said. 'I want to take you dinner. That's ok, right?'

I told him yes. At that moment, he could have asked me to a Denny's Restaurant, and I would have said yes. Then he repeated that he would be at my house at seven, and hung up the phone."

"I hope it was a special place, for you to be so excited," Pamela snickered, and made eye contact with Michie.

"I had no idea where Steven was taking me, but it didn't matter. I was going out, and I was happy. I ran to the shower. I washed and blow-dried and then put my hair in hot curlers. I put on a black gabardine dress. I wore a pearl necklace and earrings that were also a wedding present from my ex-husband."

"Is he white too?" Pamela interrupted.

"Yes, he is white."

"She got two white men!" Pamela slapped Michie on her thigh.

"That hurt!" Michie snapped.

"Well, damn. I'm sorry," Pamela said.

Lulu looked at the women. "I guess we're done with this story for now."

"No, no," Pamela insisted. "I want to hear more. Was your dress designer? Yves St. Laurent or some shit like that?" Pamela asked.

"No, but it was expensive. It was from Neiman Marcus."

"Neiman Marcus?" Michie exclaimed. "People buy shit from Neiman Marcus? I cannot step into a Neiman Marcus without them alerting security. What I want to know was if he bought you flowers, and what kind of perfume did you put on?"

"Yes. He did. I wear *Joy* perfume. You know I put perfume on my wrists and the backs of my knees." Lulu blushed as the women stared at her. "Yes, I put perfume on the backs of my knees."

"Tell it!" Pamela screamed, and Lulu laughed.

She could not remember when she had been as excited to see someone. She was dressed and waiting in front of the phone, and praying that he would not cancel the date, or say that he was going to be late. She looked at her watch: it was almost seven. She listened for the sound of a car engine. There was nothing but the patter of the rain falling on the window panes. She got up and walked into the hallway, and was about to make herself a drink when the doorbell rang, and with it her heart was beating loudly in her chest.

She waited a second, and then headed towards the door as the chime pealed again. She opened the door, and this time she knew that she looked strikingly beautiful. He too had cleaned up, with hair in place, and blazer and shirt matching his blue eyes. In his hand, he held a large bouquet of pink roses tied with a pink bow. She was once again staring, but this time Steven Flaherty was looking back at Lulu with keen new interest.

"Come in," Lulu said, as she opened the door. "Those are so gorgeous.

Such a beautiful color. And look how beautiful the presentation, not a thorn in sight. You have a very good florist."

"You look like you stepped out of a magazine. And you smell like Paris." Steven said, sniffing the air. Lulu smiled.

"Let me put these in water before we leave." Steven had not taken his eyes off of her. She felt a little uncomfortable, but she was pleased that she had aroused his interest.

"As you wish," Steven answered. His eyes followed Lulu as she walked into the kitchen to get a vase.

"I think you should put them in your bedroom," he suggested. "Flowers first thing in the morning, and last thing at night."

"I agree with you," Lulu answered. "I love flowers. The price of fresh-cut flowers of this quality are really expensive—especially roses," Lulu said, and then stopped, because she realized that she had a paying client and was technically no longer broke.

"A woman like you shouldn't have to worry about the price of flowers—or anything else, for that matter." His statement stopped Lulu in her tracks.

"That's a good philosophy, nice if you can make that happen. My coat is in the closet," Lulu continued, pointing to the closet. Steven stepped aside as Lulu opened the closet doors, and took a black cashmere coat from a wooden hanger. As she turned to put it on, Steven smoothly took it from her and helped her put it on. The touch of his hands aroused her, and she froze for a millisecond. "My purse is upstairs; I'll just be a second." Lulu smiled as she turned to walk up the stairs to the second level of the apartment.

"Your keys are lying right there on that table." Steven said, pointing to the table in foyer. "You don't need to bring your purse."

"Identification," Lulu smiled back. "I'll be just a second," she said.

"Okay," Steven said. "You might want to powder your nose," he added.

Lulu turned at looked at him.

"Yes, Counselor. I said, powder your nose."

"I'll be right back," Lulu repeated as she hurried away from the sexual tension that was rising within her. She needed a moment to calm herself.

As she walked down the stairs and down the hall to the foyer where he waited, Lulu felt like a bride walking towards her groom. Lulu smiled. It was going to be a great December, after all.

Pamela and Michie listened to the story, and had questions and comments. "So, he brought you flowers, he had a nice car, and took you to dinner. Wasn't your last husband rich? I mean, you say you are a lawyer; you can make money. Was it the coke?"

Lulu felt confronted by a question she did not know how to answer.

"No. It wasn't the coke; it was everything. The gleaming brown jaguar, the soft leather chairs, the music—everyone knew him." Lulu was flustered and confused.

"Hey, baby," Michie said. "I want to hear everything that happened. I get it. The music's playing and the champagne is flowing."

Pamela looked at Michie, and Michie stared into Pamela's eyes, and without words being said, they communicated to each other. Pamela smiled, and said, "yeah, tension. Right."

Lulu was uncomfortable in the soft, cream leather seats of the car as it sliced through the evening rain. The big engine was purring as Steven drove excessively fast over the 520 bridge which spanned Lake Washington and connected Lulu's suburb to downtown Seattle.

"Where are we going for dinner?" She asked.

"It's a surprise. Or shall I tell you, just in case I have guessed horribly wrong about you?"

"Well, I gather that we are heading towards Seattle, and that could mean anything. Don't tell me. I think I would rather be surprised."

"Fine with me," he smiled. "By the way, you look exquisite. You should really give up that profession of yours. Way too aggressive and hostile for a woman. In ten years, your face will be hard."

"Oh, really?" Lulu replied. "What do you suggest I do for a living, then?"

"Who's suggesting that you have to make a living? You know, my sister is a lawyer."

"Really?"

"Yes, she is, but she doesn't practice. It's one thing to get the training, it's another to make a living as a lawyer...there are worse ways, I suppose," Steven said.

"What does your sister do with her law degree?"

"Run the family company."

"And that's what?"

"For now," Steven said, "let's say the family makes cookies. Yes, cookies."

"That's not true. Why won't you tell me what the family business really is?"

"Because it's boring, but you'll find it interesting. I think you have a head for business and a nose for money. You'll manage to meet my sister, and go to work for the company. Then where would I be? I would be out of a girlfriend. Out of a lawyer. That is, of course, if there would ever be the slightest chance that a woman like you would be interested in a thug like myself."

Girlfriend? Lulu's heart was pounding. Did Steven Flaherty just ask her to be his girlfriend? What was happening? "I'm going to guess either the Metropolitan Grill or possibly Flemings."

"Give the girl a cigar!"

"So which is it?"

"Metropolitan Grill. I wouldn't go to Flemings without Mother. It's her favorite restaurant."

"You mention your mother a lot."

"Love-hate relationship," Steven answered. "And we should leave it at that," he said, as he pulled the car in front of the valet stand.

"Good evening, Mr. Flaherty," the valet driver said, as he reached to open the car door for Lulu while Steven threw him the keys.

"This is Mom's car, be careful or she'll get me," Steven laughed.

"I was wondering where your Lotus was," the young man asked.

"You really can't drive those things in town," Steven answered.

"That car belongs in Europe, not in Seattle traffic," Steven said over his shoulder as he steered Lulu towards the entrance of the restaurant.

"Good evening, Mr. Flaherty." The hostess smiled at Steven. "Your table is ready. Would madam like to check her coat?"

"Thank you," Lulu answered, as Steven reached for her coat.

The woman took the coat and handed it off to another woman standing nearby. The hostess picked up two menus and a wine list and said, "this way. You know John, the sommelier?" She gestured to a man who was opening a bottle of wine at a nearby table. "Can I order you a cocktail, in the meantime?"

Steven looked over at Lulu, "Will you indulge me and let me order champagne? Or is that really too corny, and you'd prefer a martini, perhaps?"

"Oh no, champagne is wonderful. I love champagne," Lulu replied.

"A wine list, then?" The hostess asked.

"Lilly, what do you think, Mums, Tattinger's, or Cristal?"

"Such difficult choices! Tattinger's works," Lulu said, as she slid into the leather mahogany booth.

"Tattinger's it shall be," the hostess said, with a professionally artificial smile.

"Steven," Lulu said, after the champagne was brought to the table, "what is this about? What do you really want from me? I feel as if I'm being played. That there's something going on, and I'm the only one who doesn't know it."

"Can't you just accept the way things are?" Steven replied.

"That just it, I don't know how things are. You came to me seeking legal representation. We smoked crack. You gave me a check from Catherine Connors."

"It cleared, didn't it?" Steven asked.

"Yes, it did clear. I talked to Catherine the other day. She seemed cold."

"Catherine is cold. Can we discuss something else besides Catherine Connors?"

"Why are you avoiding discussing her?"

"Why do you insist that she has any importance?"

"Because I believe she does. I'm not so sure I trust her..."

"Or, for that matter, me?"

"Yes, I don't know you."

"Who would you like to ask about me? Everybody in this restaurant knows me. Do you want to talk to the hostess, or the valet attendant?"

"No, I don't."

"So, what's the problem?"

"I don't know."

"Is it that nobody's been nice to you for a while? I know about your bartender boyfriend, what a loser."

"Where did you find out about him?" Lulu asked, embarrassed

that Steven knew that she had dated a waiter while she was in law school.

"He used to be a waiter before he got his job as a bar manager."

"At least it's honest work," Lulu replied.

"This conversation is going nowhere. I didn't bring you here to discuss my past or your past. Can we just have a nice time, or do you ruin everything with your questions? Put that mind of yours to better use. Read the menu. Pick an entrée, then a dessert. Honey, it's Christmastime in Emerald City. Go powder your nose," he said slipping his hand under the table to hand her a crack pipe and a packet of crack.

"In here?" Lulu asked.

"No better place for it. Upscale restaurant, they'll think you smoked a cigar. There's a woman's lounge here. You're not afraid, are you?"

"No, I just wonder if it's wise," Lulu replied.

"No, it's not wise, Counselor, but it could be fun. Remember to add the word 'fun' to your vocabulary."

"Okay, I'll do it."

"Don't let me force you."

"You're not. You're right. I'm not used to all of this. I guess I'm a little out of my element."

"No, you're not. This is where you belong. Now, hurry back. I'm ordering an appetizer."

"All right," Lulu laughed, and the rainy Seattle evening suddenly grew warm.

By the time dinner was over, Lulu was falling in love with Steven Flaherty. He was a handsome man who told funny jokes, and whose laughter was infectious. He gave everybody big tips. When the car was brought around, Steven gave the valet driver a twenty-dollar bill. The young man turned towards a cabinet of keys, and busied himself while Steven and Lulu sat in the car and Steve relit the crack pipe. He passed Lulu the pipe, and then put another rock in the pipe and inhaled deeply. When the piece of crack had turned to ashes, Steven put the pipe in the glove compartment, saying, "don't want to burn a hole in my pocket with that hot pipe." He started the car, and drove back across the bridge to Bellevue.

"Do you mind if I don't come up? I have an early meeting tomorrow, but I will call you later."

"The children come back tomorrow," Lulu said, disappointed.

"I know. Your children told me their schedule when I met them the night that we were with Catherine's children. That's why I picked Friday night, silly."

"What do you mean?"

"I knew your children were gone for the weekend. Your older son, smart kid. He told me his entire schedule."

"I did not know that." Lulu answered, her voice flat with disappointment and distrust.

"Lovely children." Steven said, as he unbuckled his seat belt and got out of the car to open Lulu's door.

"Thank you. Good night, I had a great time."

"So did I," Steven said, and kissed Lulu's hand. He stood by the car, and watched Lulu walk up the stairs to her apartment and unlock the door. When she had unlocked the door, she turned and waved. Steven waved back, and got into the car and drove away.

As Lulu finished telling the women the story, she was sad. She looked at the women, as if to ask whether they had any questions or comments.

"Damn!" Pamela said. "That can't be all that happened!"

"But that was it," Lulu said.

"He's not homo or nothing, is he?" Pamela asked.

"No, he's not," Lulu answered.

"Then what? He couldn't do it because of the crack?"

"Yeah, that could be it," Michie said.

"No, it wasn't," Lulu cut in.

"No! But, of course, another woman?" Michie slyly suggested.

"No, hold up. You can't be for real, can you? Couldn't you see that he was just playing you? Guys say shit like that all the time," Pamela interjected.

"No. I thought he was serious. Why was he asking me out in the first place? You see, lawyers are not supposed to be going out with their clients." Lulu looked at the women's faces. "It's just a rule. You know, it's meant to protect the clients, not the lawyers. Never mind, but no, I believed him."

"So why didn't you just ask him whether he was serious?" Michie asked.

"I don't know," Lulu replied. "The moment was magical. We were driving in this beautiful car to a mystery dinner date."

Both women looked disgusted. They were dumbstruck by Lulu's answers, and her next statement made absolutely no sense.

"I think I was intoxicated in some way. He was also driving recklessly. Or, at least, I thought it was reckless. I'm tired. I'm going to go to bed now."

"Sure," Pamela and Michie said. "We're going to go to the cafeteria and maybe have a smoke."

"All right," Lulu said, turning off her lamp as she watched the women leave the room. After they left, Lulu turned her face into her pillow and wept.

TWELVE

She woke up in the wee hours of the morning. Her heart was pounding and her chest and shoulders were heaving. The green silk pajamas that had been washed earlier in the day were soaked with sweat; her hair was plastered to her head and face. She looked around. Where was she?

From the bed a few feet away, Pamela was snoring. She was not home. She was in treatment. She had had the same dreams many times before. In fact, the last time she had had this re-occurring nightmare was the Friday after Thanksgiving, just two months ago, and Lulu remembered what now seemed like a lifetime ago.

She had spent Thanksgiving with her children: eight-year-old Teddy and six-year-old Christopher. She was the guest of her law school benefactor, Janine Zimmerman, and a group of Democratic benefactors who were still celebrating President Clinton's re-election.

That morning, like many before, she had bolted upright from a nightmare. To calm herself, she focused on the colors of a pale sun as it broke through the blackness of the November dawn. She was awake, and knew that she would not be able to go back to sleep. She never could. It was just as well; there was always work to be done.

That morning, she got out of bed and went into her bathroom, in which her benefactor had mirrored the entire room. The result was that Lulu's every move was reflected multiple times, and this annoyed and disoriented her. She opened a medicine cabinet, selected a bottle from which she took a pill, and swallowed it without water. She turned and walked to a walk-in closet where she peeled off her soaked nightclothes. She was shaking. She hugged herself, and waited for the anti-anxiety medication to kick in.

There was no walk-in closet and no mirrored bathroom at the rehab center. She looked around and realized that Pamela was in a deep sleep. She got out of bed, took off her pajamas, and put on a pair of pants and a t-shirt. She was cold. She knew what the dream signified. She had spent hours analyzing it with therapists.

The dream was a metaphor within a metaphor, and all of the elements of the dream had actually occurred, but not in the frenzied sequence of her dream. The dream was about her pregnancies—one that had been terminated on her fourteenth birthday day, and the unplanned pregnancy with her son Teddy when she was at the height of her television career. Her television colleagues had advised her to get an abortion. Her friends had told her that her television career would be over if she didn't. She had reluctantly scheduled an abortion. In those days, there had been a week-long waiting period before a doctor would perform the abortion.

She had always been disciplined about exercise, and being pregnant did not change that fact. During that week before the abortion, she ran her daily five miles that took her through a lower income neighborhood before she headed back to her luxury apartment on Delaware Street. One day, there was a pile of garbage sitting outside of a home. Someone had been evicted. Sitting on a pile of old mattresses and broken furniture was a pair of abandoned kittens. The bad end that someone's life had come to touched her. She was going to run past the pile when one of the kittens mewed at her. She stopped. The kittens were tiny, perhaps a day old. She walked over to the wet mattresses and picked up one of the kittens, who was orange-striped, and saw that its eyes were infected. The other kitten was gray, and its eyes were shut. Both of the kittens were crawling with fleas. She could not leave the kittens to what might be a sudden death by a dog or being run over by a car. She had to take them to an animal shelter. But as she walked back to her apartment, holding both crying kittens, she realized that taking them to a shelter would only prolong the kittens' lives for a few days. Then, as she walked home, she realized that she was going to throw her unborn fetus into the human garbage pile. She couldn't do it. So, she kept the kittens, and decided to keep her child, and vowed to take whatever the consequences would be for being un-married, black, and on television.

Now, as she sat on her twin bed in the treatment center, tears rolled down her face. Her children. They had gone through so much. Now they were so far away from her. The last time she had had that dream, she had walked down the stairs from her bedroom into the main level of the apartment.

Three doors faced her. The first door was where her children slept. Inside the bedroom, the gray light of early morning was bright enough for her to make out the white metal bunk bed where her children were sleeping. On the lower bunk, Teddy was sleeping with his arms around an old teddy bear dressed in a yellow rain coat and boots. Christopher was sleeping with a tiny blue whale next to his face.

She had tiptoed closer to the bunk beds, and stared as the blankets covering each child gently rose and fell in the rhythm of their untroubled sleep. In the silence of their peace, she became calm. She watched for a few more minutes, and then quietly tip-toed out of the room and down the hall to the next closed door that was her office.

She had hesitated for a few seconds before opening the door. She could not enter her office feeling vulnerable. She had to become a warrior, someone willing to destroy the opponent, and she had to be sure she was ready to make the transformation. She flipped on the light, and saw the simple glass desk upon which a phone and a computer sat. Stacks of law books stood as high as the computer, and another stack lay under the desk. An ergonomic black mesh chair was pushed under the desk.

She had entered the room, and sat in the chair before the darkened computer screen, waiting for it to slowly start up. She flipped through a yellow legal pad and checked a citation from an opened legal textbook. When the computer came to life, she entered her password, and the screen opened to a legal case she had downloaded the night before.

She actually loved writing briefs and researching the law. She was like a detective, seeking facts that would allow her client to achieve whatever had brought them to a lawyer. There were days where she lost track of time when working. Sometimes she wished she could stay in the world of legal research forever.

As she sat on her bed at the treatment center, she wondered if she would ever practice law again. She buried the thought, and lay back on her twin bed. But still, the images of that past Thanksgiving weekend ran through her head. Later that Friday morning, she had received a call from a friend of her benefactor. The piercing ring of the phone had shattered her concentration. It had been barely eight in the morning. She did not have any clients; she had only been admitted to practice in Washington State a month earlier. She wondered who could be calling so early; after all, it was the Friday after Thanksgiving. The phone rang again, and she quickly grabbed the receiver, hoping that the loud ring had not awakened her children.

"Lulu St. Blanc, may I help you?" was how she answered her phone.

"Is this the St. Blanc law firm?" a woman's voice had tentatively inquired. The wealthy female client had wanted to meet with her that day to discuss her case. Lulu felt obliged to meet with the woman who, if Lulu had gotten a retainer, could help her out of the deep financial hole she had found herself. But then she saw her sleepy-eyed children standing at the entrance of her office. She put a finger to her lips. The boys groggily nodded, turned around, and went into their room.

On the other end of the phone conversation, Ms. Winters—that was the woman's last name—continued relating a series of events that Lulu could barely follow or comprehend. She had allowed the woman to continue for almost a minute and then interrupted her with, "That was an incredibly aggressive and possibly illegal act on the part of the hospital. It sounds as if this situation has been going on for some time. We should probably meet, if you'd like to discuss it further." She paused and said a silent prayer. She was more than three months behind on the rent, and, but for her gracious landlord and benefactor, Janine Zimmerman, the children and Lulu would have been evicted. Although she desperately needed money, she had planned a day with her children, and that wasn't going to happen, because the woman wanted to meet that day.

When she got off the phone, she went into the boy's room and told them about the change in the plans for the day.

"Mommy, you said we could watch a video this morning. We just started it." Teddy's face turned red. He just wanted to be with his mother, who never seemed to have time. "You promised," Teddy shouted. "You promised. You always work. That's what you do. You don't care about us. You never do anything with us. I don't know why you even had us born." Tears streamed down Teddy's face as he threw himself on his bunk bed.

She felt bad. Her children had put up with her ugly divorce from their father, and then had their schedules dictated by Lulu's law school schedule. "Oh, Teddy, stop, please stop. I didn't plan this."

"You could have told the person no, that we had plans," Christopher, her younger son, said as he ran to join his brother.

Lulu did not know how to respond. She was overwhelmed. Her first resort was anger. She marched into the children's room and turned off the video machine. Both children began to cry.

"Just stop it!" she screamed.

"No!" Christopher yelled back. "You broke a promise!"

She had moved quickly towards Christopher and slapped him hard on his derriere. "Get into the bathroom and change your pajamas!" she had yelled. Christopher's mouth was open wide, but no sound came out of his mouth. His face was red as he ran to the bathroom. His hand was on his bottom where Lulu had struck him. Tears streamed down his face.

"Oh, shit." She had muttered to herself. On the bed, Teddy had curled himself up into a ball of fear. He was scared of Lulu. All she said was, "pick up those Legos off the floor."

"Yes, Mommy," he said quietly, as he uncurled his body to get off the bed.

Lulu was crying as she remembered the story. She remembered looking into the bathroom. Christopher was taking off his pajama bottoms and he was running the bath water. She saw the red hand mark on his bottom, and she cringed. She moved towards him and Christopher moved away. "What have I done?" She opened her mouth and croaked, "I'm sorry, honey."

"I know you are, Mommy," Christopher said.

In her bed in rehab, Lulu was weeping into her hands to try to muffle the sound of her tears as she recalled the memory.

THIRTEEN

Lulu could not go back to sleep after her she was awakened by her nightmare. She lay awake in her twin bed in her room in rehab, and stared out of the tiny window where she could see the stars in the blackness of the night of the mountain town of Yakima, Washington. The fog in her head became denser, as both the prescription and street drugs detoxed from her body. She was anxious and depressed. She wished that the treatment center had not taken away her prescription medication. But the policy of the center was no drugs, prescription or otherwise. She couldn't eat, either, because she was too anxious. Her time with her therapist, Terry Berkquist, became the highlight and a haven for Lulu, and a place to disclose the facts that had railroaded her life.

That afternoon, Lulu sat outside of Terry's office and waited for the current patient before her to leave.

Then, she entered Terry's office and sat down glumly in a chair. Terry noticed that Lulu wore no jewelry, and that a sweatshirt had replaced her silk blouse. She was wearing a pair of tennis shoes and a pair of slacks. "Good afternoon, Lilly. Is there anything that you would like to talk about today?" Terry asked.

"Nope," Lulu replied.

"Okay. Why don't you begin with your first memories of childhood?

What do you remember and associate with your childhood?" Terry asked.

Lulu was slow to respond. Finally, she said, "you ask me to recall my earliest memory; I will tell you what it is. I am sitting in an upstairs room, which is empty of all furniture except for toys scattered across a dark wood floor. My eyes are red and swollen from crying and the tears have dried on my face, leaving it sticky. I am living with my grandparents and a sibling, and a couple of cousins. I am in the country where I was born, which is an island on the Sea of Cortez.

The day is hot and humid, as it is on most days. The island is on the equator. My hair is damp from the heat of the afternoon, and from the heat of my temper tantrum. It has been hours."

"Were you being punished?"

"No. My grandmother was trying to wait out one of my tantrums."

"Do you recall what you were upset about?"

"It was about taking a shrimp out of my toy refrigerator."

"Did it have electricity? I don't understand the context," Terry said.

"My mother, Octavia, had sent the toy refrigerator to me as a present. I had asked my grandmother for a shrimp to put in my toy refrigerator. I wanted to keep the shrimp in the refrigerator. The shrimp began to rot and smell after a couple of days. I don't know why I wanted to keep the rotting shrimp in the toy refrigerator. My grandmother had hired a woman to clean and wash the clothes. The cleaning woman wanted to take the shrimp out of the refrigerator, and I wouldn't let her do it."

"So what did you do?" Terry asked.

"Well, I bit the woman. She complained to my grandmother. I think the woman thought my grandmother would punish me."

"Did she?" Terry asked.

"No," Lulu answered.

"Then what happened?" Terry asked.

"I could hear my grandmother talking to the cleaning woman. She said, 'I'm sorry that my granddaughter bit you.' Then the woman started to say something about me, but she hesitated because she didn't know how to say I was crazy." Lulu choked on the word crazy, but then continued. "But my grandmother finished the sentence for her." Tears streamed down Lulu's face. She gathered herself, and then repeated to Terry what she remembered her grandmother saying. "My grandmother said, 'I know.'" Lulu broke down again, but fought the tears, and continued telling Terry what her grandmother had said about her.

"'I know,' my grandmother said. 'She never speaks. She only cries. She won't wear shoes or socks. She refuses to bathe. She will only eat three or four things.' Then my grandmother said to the cleaning woman, 'she was born early, premature. Her mother did not want her. My daughter-in-law tried to abort the child. Then, when the child was about six months old, her mother almost drowned her. Her aunt saved her.' The last thing I heard my grandmother say was, 'she's troubled.'"

Lulu cried silently, and then Terry asked, "as you recall this memory Lilly, how does it make you feel?"

"You mean, besides sad?"

"Any emotions, anything you care to say or comment about," Terry added.

"Well, from that moment on, I always felt that there was something wrong with me, and that I was unwanted and unloved by my mother."

"Do you still feel this way about your mother?" Terry asked.

"Yes," Lulu said, and pursed her lips.

"Do you have anything else to say? Are there other memories from your childhood?"

"One of my therapists says, if I have recollections from my early childhood, that I can consider them to be true."

"The point is *if* you believe these memories to be true. I want to hear about it," Terry said.

"Okay." Lulu paused, and then said, "I have this memory of being under my blankets or bed sheets. I think they were crocheted, or embossed with pink and white bunny rabbits. I am pretending to be sleeping. I am waiting for my grandmother, who I call Mommy Celestine, to wake me up by kissing the top of my head. I like to hide and observe others. I do not want to play with other children. I really don't want anyone to come near me but my grandmother, Mommy Celestine."

"Why only your grandmother, and where is your mother?"

"My mother was in the United States, in Washington D.C., getting pregnant with her American-born child."

"So your grandmother raised you?" Terry asked, ignoring Lulu's sarcasm.

"Pretty much, until I was five. Then I—we—came to America, and I met my lovely mother."

"You say that with such sarcasm, Lilly."

"Do I, Terry? I think it's more dislike, or hatred, or disgust. I don't want to play the 'abandoned child' card, but my mother did abandon me for the first five years of my life. She was a stranger to me. I was a little child, and she was mean to me!"

"What did your mother do to you, Lilly?"

Lulu was silent, then said, "it's really in the past, and you have to understand my mother's actions in context. The first thing that you should know is, for the first few years of my life, I rarely spoke. My grandmother had taken me to a speech therapist, but there was nothing wrong with my vocal cords because I cried a lot, but refused to speak. The doctor recommended reading to me. Still, after months of reading aloud to me, I remained silent and watchful. One night, as my grandmother was reading a story to me, she must have fallen asleep. I woke her up because I wanted to hear more of the story. So she knew I could talk, I just chose not to. Then, from that point on I would speak only to my grandmother; to everyone else I simply said, 'no.'"

"Did you refuse to talk to your siblings, and children with whom you played or went to school with?" Terry asked.

"I don't remember any other children but my siblings and cousins. I don't really remember my siblings, or any of my relatives except for my grandparents." Lulu shrugged her shoulders.

"Go on," Terry nodded.

"Everything was difficult for me. I only ate fruit and ice cream. There were entire days when I refused to eat. I didn't like to bathe. Washing my hair was more of a complex matter. I didn't like to wear socks or shoes. I always had a stuffy nose or allergies. I was a difficult child, I guess," Lulu finished.

"So your grandmother tolerated your bad behavior as a child?" Terry asked.

"I don't know whether it was 'bad' behavior or not," Lulu replied.

"Fair enough, let's move on," Terry said.

"I guess she just accepted, or felt that she had to protect me. All of that changed when we left the island to come to America."

"And how did it affect you when your family came to America?"

"I did not like the man, Cordell II, who said he was my father. I did not like the woman, Octavia, who said that she was my mother. To me, Celestine was my real mother, and Cordell, my grandfather, was my father. My parents were strangers, and they were mean. Also, I had a baby sister named Dahlia, who demanded everyone's attention. I was the one who had once demanded everyone's attention and got it. Now, I was one of five children, two of which were babies."

"When I met my parents for the first time, my grandparents and my siblings and I had been traveling for twenty four hours. I was sick, and dehydrated from vomiting. I was in no mood to be friendly. My father and my Aunt Verna came to pick us up in two cars. We then drove to Washington D.C., to a neighborhood that was transitioning from a working-class Jewish neighborhood to a middle-class black neighborhood. The neighborhood was eclectic; blacks and non-blacks lived and played together."

"During my first hours in the strange house, owned by an aunt that I had never met, I announced that I was hungry, and that I wanted ice cream. When my grandmother told me there was no ice cream, I started to cry. The more my grandmother tried to calm me, the more I cried. I guess my mother had enough of my crying, and she suddenly grabbed my wrist and dragged me down a dark hallway. At the end of the hallway there were two doors, one led into the kitchen, and the other led downstairs into a basement. My mother opened the door to the basement. She pushed me through the door. She took my face in her hands, and then slapped it. 'Be quiet. You will learn some manners,' she hissed through compressed lips. She shoved my face to the wall. Then she turned off the light, shut the door, and then locked it. I began to cry, but my mother walked away. Why my grandmother did not come and get me is understandable now, but back then, I was terrified. I don't remember how long I stood on the top of the stairs with the light turned off, but I could hear the voice of the man who had married my father's sister. He told everyone to come into the kitchen and eat. I heard laughter, and my mother say something to one of my sisters. That was my first meeting with my mother."

"Did things get better?" Terry inquired.

"No," Lulu answered. "In fact, things got worse, but we're probably out of time."

"We are out of time."

"All right. More tomorrow at the same time?"

"Yes," Terry answered, and watched her client walk out of her office.

FOURTEEN

When Lulu was walking back to her room to change for gym—gym was required almost every day, although it could consist of merely one person showing up at the gym—she saw Pamela and Michie.

"You are not going to gym, are you?"

"I'm afraid so," Lulu replied. "Why?"

"We hate gym."

"We hate exercise," Pamela added.

"I'm going," Lulu said.

"Come with us," Michie coaxed. "We are going to smoke."

"Smoke what?" Lulu asked, suddenly tense and on guard.

"Don't worry, Counselor. Just cigarettes."

"Oh," Lulu said. "I don't smoke."

"Yeesh," Michie said. "We just wanted you to hang out with us."

"I can't. I'm sorry," Lulu said.

"You have twenty minutes before you have to be there," Pamela added.

"Why do you want to hang out with me?" Lulu asked suspiciously.

"Well, for one thing, you a lawyer. Two, nobody here come from where you do. Three, you never finished telling us how you got with that man."

Lulu laughed. "Michie, you missed your calling. I've never met a more persuasive person than you. What do you want to hear?"

"I want to hear about your husband," Pamela said.

"I definitely don't want to talk about him," Lulu said.

"Okay, I want to hear about your date with your man and how it ended. I don't mean dinner and shit. What happened next? I want the real stuff!"

"Ok,ay" Lulu said. I will tell you about what happened after our date: nothing."

"No," Michie wailed. "Y'all had to get together at some point."

"She ain't' gonna tell us about that," Pamela sneered.

"There's nothing to tell," Lulu countered.

"Okay, okay," Michie said. "Tell us about the next date."

"Will you go outside with us while we smoke?" Pam asked.

"Okay," Lulu said, and the three walked to the picnic tables outside in the common area near the gym. And Lulu began telling the women about the next time she met with Steven Flaherty.

After the dinner of champagne and cocaine, the next few days dragged by. The children were with their father, and Lulu took the opportunity to do as much work as she could. She relaxed a little, made herself dinner, and went to bed early. Then, all too soon, the boys were home. It was Friday night. There was dinner to be made, groceries to be bought, and two loud and happy children. Lulu was glad to see them. She was happy to spend time with them instead of watching the clock and waiting for Steven Flaherty to call her.

The children had awoken early as usual, and Lulu was awake before they were. She made them breakfast, and they were planning what to do, when the phone rang. It was Steven Flaherty finally calling, four days later.

Lulu grabbed the phone and answered, not knowing who it was, but hoping with all of her heart that it was Steven.

"Do you have a Christmas tree?" He had asked.

"No. We usually buy our tree a week before Christmas. I don't know why. I am not one of those people who puts a tree up as soon as the turkey is off the table." She frowned as she said the words. Just where had that twist of language come from? she asked herself.

The boys had stood and listened to her talk about a Christmas tree, and they were happy when she got off the phone.

"Was that Daddy?" Christopher asked.

"Nope," Lulu replied, with a smile on her face.

"Are we getting a tree?" Teddy asked.

"Yes," Lulu said, and the boys jumped up and down until Lulu quieted them down.

"He will be here at noon," Lulu said. "So, clean faces, clean clothes, and clean rooms," she yelled, as the boys ran to their rooms to do what their mother had asked. Lulu was close behind them as she ran up the stairs into her walk-in closet. She scanned the suits and the dresses, and chose dark blue jeans and a crisp white shirt. She smiled to herself as she changed from her green sweat pants into the jeans. She was happy. Steven Flaherty was coming to take her and boys out to buy a Christmas tree. She was delighted.

The boys heard the car in the parking lot, and ran to the window. "He's here, Mommy!" They sang out. Lulu looked out the window and could see the gleaming brown Jaguar. Either his mother had another car, or she rarely drove the one Steven was driving.

The boys had been eating snacks because Steven was arriving at noon, and Lulu wanted to make sure the children were not hungry while choosing the tree. She was nervous as the boys hurried to the hall closet to get their coats. Lulu helped each of them, and they bounded out the door and down the steps. Lulu barely had time to grab her black coat and her hand bag before the boys were almost down the stairs. She stood at the top of the stairs and locked the door. To her surprise, the boys had met Steven and knew his name, and treated him like a long-lost friend.

"Did you guys ever finish seeing that Mummy movie?" Steven asked.

"No, we fell asleep, and Mom doesn't have cable, so we can't see it unless we go back over to your house."

Lulu slowly descended the stairs and hoped that her mouth was not open in surprise. She heard Teddy clearly say that they were at Steven's house. Steven had not corrected Teddy, and Lulu was immediately suspicious and on guard.

"All right, gentleman," Steven said, addressing the boys. "Everybody under the age of twelve needs to sit in the back seat." The children laughed, and Teddy helped Christopher fasten his seat belt. It was then that Steven turned his attention to Lulu. "You look great in jeans." He inhaled my fragrance. "*Joy?*"

"Yes," she said. "An expert of perfumes, as well?" Lulu replied in a somewhat rude way, as Steven opened the car door for her.

"How about of beautiful women?" Steven replied. The statement was supposed to be a compliment, but it sent a shiver of fear up Lulu's spine. It was like high school all over again. Steven was the nice boy who danced with her at cotillion because his mother had ordered him to. Lulu's head began racing.

Steven probably did know lots of beautiful women, Lulu thought to herself. She was probably one of a long list of women that Steven Flaherty squired about town in his mother's car. She silently scolded herself, and told herself to stop fantasizing about Steven Flaherty. He was a client who was being nice. He had no romantic interest in her. He was being nice to a woman with two kids with limited funds. Steven Flaherty was probably romantically interested in his "friend" Catherine Connors, and her big house in the hills. *Put your dreams away*, Lulu warned herself. This man was not going to be a boyfriend. She forced a smile. "Where are we going?" she asked Steven. "And thank you for being so generous to me and my children."

"To a little farm," Steven said. "It's a bit out of the way, but I think that your kids will like it. I used to like it when I was a youngster," he added.

"This is someplace that you used to go as a child?" She asked.

"Steven turned to Lulu and said, "shush, don't tell anybody, but my family owns the piece of dirt that the trees are on." Then he smiled, started the car, and expertly turned around and headed north to what might be considered a more rural part of the Eastside. In about twenty minutes, they arrived at what looked like a classic country farm. There was a hay wagon with a horse next to a small wooden building. A cider pot was boiling on a table on the front porch, and candy canes and Christmas lights wrapped the building. There was the smell of pine and hot chocolate in the air.

"This place is great," Lulu said, taken in by the charm of the little building.

"Yeah!" The children yelled from the back seat.

"Can we get out?" Teddy asked.

"Can we get a ride in the wagon?" Christopher asked.

"Yes, and yes," Steven laughed as the boys unbuckled their seat belts and ran from the car.

"Come on, Mom," they cried.

"I'll be right there," Lulu said, as she unbuckled her seat belt.

"Hey, Mr. Flaherty," an old man said, as he and an old woman came out of the building.

"Francis, Lizzy," Steven said. "You're both looking great!" Steven smiled.

"We haven't seen you for a month of Sundays," the old white-haired woman said. "Saw your sister and your mother here a week or two ago. Cutting trees for the charities, you know. Your mother was always good about that. Still is. Good to see you."

"Mom's great, yes she is," Steven said.

"Who are these young fellas?" the old man asked. "These aren't your kids, are they?"

"No," Steven said, "but I wish they were. Here's their mother, Lilly St. Blanc."

"How do you do, miss?" the older couple asked, each taking one of her hands within one of theirs.

"I'm fine. This is great. Are you here year-round?" Lulu asked.

The old couple looked at each other. "No, we're only here from October to a week or so before Christmas. The tree business is short."

"Oh, I see," Lulu said. "What do you do the rest of year?"

Once again, the couple looked as if Lulu were asking them if they were from Mars. "We work for the Flaherty family."

"Oh," Lulu replied, as if she knew what their statement meant.

"I told her we made cookies," Steven said.

"Aye, you're a wicked one, Steven Flaherty," the old woman said.

"Speaking of cookies, I've got gingerbread men and women, you know. Ms. Colleen said we should make them both, now that the times have changed. Do your children want some cider and cookies, miss?" the woman asked.

"Yes, yes," the boys answered, without bothering to get permission from Lulu.

"Can we ride in the wagon?" Teddy asked the old man.

"Sure you can, if it's all right with your mother," the man answered.

"I guess it's all okay," Lulu replied realizing that the scene was out of her control, and that Steven Flaherty had managed to take control and make everyone happy. Yet, a trickle of anxiety ran through Lulu's heart. She was missing something that was important, but she couldn't fit the pieces together. There was too much going on.

"It's fine with me," Steven said. "I haven't had one of Lizzy's gingerbread cookies in…"

"Five years. It's been five years, Mr. Flaherty. Five years," the old woman sadly repeated.

"Now, now, Lizzy don't be making your Irish eyes a-crying," Steven said mimicking the elder couple's Irish accents.

"Don't you go making fun of me, Steven Flaherty, I can still whip your bottom at any time," the old woman said.

"Francis, boys," Steven laughed. "Save me from old mother Lizzy here," he said as he wrapped his arms around the old woman.

"Come, children, come have some cider. And, miss, it will do you no good, but this Steven Flaherty is one to watch. I've been knowing this lad since he was wee tall, smaller than your lads. So, I'm warning you. He has the charm of a snake, that Mr. Steven does. Beware, miss, he can charm the best of us," she said. The old woman had turned from Lulu and began to address the boys. "Now, do you want a boy gingerbread boy or girl gingerbread?" she asked. "Shall you have one of each?" she asked, before the children could answer.

"We'll take one of each, unless you need to save some," Teddy answered, for himself and his brother.

"We've got plenty," the old woman replied.

Lulu was left standing with Steven and the old man. "Getting a tree for the lads?" the old man asked.

"Yes," Steven said and slipped his hands into his pockets and pulled out a bill and handed it to the old man.

"That won't be necessary, Mr. Steven," the old man said.

"It's for Christmas," Steven said and pressed the unseen bill into the old man's hand.

"Thank you, Mr. Flaherty. I'll go check on Betsy," he said, referring to the horse attached to the wagon.

"How's the old girl doing?" Steve asked.

"Not much life left in her, but she's good with the kids. You know, your mother brings down lots of children from the different homes and societies, and the children love old Betsy. The rest of the year she sleeps in the barn and eats hay, but she's been a good pet, right, Mr. Steven?"

"Yes," Steven said. "We have a good retirement plan for horses."

"Aye, that's true," the old man said.

"Who are these people?" Lulu asked Steven, when the old man was out of earshot.

"People who've worked for my family for years."

"I gathered that much, but in what capacity?"

"Nosy, aren't you?" Steven said.

"Well, they alternate between calling you Mr. Steven and Mr. Flaherty as if they can't decide what to call you."

"The driver and the house keeper," Steven said, as if the subject were bitter to him. "Let's see what old Lizzy is feeding your kids," Steven said, walking to where the old woman and the boys were standing. "I see you're up to your old tricks, Lizzy," Steven said. "Got any soft gingerbread?"

"Of course, I do. Your father, God rest his soul, loved my Christmas gingerbread. I always make a batch and think of your father," the woman said, going into the little wooden building. She came back out with two pieces of gingerbread and two shots of Irish whiskey. "Here's something to keep you warm, miss," the woman said, offering Lulu the shot glass.

"Why, thanks," Lulu said, and sipped the whiskey from the shot glass. She felt the whiskey immediately in her head and in her stomach.

"What kind of lass is this that sips her whiskey from a shot glass?" the old woman asked.

"A gentile woman," Steven said, and turned to the boys. "Drink up, boys, we're going in the wagon with Betsy to find the best Christmas tree in Seattle." The boys, their mouths full of gingerbread cookies, nodded their heads, and headed towards the wagon.

When the children had settled on an eighteen-foot noble fir, Steven laughed, and told them that they could certainly have that tree, but he would have to cut off about four feet off it in order for it to fit in the living room. Then he helped the children pick out a tree that would just barely scrape the ceiling of the apartment. He took the saw that was in the wagon and cut the tree down. With the old man's help, they loaded the tree on the wagon, and then to the car. Soon, the tree was tied to the top of the car, and Steven and Lulu and her children were saying goodbye to the elderly couple.

"Don't let it be so long," the old woman said.

"I won't," Steven said, and turned the car out of the tree farm. "This entire tree cutting has made me hungry and thirsty."

"Me too! Me too!" chorused Lulu's children.

"They can't be hungry," Lulu said to Steven. "We had a snack right before we left."

"But Mommy, I am hungry," Christopher said.

"Me too," Teddy echoed.

Steven looked over at Lulu and said, "three against one. That settles it for me. What do you say to burgers and fries and hot chocolate?"

"Yeah, burgers and fries and hot chocolate," the children sang out from the back seat.

The rest of the car ride to Bellevue proper was mostly silly dialogue between Steven and the boys. In about ten minutes, Steven pulled into a Red Robin restaurant. He was heartily welcomed, and he and Lulu and her children were seated at a round table near a roaring fireplace. The orders were taken, big mugs of hot chocolate with mounds of whip cream were placed in front of each of them, and were followed by burgers surrounded by fries. Lulu shook her head as the plates and the mugs went by, but said nothing. She sipped her hot chocolate and nibbled at a French fry or two; she didn't want to look as if she were hungry and in need of a meal.

The chatter between Steven and the boys continued, but during a moment of quiet, Steven turned to Lulu and said, "I hope I haven't ruined their dietary plans for the day."

"Of course not," Lulu answered. "They are such good children. They have marched like little soldiers over the past three years since I was in law school. We have not had an easy time. We have been up at six, out the door at seven. Of course, there has not been a lot of money. But let me stop. I'm ruining the festive mood here." From the look on Steven's face, she could see that she was ruining his mood. He had no response to what she had said, so he reached under the table and squeezed Lulu's hand.

"Anything else, fellas?" He asked the boys.

"No, we're full." Teddy replied. "Aren't we, Christopher?" Teddy asked his younger brother.

"Yes, I'm stuffed up to here," Christopher said, raising his hands to the level of his eyebrows.

"Good," Steven said. "Do you boys know how to ski?" Steven asked. The children shook their heads in unison.

"How about snowboarding?"

Again, they shook their heads.

"All right, tobogganing? Everybody's been tobogganing before."

"We haven't," said Teddy.

"That's true," confirmed Christopher.

"We will tomorrow, if it's okay with your mother. I say we send her off to buy some Christmas decorations to add to that tree we bought today and we go tobogganing. Then we can all decorate the tree. What d'you say, Mom?"

"Yes, Mommy, say we can go," Teddy asked.

"Yes, Mommy, let us go," echoed Christopher.

"Once again, three to one. I guess I lose," Lulu said. "Of course you can go tobogganing with Mr. Flaherty."

"He said we can call him Steven," Christopher said.

"You may call him Mr. Flaherty."

"Yes, Mommy," both boys replied.

"Perhaps you were not as gracious a loser as I thought," Steven commented. Lulu did not respond. In the absence of a reply, Steven said, "let's round up that waitress and make tracks out of here and get you home before your mother puts me in time out." The boys looked at each other and giggled.

As the four walked back to the car, when Steven opened the door for Lulu, he slipped two crisp one hundred dollar bills into her hand. "For the decorations," he said, as Lulu slid in the front seat and slipped the money into her coat pocket.

As Lulu recalled and told Pamela and Michie about the day buying the Christmas tree, Pamela interjected, "now that's what I'm talking about," and high-fived Michie. The women stopped when they saw the look on Lulu's face. "What?" Pamela asked.

"I was bothered by the fact that Steven had given me money. I was wondering whether I should return it. Would that be ungracious? Did I look cheap by taking the money?"

"Girl, are you crazy?" Pamela said. "Some man give me some money, and I'm wondering whether I should give it back? Girl, you crazy."

"And didn't you say you was broke, you told him a few minutes before that money was tight?" Michie added.

"All that was true. But, I don't know, the money made me uncomfortable."

"So you gave it back to him?" Pamela asked.

"I tried to," Lulu answered, and her face grew hot as she recalled the scene which had occurred just a few weeks ago.

As they neared the exit to where Lulu and the children lived, Lulu had decided that she would give the money back to Steven. When they arrived at the apartment, Lulu gave Teddy the keys so that he could let himself and Christopher into the apartment. The children did as they were told, but they looked at Steven, and Christopher asked, "we'll see you tomorrow, right?"

"Yes and yes," Steven answered. "Now, you boys do what your mother said, and I will see you tomorrow afternoon, about noon?" he said, looking at Lulu, who nodded. "Then it's a date."

"Yeah," the boys shouted, as they ran towards the stairs leading to the apartment.

"They are great kids," Steven said, as he watched the children run up the stairs.

"You are spoiling them," Lulu said. "I can't take this money for decorations," Lulu blurted, reaching into her coat pocket for the money.

"Why not?" Steven asked. "It's Christmas. You're a single mother. I'm a rich guy who has lived off a trust fund since I was a teenager, and you look like you haven't had any fun since you were a teenager," Steven finished.

"Absolutely untrue," Lulu replied. "I had lots of fun this past Tuesday. I drank champagne."

"Yes, I forgot about that," Steven joked. "Well, let's say except for that one moment in time this week. Take the money. It means nothing to me. I'm sure you'll buy great decorations."

"All right," Lulu hesitated. She reached to open the car door, and Steven reached across and put his hand on hers.

"Let me get that," he said. The touch of his hand on Lulu's sent a wave of electricity through her. She looked into his eyes and saw that Steven felt it as well. Steven removed his hand, and, in a deft move, unlatched his seat belt and swung out of the car to open Lulu's door. She stood still for a moment, expecting to be kissed, but Steven merely opened the door, squeezed her hand for a moment, and said, "let me cut the ropes and carry the tree upstairs for you."

"Can I get you a knife?" Lulu stammered, embarrassed that she had not been kissed.

"No, I have my Swiss army knife right here," Steven said, as he took the knife out of his pocket and began to cut the cord that held the tree.

"Can I help you at all?"

"No, I'll just take it up and set it in a stand. You do have a tree stand, don't you?"

"I think I do, but I can set it in a bucket on the patio. You don't need to wait while I find the stand."

"Not a problem," Steven answered, as he lifted the tree over his shoulder.

"Lead the way, Madame Lilly," Steven said. Lulu stiffened. Madame Lilly? Was he teasing Lulu, or was he saying something else? Steven did not appear to notice. He was lugging the tree up the steps and squeezing it into the door as the children stood by and watched with delight.

When Steven had set the tree on the patio, he rubbed each boy's head and said, "I'll pick the boys up tomorrow about twelve."

Lulu could only manage to say thank you as she watched Steven run down the stairs and out to the car. She continued to watch as the taillights disappeared down the driveway.

"No, no, no. This story makes no sense. Hold up," Pamela interrupted. "What the hell is 'cotillion,' or whatever you just said?"

Lulu stopped. "Cotillion? Let's just say that it is organized dance lessons."

"Why would anybody ever do that?"

"Well, I suppose back when I was growing up, it was important to know how to ballroom dance. I guess. I don't know," Lulu finished.

"Okay, okay," Pamela said. "Sometimes half the shit that you say makes no sense. At least, not to me. Huh, Michie?"

"That's true, but who cares? It's interesting. So was she really warning you?" Michie asked, referring to the old woman in Lulu's tale.

"Yes, I think so. Somehow I knew that the old woman was telling the truth. She didn't even bother to see my reaction. She didn't care. The warning had been issued and she turned to concentrate on the children."

"Why did he do all of that? I don't get it," Michie said.

"I didn't get what was going on either," Lulu sadly smiled. "I'm going to the gym. Anybody going to join me?"

Both Michie and Pamela shook their heads as Lulu walked towards the gym. Pamela turned to Michie. "Times running out."

"I know," Michie said. The women looked at each other.

"She's made it amusing," Pamela said. "Who ever heard of co...till or whatever she called her dancing."

Michie smiled weakly, threw her cigarette to the ground, and smashed it with her shoe. "Let's go inside. I can't stand the cold, and I have to stop smoking."

"I know," Pamela said, and she threw her cigarette to the ground and kept walking.

FIFTEEN

As Lulu walked towards the gym she felt confused and unsettled. Why did Pamela and Michie make her feel left out? Why did they make her feel that she was lying about her life? She knew why. Gender and color were the only things the three women shared. Then Lulu thought about the trauma that Pamela and Michie had shared, and she knew that was what connected the three of them. The truth of this statement overwhelmed her, and Lulu turned her eyes towards the black mountains now glistening in the cold February sun.

She inhaled as she had learned from another patient she had met while in rehab. The smell of the pine pricked her nose and reminded her of that day with Steven when they went to his family's Christmas tree farm. As she walked into the gym, Lulu was trying to make sense of her relationship with Steven Flaherty. Had she been so misguided, so lonely, or had Steven Flaherty actually courted her? She would have to say no, except for that day after tobogganing.

The children's faces were flushed and sunburned from the reflection of the sun off the snow. They were giddy and happy, and Steven had walked them up the stairs and knocked on the door. When Lulu answered, Steven and the boys were grinning, and Steven had two bags of food containing a six-course Chinese meal. It touched her heart to see her children so happy and being children. She had made Steven and the boys remove their boots and coats in the foyer while she took the food into the kitchen. She brought out plates and silverware and laid them on the glass dining table.

They ate family style, with the boys eating anything that was fried or covered in a sauce first, and then picking out their favorite vegetables from the black mushrooms and chestnuts that were sautéed with sesame seeds. Yet, while Steven told silly jokes and the boys laughed out loud with Steven joining in just as boisterously, Lulu felt sad. She was thinking that Steven would leave and take his car and his money and his crazy antics, and she and her boys would be back to counting pennies and having to choose between something the boys wanted and something they needed.

After dinner, Lulu tried to join in the fun as they decorated the tree, and the boys brought out the decorations that they had made in school over past years and that Lulu had kept. They showed their favorites to Steven and competed for his attention, but as it neared nine o'clock, the excitement of the day could not keep the boys awake, despite their desire to stay up. Despite their protestations about not being tired, Lulu excused herself while she put the boys to bed. When she was done, she returned to the living room where Steven had been sitting.

"Well, it's just us," she said.

"I need to go outside for a minute," he replied.

"What, you have to leave?" Lulu asked.

"Yes and no, but I want to get something out of the car."

"Oh, you want..." and Lulu didn't finish the sentence.

"Stop being paranoid. I'll be right back. You can even watch from the door," he laughed.

"Okay. I can see the carport from the back window," Lulu replied.

He had gotten up, run outside, and returned with two bottles of Chardonnay. "You forgot the wine that was supposed to go with dinner?"

"I did," Steven laughed. "I also have a present for you."

"What? You have a present for me? Where is it?" Steven reached in his breast pocket and pulled out a small box wrapped in gold foil paper. Lulu had recoiled, wondering what it was. She took the box and asked Steven whether she should open the box or wait until Christmas. He had laughed, and said that Christmas was days away and that she should open the box then. There was a tiny card in a heavy vellum envelope. Lulu opened it, and the card had read "New Beginnings." When she opened the package, there was a bottle of expensive perfume.

"I believe that new beginnings should be represented by something. You joked that I was an expert at perfumes. In a way, I am. I like it, and I buy it for the women I love." She was left speechless, then he brought her back to the present by saying, "let's have a glass of this expensive Chardonnay that I borrowed from my family's wine cellar."

As Lulu began walking along the track inside the gym, she thought that they would smoke crack again that night. They had not. She then realized that the whole time she had been with Steven, even though her children were with her, she had wanted to smoke crack. She knew that she had made too much of the bottle of perfume. Had she always set such a low bar for men? She involuntarily shook her head. No, there had been David Hughes.

SIXTEEN

Terry Berkquist sat reading the long analysis of Lulu's troubles with her former husband, David Hughes. Terry thought that it would be helpful if she had another therapist's opinion on Lulu.

"The other issue that would create a distance between David and Lulu was sex. There was no one to blame. Both David and Lulu had sexual issues. Sex for Lulu was a traded commodity, and men were tools to get her from one point to another, but she is not consciously aware of this.

Lulu's issues run deep, and permeate her entire way of life. Unfortunately, neither Lulu nor her husband David Hughes had ever satisfactorily addressed those issues. Lulu, however, was too emotionally immature to accept accountability for her part and blamed all of their problems on David. Lulu felt that while David was a brilliant man, he was insecure. Lulu would point to David's signature as an example of this. David's handwriting was tiny and child-like. In Lulu's analysis, because David was extremely tall and white as a teenager on an island of short brown people, he felt awkward and left out. He was a loner, and had few friends. As a result of his teenage inexperience, David remained sexually inexperienced as a young adult until he met and married Lulu. It is Lulu's opinion that David had never been comfortable with women. She feels that David loved women in the way a teenage boy idolizes a movie star or pin-up.

On the other hand, Lulu had been promiscuous as a result of her poor opinion of herself and her scarred past. Lulu has a deep-seated hatred towards men and at the same time feels as if she cannot survive without them. This conundrum fuels her rage towards men in general and David in particular.

With this historical backdrop, it was not surprising that Lulu and David would use the bedroom as a battle ground to express unresolved fears. Neither of them was mature enough to talk about these issues and instead of communicating and teaching each other, Lulu became critical and ridiculed David's sexual performance. As the barrage of invectiveness continued, David had become more repressed, and became a premature ejaculator.

Lulu emotionally distanced herself from David, triggering all of his fears of abandonment. David, normally a wise man, agreed to begin using illicit drugs to improve their sex life. This was the beginning of an inevitable end of the relationship. Lulu began using the drugs on a regular basis, until there came a time when David would come home to find Lulu in the bathtub with a gin and tonic on the side of the tub and a marijuana joint smoldering in an ashtray. Teddy was either left in his crib or left playing with his toys, or, worse, he would be wet and hungry and crying, and Lulu seemed not to care.

David had little experience in being a good father or husband. It was not that he did not want to remedy the situation; it was that he did not know how, and did not know where to turn. David loved Lulu and her little boy, and he was helpless to help either of them. A few months after their marriage, David thought that if he and Lulu had a child of their own, that it would solidify the relationship. This turned out to be troublesome as well. After months of trying, Lulu and David were unable to conceive. Friends suggested a fertility expert. Lulu had declined, and, as usual, Lulu blamed David. Her thoughts were that she had become pregnant before, so it must be David. The bedroom became more volatile and the sex act more desperate. The act of sex became tainted with frustration and tears and anger.

Finally, right before Thanksgiving Lulu went to her doctor and was told that she was pregnant. She was happy, and told all of David's friends who found it less than tasteful for a woman who had just recently found out that she was pregnant to broadcast it in the way that Lulu had. David's friends thought that Lulu should have waited at least a month after the first trimester before she made such an announcement; Lulu had never been one to comply with social norms and had laughed at 'those proper friends of David's.' Lulu also took advantage of this pregnancy to be particularly lazy and demanding. When David's friends invited them over to dinner, she was often known to call the hostess or host and tell him or her which foods at that moment made her nauseous, so that they were sure not to serve that item for dinner. When she arrived at the home of her host, Lulu would kick off her shoes and sprawl on their sofa. She would demand to be waited upon, either by David or the host or hostess. Oftentimes, if they had brought Teddy with them to dinner, it was David who tended to the little fellow while Lulu indulged herself with whatever made her happy at the moment. As a result of Lulu's behavior, David's friends who had known him for a long time began to either only invite him without Lulu, or to invite David with little Teddy. While David was embarrassed for Lulu, he never told her that his friends thought that she was too fixated with her pregnancy. Lulu never did anything to change her behavior. Slowly, David's friends, all of whom were childless by choice, began to dislike Lulu, and privately told David as much.

"Although no one ever actually told Lulu that they did not like her, it was apparent to her that more and more she was left out from invitations from David's friends. She knew that she could not survive long in the atmosphere where she was clearly not liked or wanted. She knew that her marriage would never survive with David's friends feeling the way they did. So, when Teddy was two and before her second child, Christopher, was born, Lulu decided that it was time for them to move away from David's meddling friends. She picked the Pacific Northwest because it was the geogarphic area farthest west from the east coast, and still on the North American continent. She asked David to see if he could find a job in that area.

Lulu also told David that she did not like the weather in New York, and, in truth, the cold weather aggravated Lulu's allergies. She was also terrified of driving in the snow. When not quite a year old, he and Lulu were in a car accident during a sudden snow storm casuing Lulu to drive the car off the road that led from their hilltop home. Both she and Teddy were taken to the hospital and checked for injuries, and, luckily, both were unharmed. But after that accident, Lulu would not leave the house without checking the weather forecast. She had become terrified of driving in the snow, and desperately wanted to move before the first snow fell.

David, being the ever accommodating husband, began to search for jobs in Seattle and Portland. Because of his impeccable credentials, he found a job with a company that was a peer to Microsoft. Lulu, Teddy, David, and their brand new son Christopher, moved to Portland, Oregon.

Terry put down the neatly written notes. She wondered how someone who seemed to have it all ended up in a drug rehab facility, but she knew that Lulu only looked as if she had it all. Lulu, besides being an addict, had been traumatized at some point in her life—or better yet, throughout her childhood—yet during their almost daily sessions, Lulu had only shared excerpts from her life, as if she were a star in a soap opera entitled, "Lulu." Terry sighed. Hopefully, Lulu would start talking about the real issues in her life.

SEVENTEEN

From the street, the house was an unassuming two-story three-bedroom home, with a sun porch and neatly trimmed hedges that carved out the front yard. Over the years, the hedges would be chopped down, the front yard filled with weeds, and the house itself destroyed from its foundation to its roof, which was burned by fire and never fixed. But in the beginning, the little mint green home with white trim and shutters was Lulu's first real home; it was also the first real break Lulu would have with her grandmother, Celestine.

The interior of the house was beautiful and filled with antiques left by the former owner, whom Lulu could never recall, although she had lived next door to them for almost two years. The floors were wood, the rooms were separated by wooden pocket doors, and the kitchen led to a beautiful glass sun porch that looked out into a back yard where rose bushes lined one long side of the property, and then turned sharply to define the back of the property. Two large flowering trees occupied the other side of the property, and a neat layer of grass covered the long, narrow backyard.

Lulu had been coaxed to look inside the house with the promise of her own bedroom, but that turned out to be a lie. Her sisters, now four of them, were jammed into what would have been a living room. Her parents took the large front master bedroom, and the other two rooms were rented out to medical students. Everyone shared a single upstairs bathroom.

One night, shortly after Lulu had moved into the house, she woke in the middle of the night, but thought it was morning. She stumbled up the stairs, and saw one of the medical students urinating in the toilet. The man had left the bathroom door open, and Lulu had stared at what she thought was a continuous stream of water. The man did not see her at first, but he felt her stare. Lulu continued to look at the man, and wondered whether she was still sleeping and what she should say to him. Instead, he asked "what are you doing up?"

"It's morning," Lulu said.

"Yes, it is morning, but much too early in the morning for you."

"I have to pee," Lulu said.

"Well, come in when I am finished," the man said. Lulu walked into the bathroom to take a closer look at what the man had in his hand. The man laughed. "Never seen one of these before?" he asked. Lulu shook her head.

"Do you want to feel it?" the man asked. Again, Lulu shook her head.

"Well, then," the man said as he put his penis back into his pajama pants. "Come sit and pee."

"Okay," Lulu said. She pulled down her pajama pants, sat on the toilet seat, and urinated. She wiped herself, and the man watched. She washed her hands and dried them on a dirty towel that was hanging on the towel rack.

"Good night," she said, and left the man in the bathroom.

The next day, the man bought Lulu candy. The man had a television in his room, and Lulu and her sister loved to watch television. Their mother, whenever she was around, would warn the girls to leave the man alone, but the man smiled and said he liked them. Lulu liked this man as well. She liked to lie in his lap while he stroked her hair. The man would also carry her around on his back, and Lulu loved this. In fact, the handsome young man paid Lulu a great deal of attention, and was as much fun as anyone she had met since moving to America. One day, while Lulu was riding piggyback, the man felt her bottom. "You have no panties," the man said to her.

"Is that wrong?" Lulu asked the man.

"No, "he said. He continued to touch her bottom, and, finally, touched her anus. She flinched. "Has anyone ever done this to you before?" the man asked. Lulu shook her head. The man and Lulu went into his bedroom. Years later, Lulu's father would accuse her of not being a virgin; one of the very worst things one could say of a Catholic girl.

The year the house was purchased was also the first time that Lulu was in a group where there were rules to be followed. She did not understand her role as a pupil and the role of her teacher. Lulu thought that the teacher was a substitute for her grandmother. She also thought that the woman should entertain her, and she was not happy with the fact that there were other children. She didn't understand why she had to listen to the woman talk about numbers and colors. Lulu wanted fairytales, and stories about princesses.

Because she was bored, Lulu squirmed in her seat, got out of her seat, failed to raise her hand, and could neither sit still nor pay attention. Her mind wandered, and she sang to herself, and was not interested in playing with her classmates. She blurted out whatever thoughts came into her head, and wanted to see what was down the hall. Within the first few hours of kindergarten, she was put in time out.

By Lulu's second week, she was labeled a troublemaker. Daily, her teacher sent home notes about her behavior, and every day either Octavia or Cordell would whip Lulu for misbehaving. Sadly, Lulu did not understand why she was being beaten, she only knew that she hated the woman known as Octavia, and the man who shared grandpa's first name.

Still, Lulu tried to behave. Lulu's mother, Octavia, had told Lulu to sit still and say nothing in class, so that was what Lulu decided to do. Each day while in school, she stared out of the window. She thought she could see the heat rising from the windowpanes and float into the sky. She looked so intently she believed that she could see individual colors rising with the heat.

By the time Lulu entered first grade, her teachers thought that she had learning disabilities. She would have been placed in a special education class, except for a tiny French woman named Madame Rosenbloom. This teacher, one of the few white teachers still remaining in the predominantly black school system, realized that Lulu was not learning disabled. She realized that Lulu was not being engaged. So, instead of Special Education, Lulu began taking French lessons.

Madame Rosenbloom was the first of Lulu's teachers to make a difference in her life. Lulu was charmed by Madame Rosenbloom's accent, and she tried to copy it as best as she could. Madame Rosenbloom saw Lulu blossom, and suddenly the sullen little girl was counting and reading and spelling in French, and translating it all for Madame Rosenbloom.

Madame Rosenbloom was charmed by Lulu St. Blanc. Yet, Madame Rosenbloom did not understand why Lulu's parents paid so little attention to such a bright and curious child. Occasionally, one of the teachers saw Lulu's father, but all he did was flirt with them, and tell them how wealthy he was going to become. Neither parent came to teacher-parent conferences. It seemed that no one cared about Lulu St. Blanc.

One afternoon, Madame Rosenbloom walked Lulu home. She wanted to speak to someone, anyone who could or would support Lulu by helping with homework. Grandma Celestine was the only adult home that afternoon. As she and Madame Rosenbloom sat on the front porch, they plotted Lulu's future.

"She must be sent to a private school—a Catholic school. She will be thrown into the dust heap if she remains in the local elementary school."

Grandma Celestine looked at Madame Rosenbloom. "You are a Jew, are you not?"

"Yes." Madame Rosenbloom fiercely whispered. "I am a Jew, but foremost, I am a teacher. This child has a great mind. If a Catholic school will save her mind, my soul will be fine."

Grandma Celestine nodded. "I understand. She will go to Catholic school." The plan had been set in motion.

Besides the fact that there were no Catholic schools in Lulu's neighborhood, she had never been baptized as a Catholic. Except for her grandfather's funeral, Lulu had spent her first three years in Washington D.C. without stepping into a church. Octavia had left Lulu with her mother-in-law so that she could be with Lulu's father. Lulu had only been six months old. In those days, and within that culture, children were usually baptized before they turned a year old. To Celestine's dismay, her husband, Lulu's grandfather, had baptized Lulu in the Lutheran faith. As far as Octavia was concerned, it was of no importance, as

Lulu was a child that she would rather not have had. Unfortunately, being a Catholic was the baseline for any parochial school, as it was for the Catholic school that had accepted both Lulu and her sister Iris. So, besides her school work, every morning at seven o'clock Lulu had to attend special classes to learn what it meant to be a Catholic.

In many ways, Lulu fell short of the way a Catholic girl should behave. She was often kept after school in order to think about her behavior. It was the beginning of the school's more accelerated program to remove ungodly impulses from the heart and soul of Lilly Marie St. Blanc.

On one of those early school mornings, Mother Marie interrupted Lulu's mandatory time of prayer and reflection. "Lilly St. Blanc, are you praying for your soul, or are you just kneeling and daydreaming—or worse yet, sleeping?"

"I was praying, Mother Marie."

"What are you praying about?" Mother Marie asked, as she looked at Lulu's navy blue cardigan that was covered with lint, and the dingy white collar of her Peter Pan blouse.

"I was praying about...." Lulu started to lie, but because she had been called by her proper name, it had startled her, and she could not make up a story, as she had learned to do without effort. "I was praying about...." Lulu started again, and then told the truth: "I was looking at the colors in the stained glass window, Mother. I was thinking about how sad Jesus looked as he hung on the cross. I really love the way the sun shines through the glass and how the reds in the stained glass make red shadows on the alter cloth." Lulu lowered her eyes, and awaited a rap on her hands with a ruler and a punishment of Hail Marys and Our Fathers, but that day Mother Marie had other concerns about Lilly St. Blanc.

"Lilly, I need you to come into class right now and bring your notebook and books." Lulu rose from where she was kneeling, and followed Mother Marie out of the chapel and to the school across from it.

Mother Marie had found pictures of naked women. The culprit was Lulu. It was never clear whether the Sisters of the Holy Cross understood the implications of Lulu's nude drawings. She was not punished; instead, she was given art lessons. From that day, Lulu was taken under the collective wing of the nuns. They made sure that Lulu and her sisters, Iris and then Dahlia, had enough to eat. Each year, the Sisters gave Octavia a set of uniforms for each of her daughters, and loaned them used textbooks. While the Sisters loved each of the St. Blanc girls, it was Lulu St. Blanc that had stolen their hearts and caused them great worry. The Sisters puzzled over Lulu, who was bright and beautiful, and yet insecure and preoccupied. At times, the Sisters could not help but laugh at Lulu's antics; at other times they worried that, for a pre-teen, Lulu was far too knowledgeable in the ways of the world. "Pray for her," Mother Marie urged. "She is God's child. She is our child. We have her for a few more years. Let us do the best that we can."

Now, years later, as Lulu sat in the office of Terry Berkquist, she wondered how she could convey to the therapist how intertwined her life and her thoughts and her beliefs had shaped her life. It was far too subtle. She had been trained from her earliest years in the rules of good Catholic behavior, and had had years of that belief system trampled by her father. Now, she sat and heard Terry's voice asking about childhood memories. Yes, there was more...

It had only been six months since Lulu had arrived in Washington D.C. when Daddy Dell, her grandfather, had died. Lulu's parents told her that Daddy Dell had died of pneumonia. When Lulu asked her mother what pneumonia was, Octavia told Lulu that pneumonia came from cold temperatures. From that moment on, Lulu hated cold weather. In her adult life, Lulu would own many fur coats, and coats in general. She would jokingly tell people it was because she was born in the Banana Belt, but she had long forgotten that she was trying to avoid dying from pneumonia and the cold. Many years later, Lulu learned that her grandfather had not died of pneumonia, but that his lungs had filled with vomit because he had been drunk. He was an alcoholic.

It was right after Daddy Dell died that Lulu's parents had bought the house next door to her Aunt Verna. Although Lulu's grandmother lived just next door, Lulu was no longer living under the same roof as Celestine. Every chance Lulu got, she would run the fifty feet or so to the house where her grandmother lived. It was only with her grandmother that Lulu would feel safe.

One early spring day, it happened to snow. Lulu was struggling with first grade, having failed to color in between the lines in kindergarten. She and her grandmother were standing together, looking out of the back door of the kitchen. Grandmother and granddaughter silently watched the falling snow. Lulu was pensive. She turned to her grandmother, and asked whether she would put her in a box in the ground, as Lulu's parents had done with her grandfather. "No, darling," Lulu's grandmother answered. When Lulu realized that her grandmother wasn't going to say anything else, Lulu asked her, "why can't I come and live with you?"

"You know why. You have a mother and father, and it's important that you respect and obey them," her grandmother said.

"But I hate them," Lulu shouted back.

"No, you don't hate them, Lulu. They are your parents."

"Well, I wish they would die," Lulu replied.

"No, you should not wish that, Lulu. That is the worst thing that you could wish. It is terrible to grow up without a mother."

"But I would have you," Lulu answered.

"You will always have me," her grandmother replied, and then she tried to distract Lulu from the conversation that they were having. "Lulu, look at the birds sitting on the telephone lines, don't they look like little old men in black coats?" Her grandmother laughed.

"Yes, Mommy," she answeres, and then Lulu stopped and corrected herself. "Yes, Grandmother Celestine."

"And look over there, darling. Do you see the irises poking their beautiful purple heads out of the ground, even though there is snow?"

"What does that mean, Grandma?" Lulu asked.

"It means that there is the promise of spring in those flowers," Celestine smiled at Lulu.

Lulu wrestled with what her grandmother had said. When she couldn't figure it out, she asked another question. "Grandmother, will you ever marry again?"

"No, child, never again."

"Why, Grandma? Mommy Octavia says that you are still young."

"I have married the only man that I have ever loved, so there is no need to marry again."

"Mommy Octavia says you were married three times. Is that a lot, Grandmother?"

"To some people, yes, it is a lot."

"Why did you marry so many times?" Lulu asked.

"Because my first two husbands died, Lulu."

"Mommy Octavia says that you are a black widow. What does that mean, Grandma?"

"I don't know what your mother means about that, but we won't say that again."

"Is it a bad thing?"

"No, black widows are spiders," Celestine answered.

As Lulu sat silently, refusing to answer Terry's questions and remembering her grandmother, she began to cry.

"Why are you crying?" Terry asked.

"I don't know," Lulu answered. "My grandmother would be so disappointed in me. Here I am, a drug addict. She would have expected better of me," Lulu sobbed.

Terry was silent, except to say, "I'll see you tomorrow."

"Sure," Lulu answered. She got up and left the room as she held back her tears.

EIGHTEEN

Finally, it was the fifth day. She could use the phone. She realized that she had no money, but she quickly learned the ways of the system, and for a gray cashmere sweater, she had gotten a phone card with twenty five dollars on it. The first call she made was to her children. Christopher answered the phone. At first, all Lulu could do was sob silently. Then, in a cracked voice, she said hello.

"Mommy, where are you?" Christopher asked.

"I'm not well. I'm in kind of a hospital," Lulu said.

"When are you getting out?" Christopher asked.

"In a couple of weeks," Lulu said.

"Oh, Mommy, I miss you so much," Christopher said.

"I miss you too, baby," Lulu said, controlling her tears.

"Mommy, do you know where my hand is?" Christopher asked.

"No, baby, I don't," Lulu answered.

"It's on my heart," Christopher said. "Because I love you."

"I love you, too," Lulu said, as tears streamed down her face.

"Mommy, Carmen says I have to go, but Teddy wants to speak to you too."

"All right, sweetheart, you be a good boy. I love you, and I will see you soon."

"Bye, Mommy. I love you," Christopher said.

"Mommy," Teddy said, as he got on the phone line. That's all he said, because he was sobbing.

"Oh, Teddy, please don't cry. Mommy is going to be ok. I'll see you soon. I promise."

"Mommy, I'm afraid you won't come back. That you won't get better, and I'll never see you again."

"But you will, Teddy. You will see me again. I love you, darling. You are such a good boy."

"Mommy," was all Teddy said.

"Teddy, Mommy loves you. I am on a pay phone. There are other people who need to use it, so I will have to go soon, but remember that I love you, sweetheart."

"I love you too, Mommy," Teddy said, and Lulu could hear Carmen's voice in the background. The phone went silent, and then there was a dial tone. Lulu hung up the phone and headed back to her room.

When she got there, she was alone, thankfully. She lay on her bed and sobbed until she could not cry any longer. She knew that Steven had grown tired of her. And she wondered whether she was better off without him in her life. She reflected upon how terribly hard it was to be away from him. As she lay in bed at the rehab center, Lulu recalled the days after Steven had taken the boys tobogganing.

The pain of withdrawal from him had to be managed, and therefore the time away from Steven did not go well for Lulu. She awoke each morning and craved Steven. She woke up anxious and desperate, and throughout the day she compulsively thought about him. In her mind, she replayed each moment that she wished things had turned out differently. Each night, she smoked some of the crack he had left her on the night that he had given her the perfume. By the third day, she was irritable and cranky. She missed a deadline to do work for her partner, and she had lied to cover why she had not delivered the work. By the fourth day, she had smoked all the coke. On the fifth day, she had slept through a meeting and was late to pick up the children, but her weariness was a relief from the high pitch her body had been in for the past few days. Finally, on the sixth night, she was still craving the combined effect of Steven Flaherty and cocaine, but she was able to work.

On the evening of the sixth day, it took iron discipline to work after putting the children to bed. Lulu forced herself to sit at her computer. Even if her fingers just moved across the keys, she would stay in front of the computer. Soon, her brain would click on, and she would accomplish writing the brief, which was the basis of the defense for Fiona Winters. Because she was far behind in her work, Lulu pushed herself to continue writing and editing her research and fact section until the digital clock on her computer edged towards 2 a.m. Finally, she was focused, and finally feeling that she had made up for lost time, when the doorbell rang. Her heart skipped a beat. It had to be Steven.

Lulu quickly walked to the front door and hoped that Steven would not ring the doorbell again, because she was afraid that he would wake up the children who were sleeping. "Steven?" she called, when she got to the front door.

"Yes. Open the door."

"My God!" Lulu said, as she opened the door.

"What happened to you?" Steven's face was scratched, and his lip was puffy.

"Are you going to let me in?" he asked.

"Let me get some iodine and a band aid for that cut on your face," she said, as she let Steven into the apartment.

"No, it's all right," Steven answered.

"Shh," Lulu warned. "The children are sleeping."

"I'm sorry," Steven said. "Maybe I should just go."

"No, it's alright. Please come in. We just need to be quiet. Sit down," Lulu said, as she led Steven into the living room.

"What happened?" Lulu asked.

"I never really went out of town," Steven said. "I just told everyone that. Instead, I went to the Holiday Inn. Tonight, Catherine left her children with a babysitter. I went back to the house and forced the babysitter to tell me where I could find Catherine. Catherine can never leave the house without someone knowing where she is."

"Let me interrupt you," Terry said. "Now, Catherine was a woman that you had met because each of you had children that played soccer, right?"

"Yes," Lulu answered.

"Okay, go on. I just needed to clarify we weren't talking about last night's Catherine."

"No," Lulu replied. "Very different Catherine, but she was blonde as well."

"Alright, let's continue," Terry said.

"Okay. I then asked him why Catherine...should I say her last name?" Lulu asked.

"No, it's not necessary, and I don't need you to identify her except as to how she relates to your addiction."

"You mean, besides setting me up with Steven Flaherty?"

"I didn't know that she did that."

"I might not have told you, but he says that she had sent him to my home office. That's how I met Steven."

"Okay. Clarified," Terry said, and then nodded her head, signaling Lulu to continue where she had left off.

"I asked Steven why Catherine could not leave her house without someone knowing where she was going. He said he would tell me in a minute, and he sat down on my sofa. I sat next to him, and he began to tell me a crazy tale about Catherine."

"The babysitter told me that Catherine was at the West Coast Plaza Hotel in Bellevue," Steven began. "I went to her room and knocked on the door. I pretended I was room service. She opened the door in a bathrobe. When she saw it was me, she tried to shut the door. I pushed it open, and there was an older guy, naked, in bed."

Steven fought back a wave of emotion as he recalled the sight. "It is not that I was so much in love with Catherine, but her betrayal reminded me of my mother's betrayal of my father years ago. Most of my issues with women and with drugs stem from my unresolved anger at my mother. At the same time, I want to feel loved by a woman who is strong and authoritative, like my mother. Unfortunately, although I have had years of therapy, I simply cannot get it in here," Steven said, pointing to his heart, "that my mother is incapable of loving anyone, not even her own children."

Lulu was silent, and waited for Steven to continue.

"I don't even love myself. At my core I feel unlovable. The only thing I have going for me is my money, and my mother controls that through her lawyers.

Steven took a handkerchief from his pocket, blew his nose, and wiped his eyes.

"I went after the old guy, and Catherine got in the middle. The door was left open, and a couple walking by the room yelled out that they were going to call the police. I thought to myself, why the hell am I going to go to jail for a two-bit whore and a convict? So, I got out of there, and I came here."

"Do you need a place to stay?" Lulu asked.

"No," Steven answered, "I still have the hotel room."

There was a heavy silence, as both Lulu and Steven pondered over the course of the conversation and the events related. Lulu broke the silence. "You still have not told me why Catherine could not go anywhere without somebody knowing where she is?"

"She's under house arrest," Steven mumbled, in an off-handed way, as if what he had just said should have been common knowledge, and expected of Catherine.

"House arrest?" Lulu asked.

"Yes," Steven said flatly.

"You've got to say more about that. Why is she under house arrest? What did she do? I mean, I saw her almost every week for months and she never let on there was anything wrong with her life. My children have spent the night at her house!" Lulu finished.

"It's such a long story," Steven replied. "And I really don't want to get into it now."

"Oh, no," she said. "That's simply not fair. You can't drop a bomb like that and then say that you don't want to talk about it. If you don't want to tell me, perhaps I should ask her about it. I'm an attorney. I can't be consorting with known felons. So please tell me what this is about."

"You're right. I have been unfair and untruthful to you. I guess I should start by telling you that Catherine wanted to use you to set up a call girl service for her. She's currently broke. She's got a streak of criminality in her that is a mile wide. She was hoping to use you to set up a corporation so that she would not be held responsible for the actions of her so-called employees. The reason that that was crucial to her was that she already has two felony convictions. A third conviction, and she could possibly go to jail for life under the three-strikes law."

"Oh, my God," Lulu said. "I think I need a drink, or a drug or something. You just never know who you meet, do you?"

"Do you want some coke?" Steven asked.

"Oh, hell," she answered. "Of course I do. I have the most addictive personality. I always have. If it's there, I will do it. That's why I limit the amount of alcohol I have in the house. I know I shouldn't be doing this, yet sometimes, when I'm under pressure, I need a glass of wine or something."

"Perhaps you're an addict," Steven said. "Do you know the definition of addiction?" he asked.

"No, but I don't think that I am an addict because I have always been able to quit or stop."

"I'm certainly not the one to lecture to anyone. Lilly, I'm going to tell you the truth. You won't believe it, because you will want to think otherwise, but I am an addict. Sure, I look like a nice guy, and I am, but at my core, I'm an addict. I know that you will forget what I have said tonight, because you will want to. The reason you will want to is called denial. You will not want to believe that all I care about is my next hit of cocaine. The reason that you won't want to, is because you are an addict."

"Oh, please," she said. "Must I listen to this?"

"No, but at some point, I want you to remember tonight. I'm not going to say anymore. I think that you are one good-looking woman. When I said I thought that we could be friends and help each other, I meant that. You just have to know that I am not what you think I am. Yes, I'm rich. Women tell me that I'm good-looking, and funny, and charming. I can be all that. Just remember what I said. Now, here's a hit of cocaine. Enjoy it, but remember what I have said tonight."

Steven took a baggie of cocaine out of his pocket. He put a large piece of cocaine in a glass pipe, took a lighter from his jacket. He held the pipe and lit it for her.

She looked at him. The cocaine in the pipe was sexually arousing. She inhaled deeply. "I guess I am a hypocrite," she said.

"Perhaps you are, but I think you're simply an addict, and you don't know it yet."

"Do you think that I will find out?"

"Sooner or later, we all do," Steven said. "Just remember, I'm not your keeper."

"I've been duly warned," Lulu said, as the drug penetrated her body. "Now, tell me more about Catherine." She curled her legs under her and looked longingly at him.

"Five years ago, Catherine Connors' husband died suddenly of a heart attack. The insurance company conducted an investigation, but nothing incriminating was ever found. Her husband was thirty five years old, and, according to his medical records, he was as healthy as a horse. He had a huge insurance policy. Why he had such a large insurance policy was never really explained to me, but Catherine said it was because his family believed in insurance policies. His grandmother had bought him his first policy when he was born. Whatever the reason, we may never know. Of course, the insurers were troubled that such a young man in apparently good health would drop dead, and they investigated. After a couple of years of trying to withhold the money, they finally had to pay out on the policy. The insurance company even had to pay a penalty for unreasonably withholding the funds, after an autopsy showed that there was no external reason for his death. Catherine's family, according to her, never liked her husband. He was a black man. She says she married him to hurt her father. Anyway, according to Catherine, her family was not at all unhappy that her husband had died. Apparently, neither was Catherine, but, then again, I believe that Catherine has an anti-social personality. Do you know what anti-social means?" Steven interrupted his story to ask.

"Not really," Lulu answered. "I think it means someone that was against society?" She hazarded a guess.

"No, not quite," Steven answered. "An anti-social personality is a character disorder. Psychology is a hobby of mine, particularly since I've spent so much time with Madame Connors." Steven laughed at this. "By the way, Catherine really wants to be a Madame. It's so perverted, but let me continue with my clinical analysis," Steven said. "A personality disorder is something that cannot be affected by therapy, or, at least, it is difficult to affect with therapy. An anti-social personality commits 'crimes,' without regard to the victims. Their only concern is whether they get caught. Of course, this is a very simplistic definition, but it would fit Catherine."

Steven turned to Lulu and asked, in wonder, "I mean, you two have talked about a lot of things, yet she never told you that her husband had died, leaving her with three young children. Don't you find that rather interesting?"

"She did say that her husband had died. She never said how he had died. But I think this entire conversation is more than interesting.

I think it is amazing, in the full sense of the word. Please continue," she said.

"So, Catherine's husband dies. Her family is extremely Germanic and controlling, particularly Catherine's father, who, by the way, I think molested Catherine when she was a young girl. Of course, Catherine would never admit to this, but that's part of her psychopathology as well. When Larry died—that was Catherine's husband's name—it was an opportunity for Catherine's parents to once again manage Catherine's life.

Catherine's father was a college professor, and he insisted that Catherine go back to school, which Catherine did. And guess what Catherine became? She got a degree in social work." At this, Steven laughed. "Don't you think that that was funny? I mean, she is such a self-centered person who could not care less about underprivileged people. But, you see, Catherine is absolutely committed to looking as if she cares about people. To Catherine, people are just objects to be manipulated. But let me continue with the story of Ms. Connors.

Catherine used some of her insurance money, or, at least, her new financial position on paper, to lease a huge office complex in Bellevue. She then leased the office space out to therapists. Catherine also started a bookkeeping service, and offered that to her tenants as well. She has an uncanny ability to detect other people's weaknesses very well." Steven paused, put another piece of cocaine in the pipe, and held it toward Lulu. She took it while Steven lit it, then took a drag off the pipe and handed it back to Steven.

"So Catherine has herself a sweet deal. She's making money as a landlord and as a bookkeeper. She's doing well financially. But that wasn't good enough for Catherine. She's greedy, and she thinks so little of other people. She thinks that they are stupid. Anyway, what Catherine did was use her tenants' patient lists and information. She created a series of fake clients, and then billed their services from her to the state of Washington. She had billed over two million dollars before she was caught."

"Oh, my God," Lulu said. "Two million dollars?" How was that possible? How can a person get away with that?"

"She did not get away with it. She finally got caught. Catherine simply made up patients and social security numbers. She joined a church downtown, and met lots of poor people. She took their phone numbers, and befriended them. It was a masquerade, and it made her look good in the eyes of the community. Finally, one or two of these poor people did end up receiving drug and alcohol treatment imposed by the court. Coincidently, the State found out that these same people were also receiving treatment in, of all places, Bellevue. Oddly, there were lots of indigent people that all seemed to prefer Bellevue and high-priced psychoanalysis. When the State began investigating, there was another unusual coincidence; all of these poor people managed to find their way to one large consortium of therapists. When subpoenas were issued, the therapists all pointed to Catherine. It didn't take much after that."

"So, I gather, she was charged with two felony counts and convicted on both? Right?"

"No, that's not quite right. Catherine hired an excellent attorney, and paid back about 250,000 dollars in restitution. She was put on probation for three years, and was ordered to do two hundred hours of community service. It was actually a slap on the wrist. One would think that she would have learned her lesson, but Catherine did not. She seems compelled to break the law in stupid ways. The worst part was that she doesn't need the money. Anyway, less than a year later, she forged a series of names on an insurance policy. She was charged with forgery. This time, the courts were a little harder on her. She lost her license as a therapist—which she never used anyway, but it gave her the right to consort with therapists and to be in business with them. Instead of going to jail, because she had three children, she was placed under house arrest for two years. She can only go outside of her house to work, or to take the children to school or after school activities, or to church."

"There's more," Steven wearily said. "I'm going to take a hit of cocaine. I need one." He inhaled deeply on the glass pipe, and offered it to Lulu.

"Who wouldn't need something, after a story like that?" Lulu also took a deep drag on the pipe, and passed it back to Steven. "So, go on," she said. "What's the rest?"

Steven took the pipe, and said, through a thick cloud of smoke, "she bought that monstrosity of a house in Laurel Hill mostly with cash from the insurance policy. Why somebody would need such an outlandish house is only a testament to her ego. Remember that I said Catherine befriended poor people at an inner city church? Well, she also drew attention from people who were trying to 'reform' themselves. One of these people was a drug dealer who called himself Buddy Oz. The 'O' and 'Z' were acronyms for ounces, of cocaine. Whatever the reason, Catherine genuinely liked this Buddy fellow. She's attracted to black men who abuse her, but that's another story for another night.

Whether Buddy Oz talked her in to it, or how it really happened, only Catherine and Buddy will really know for sure. They decided to be partners on a big cocaine buy. Catherine said that both she and Buddy Oz put up fifty thousand dollars in cash, but somehow I can't believe that a low-life like Buddy could come up with five hundred dollars, much less fifty thousand. Catherine said that the money was the last of the insurance money. After Catherine had paid for two lawyers and two trials, and paid back that restitution money, she was a little low on cash. Buddy told her that she could quadruple her money, so she went for it. Of course, Buddy was just scamming her. He did not even have the good taste to disappear for a while. Buddy took Catherine's money, and said he wasn't giving it back to her. The next thing you know, Buddy's driving a new Cadillac, and his girl's got a new BMW." Steven chuckled.

"Did she ever get any of the money back?" Lulu asked.

"Of course not! This was actually the funny part. Catherine went to the District Attorney, and told them that Buddy defrauded her! Can you imagine, a woman who had been twice involved with the criminal court had the nerve to tell the police that she was defrauded?"

"So, what did the police do?"

"Exactly what they were supposed to," Steven answered. "Nothing."

"Nothing?"

"Oh, come on. Don't be naive. She's a criminal. The police know Buddy's a dealer. What, they should arrest him for driving a new car? Of course, they knew Buddy had scammed her."

"I guess you're right," Lulu conceded. "So, where do you fit in?" She asked.

"I'm the dumb schmuck who fell in love with her kids, and then sort of liked her," he laughed.

"No, really, where do you fit within this time line?"

"You really want to know?"

"Yes, I do."

"I met Catherine in the parking lot of the building that she leased. I actually believe that she might have set that up, as well. She's an attractive woman, tall, blonde, and thin. She had a nice car. She seemed to be fun, and then I met those kids. There is something about children, Lilly, that just melts my heart." Suddenly, Steven became animated. His eyes sparkled and became wet with tears. "I had the greatest father. He was full of life. He looked and lived like Ernest Hemmingway. My Dad had the biggest and deepest laugh you've ever heard. He was like a Santa Claus. He was the best father a son could have." Steven stopped as suddenly as he had started, and paused, as if reflecting upon his father.

"Is he still alive?" Lulu asked.

"No, he died of cancer about eight years ago. I went to school back East, private college, and graduate school. I wasn't always a complete loser." Steven laughed again. "I was working for a big company back in New York. I was a vice-president. I thought I was all that, and more. When Dad got sick—lung cancer—I just knew that he would make it. I knew that he would beat the cancer. He didn't. I could not bear to see him wither away like that. I wanted to remember him being big and strong and healthy, and not a pathetic man in a bed with tubes coming out of everywhere. I refused to come back home before he died. My mother never really forgave me." Steven's face was bitter.

"Is that the reason that you said that I was a love-hate story?" Lulu asked.

"No, that started when I was a teenager. I caught her in her bedroom with a man. I never told anyone that I had seen her. She never said anything to me, except to say that my father was a difficult man. She had affairs through the entire marriage. She did not even bother to hide it."

"Did your father know?"

"If he didn't know, he was a fool. If he did know, it never changed the way he treated her. He loved her. He always had."

They were silent for a while, and then Lulu asked the question that had been plaguing her. "Was it your mother or your father who was rich?"

"It's the usual question—or, one of them," Steven answered. "But isn't the real question how much I'm worth? Isn't that what all you ladies want to know, so you can calculate whether it's worth your time to hang out with a guy who is functionally an addict? Isn't that really the question you want to ask, Counselor?"

"I'm sorry; I didn't mean to make you angry," she said.

"Don't be sorry. Being sorry is a pathetic way to be."

"I really just wanted to know how your family became wealthy, that's all."

"Oh, Lilly, my money is a burden. I know that you may not believe that, but it is. You see, I don't think anybody really likes me. I want somebody to really like me. Not my money, not what it can buy. You can't understand that. It's worse than being pretty, Lilly, and that's your curse."

She looked at him. "What do you mean, that's my curse?"

"Oh, come off it! Your life has been about your looks. Or, more precisely, proving that you are not only what you look like. At the same time, every time you pass a mirror, you check to see if that lovely face is still as pretty today as it was yesterday."

Lulu grew warm and embarrassed, and said nothing. What he didn't know was that she was not checking to see if she were still pretty, but to see whether she still looked like her mother. "When I look in the mirror, I don't see my face. I see my mother's face."

Terry scribbled a note. "Well, do you look like your mother?" She asked.

"Yes, and no. I don't want to look like her. I don't think she's very pretty. I don't think she ever was, even when she was young. The very thing I did not want to be was to be anything like my mother."

"That's a pretty strong statement. I'm sure your mother has good qualities."

"Well, if she does, I haven't seen or found them. And I thought you wanted to hear how Steven and I became intimate, didn't you?"

"I still do, but I gather you are telling me that on this evening the two of you had an intimate conversation that led you to..."

"Yes, he spent the night. Yes, we slept together."

"So he had 'come clean' with you. And did you open up to him?"

"No."

"Was there anything that he said to you that made you want to be sexually intimate with him?"

"Not really."

"So how did you transition from this long discussion to end up in bed?"

"He said that some people say cocaine is truth serum, and that he had slept with more women than he could count, and all of them thought that they could save him. And he said, 'you think you can too, don't you? You don't have to answer that question, because I already know the answer. I know the end of this story, now. I can start by asking you to marry me. Isn't that what you want? Marriage? Money? Of course, you might actually be worth it. Look, I'm keeping you awake. I'm going to go back to my hotel room.'"

"No, don't go," Lulu said. "You are in no condition to drive."

"You need not use my condition, Lilly. You can ask me to stay. I'll give you a little comfort, if you'll be so gracious as to show me to your bed. It is to bed that you want to go, isn't it?"

"Yes," she answered, and took his hand to lead the way to her bedroom.

NINETEEN

She had missed dinner that night, and she was ravenously hungry. She went into the rehab's cafeteria. It was ten o'clock, and there was a party atmosphere. Men and women sat together drinking coffee and chatting. Lulu was self-conscious because she had never been in the cafeteria, except during meal periods. She was uncomfortable, and she was hungry.

There was leftover sheet cake from dinner, and the ever-present coffee. It was all there was. Lulu cut herself a large piece of the white cake with gooey frosting, and poured herself a cup of coffee. As she turned to see if she would sit in the cafeteria or take the cake back to her room, a man with dark hair and green eyes said, "why don't you sit here?" She was startled.

"I, um," she started, and then said, "why not? Hi, I'm Lilly."

"Chuck," the man said, and held out his hand.

"Don't you mean Charles?" The man smiled. "Just let me put these down," Lulu said, embarrassed at the size of the piece of cake she had cut for herself. "Gee, I don't know how to start a conversation with someone..."

"Who is an addict?" He finished for her.

"Well, I guess I was going to say that." She toyed with her cake. "I'm hungry all the time. I feel so lonely."

"Visiting day is two days away."

"No one is coming to visit me. I called my boyfriend, no answer."

"That's too bad. You're a pretty woman."

"Why, thank you," Lulu started to say, when a blonde-haired woman came to the table and said, "what the fuck are you doing here with this bitch?" Lulu pushed her chair back.

"Nikki! I'm just talking," Chuck replied, unruffled.

"Well, where were you after dinner?" the blonde yelled.

"I think I need to go," Lulu said.

"You shut your fucking mouth, bitch, no one is talking to you."

All of a sudden Lulu reared up and said, "who do you think you are talking to, cunt?" She was angry, very angry, and it felt good.

Chuck stood up, and pushed Nikki backwards away from Lulu. "Let's take this outside, before we both get written up."

"I don't care about that. We only have a little time together." Nikki locked eyes with Chuck.

"Both of you are in rehab together?" Lulu asked, her chest still heaving from anger. Suddenly, the woman turned and ran out of the cafeteria. Lulu stared as the man ran after her. "What had just happened?" she asked herself, when Pam, her roommate, came up to her.

"You shouldn't be shopping for a boyfriend in the junk yard," Pamela said.

"I don't know what you are talking about. That woman just came up and screamed at me."

"That's her man," Pamela said.

"Just how was I to know that?" Lulu shouted at her. When Pam did not reply, Lulu said, "this place is fucked up. What am I doing here?" She cried as she left the cafeteria, without her coffee or cake.

"They are going to write you up!" Pam hollered as Lulu left.

"Fuck them!" Lulu shouted back, and walked briskly to her room. She had to get out of the rehab. It clearly had not worked for many of her fellow addicts in treatment. It probably wouldn't work for her. She had to go.

Lulu removed the key from her wrist, and opened the drawer where she had locked her purse almost two weeks ago. She grabbed it from the drawer and dumped make up into it. She looked at her suitcase, and decided to leave it behind. She walked out of her room and out of the rehab center. She kept walking down the long driveway to the entrance of the facility. When she got there, she saw Chuck.

"Oh, shit." This must be an omen. Lulu said, "you wouldn't happen to have a car, would you?"

"No," he said, green eyes glittering under the black sky. "Sorry about what happened."

"Yeah, that was some shit. Who is that woman anyway?" Lulu asked.

"My girlfriend of many years."

"Why was she so crazy?"

"Because I'm leaving tomorrow."

"Well, what are you going to do? Break up with her? How much longer is she here?"

"Whoa," Chuck said. "You are riled up."

"I hate this place. If I could leave, I would. Where are you going tomorrow?" Lulu asked.

"To serve ten years in a federal prison." Chuck said.

"Oh, my God! Really? What did you do?"

"Not that it matters, but I stole and sold a bunch of guns."

"I'm sorry." And suddenly she was deflated and wanted to cry. Chuck said nothing, and, for a moment, the two looked into each other's eyes.

"Finish treatment. At least try. It could be worth it for you."

"Are you going to make a run for it?" Lulu asked.

"No. I'm done running. They pick me up in the morning and transport me to a federal prison in Washington." There was silence again.

"Will you walk me back to the center?" Lulu asked.

"Sure will," Chuck answered, and Lulu took what seemed like one of the longest walks of her life. When they reached the entrance of the rehab, Chuck said, "good night, and good luck."

"Thank you," Lulu said, and they parted. Each of them went to their designated area of the center.

TWENTY

The next day, Lulu and Nikki were each escorted to the office of the rehab's administrator. They each had an opportunity to say why they had violently confronted each other, calling each other vile, gender-disparaging terms. Both women were deflated, now that both had expiated their anger. The women understood and recognized Nikki's jealous reaction. Lulu had behaved that way when another woman had captured Steven's attention. Both were women emotionally bound to men unavailable on many levels, which now, for both of them, included physical unavailability.

Dr. Patricia Carmichael looked at Lulu, then Nikki. Both women were dealing with multiple stressors and loss. She encouraged them to voice their fears to each other. When they had, Dr. Carmichael asked the women to shake hands. Both women reached out their hands to each other, and Lulu reached over and hugged Nikki. "I'm sorry," Lulu whispered into Nikki's ear, and looked into her eyes. Lulu wondered if Nikki could see that she was fearful as well. Then, each woman went to her scheduled activities, which for Lulu was her therapy session. Dr. Carmichael wrote in both of the women's files, recommending that each woman be allowed to remain in the treatment center. She sighed as they left her office.

When Lulu arrived at Terry Berquist's office, she was reading the notes from the night administrator's office. "Good morning," Terry said.

"Hi," Lulu replied.

"Do you have anything to say about last night?" Terry asked.

"No," Lulu answered.

"Did you really call Nikki a cunt?" Terry asked.

"Yes," Lulu answered, and then laughed out loud.

"Why are you laughing?" Terry asked.

"Because I've never cursed at anyone before like that. It was very unusual of me."

"Well, your language was surprising," Terry admitted.

"I guess I'm getting angry," Lulu replied.

"Angry about what?" Terry asked.

"Everything. Nothing," Lulu replied.

"Lilly, I understand that you were taking antidepressant medication."

"Yes." Lulu looked up quickly. "Are you going to allow me to go back on it?"

"No drugs of any kind are allowed here. We believe that drugs of any kind numb us from what's really happening inside. This is an opportunity to really get in touch with your feelings, and to allow feelings that have been suppressed to bubble up. There will be times you will feel low, agitated, angry and anxious, or any number of emotions. We encourage that, but we ask that you be responsible for those feelings, and to act appropriately." Lulu cocked her head, but Terry continued. "When I say 'appropriately,' I mean, if you are so depressed that you have suicidal or homicidal thoughts, then you will alert a staff member."

"Well, I'm certainly not going to kill myself—or anybody else, for that matter."

"Alright, that's probably true."

"What do you mean, 'probably true?'" Lulu asked.

"You could have gotten into a fight last night. You could have gotten hurt, or hurt someone else. You will have to confront your anger and your reactions to others in a less aggressive manner."

"Well, she started it," Lulu replied.

"That may be true," Terry replied. "But you will at least admit that incident last night could have escalated into violence."

"Yes," Lulu admitted.

"Alright. Is there anything else you want to say about the incident last night?"

"Yes," Lulu replied. "It won't happen again."

"Alright, I've been reviewing your files and I have derived insight into your behavior, especially as it relates to men. I understand your relationship with David Hughes—or what might have motivated you to become his wife and to have a child with him. What I don't understand is what you saw in Steven Flaherty."

Lulu looked at Terry. She thought for a long time, and then shook her head. "I don't know. I really don't know. I think it was because I believed that he was very wealthy, and I was sexually attracted to him. He is one of the few men that I was actually sexually attracted to, and I wanted to explore that." Lulu remained silent for a long while, and then she told Terry about the first night that she had had sex. As she told Terry about Catherine Connors, Steven Flaherty's "friend," what Lulu was really thinking about was the morning after.

A December sun sparkled in a cloudless sky, a welcome change from the rain that fell daily in wintertime in Seattle. Lulu could almost feel the sun's warmth on her closed eyelids, and her inner alarm told her it was time to open her eyes. Her eyelids fluttered. The sunlight streaming through the panel of windows in Lulu's loft bedroom was too bright. What time of day must it be? Suddenly, Lulu sat upright in her bed, and forced herself awake. Standing at the foot of her bed, dressed in his pajamas, was Christopher. "Christopher, what are you doing up here?"

"I woke up, Mommy, and I was hungry."

Lulu looked at the clock: it was after nine o'clock in the morning. "Oh, my God," she said. Her comment was meant, not only for the lateness of the hour, but for the fact that she realized that Steven was still in bed with her. Lulu exchanged looks with her son. She did not know what to say.

Instead, Christopher said, "Mommy, just because you sleep with him doesn't mean that you don't love me anymore. I know that."Her little boy's words tore at her heart. "Come give Mommy a hug, Christopher." As she was hugging Christopher, Teddy came into the bedroom. He was shy. "Let Mommy hug you, Teddy," Lulu said. The older boy came and stood stiffly while Lulu gave him a hug. "Both of you run downstairs and put your clothes on. I'll be down in a minute to make you breakfast," Lulu said.

"Can we have French toast?" Teddy asked.

"Sure," Lulu answered

"And hot chocolate?" Teddy asked.

"Yes, Teddy, but you're pushing it, kid. Now, go get dressed."

The boys ran out of the room, and Lulu looked at Steven Flaherty. She was embarrassed, and she could feel her face turn bright red. She had revealed way too much of herself last night—or was it this morning? What had she been thinking? It was a terrible mistake, brought on by the cocaine and her loneliness. She had better correct her mistake, and soon. She slipped out of bed to her bathroom, brushed her teeth, and put on her bathrobe. From the bed, Steven began to move. He opened his blue eyes, and stared around him.

"Good morning," Lulu said from the bathroom doorway.

"I've been kidnapped by aliens," Steven said. "I think I heard two small aliens come in here this morning."

"Yes, Teddy and Christopher were here. I can't stand around and chat. I've got to make breakfast and lunch for the kids."

"Hey, wait a minute, Lilly. Don't snap at me because you woke up late."

"I didn't intend to snap, but I do have two children who are late for school and need breakfast and lunch."

"Well, hold your horses, madame. Let me get my pants on, and I'll take you all to breakfast, and I will have the restaurant order a couple of lunches to go."

"That's not necessary, Steven. It'll make us later."

"Oh, come on, Lilly, grab some jeans. I'm out of bed. Can I borrow a toothbrush? Come on, Lilly, stop standing around and get dressed or help the kids get dressed, we're late!" He laughed at her. She fought to resist his beguiling smile, but she had to.

Alarm bells were ringing in her. She had made a terrible mistake. "Steven" she said, "This was so wrong. I'm confused and upset, and troubled, and embarrassed. What's happening here?" There was silence in the bathroom. She heard Steven looking for a toothbrush and toothpaste.

"Oh, lots of nice drugs in here," he said, looking in her bathroom cabinet.

"All prescribed," Lulu answered.

"I'm not saying anything," Steven said.

"Do you make fun of everything?" Lulu asked.

Steven stuck his head out of the bathroom door. "Look, we can be heavy and serious about this, or we can be light. The choice is yours. Right now, your kids are hungry and need food. We can dissect this later this morning."

"No, we can't, Steven. I have work to do. I work for a living. I don't have a trust fund."

"Oh, we're back to the trust fund? I'm willing to share with you, if you can get a court to dissolve it. You can tell them that I am not a spendthrift."

"Oh, Steven," Lulu began, but was stoppd from a voice downstairs.

"Mommy, come help me tie my shoes," Christopher said. She heard Steven humming in the bathroom, and Lulu thought how nice it must be to never have to worry about being any place on time, or having children. It was easy for him to turn everything into fun. It was one of the things that his money bought. Lulu knocked on the bathroom door. "Just this once," she said. "I can't have the children being late for school. Their father looks for every reason to take them away from me. We had a week-long trial when we got divorced. Mostly over the kids."

"No, I did not know that, Ms. St. Blanc, but I do now, and I will make every effort to keep you on time from now on. So, let's hustle, your kids are hungry."

Lulu shook her head, and went into her closet for a pair of jeans and a sweater. She pulled on her clothes, and found a pair of old penny loafers. In the bathroom, Steven was using her toothbrush. She sighed, and went to check where her children were in their preparations for school.

Downstairs in their room, the video machine was on, and the children were playing with toys. Each had taken off an article of their pajamas, but, for the most part, they had done little else.

"Boys!" Lulu said. "Come on, get dressed. Christopher," Lulu said, "I thought you needed help with your shoes?"

"But you didn't leave any clothes out for us, Mommy," Teddy interjected.

"Yeah, that's right," Christopher agreed.

"But you know where your clothes are," Lulu said. "Alright, this room is a mess. At some point, you are going to have to deconstruct that Lego tower," Lulu said.

"Yes, Mommy," the boys said in unison, but they were watching the video playing on the screen.

Lulu opened a white plasterboard chest, and pulled out two pairs of underpants, followed by two pairs of socks. From a lower drawer, she found two pairs of neatly-folder corduroy pants, and two long sleeved polo shirts. She laid a set for each boy on his bed, and then turned off the video machine. "Okay, get cracking, boys. We are late." The boys could see that Lulu was cranky, and chose not to push her.

"We're getting on our clothes, Mommy," Teddy said. "I'll help Christopher with his things so you can make lunch."

"Thanks, Teddy, but we're going out to breakfast, and then I'm taking you to school."

"Is Steven coming with us?" Christopher asked.

"Yes, he is," Lulu answered.

"Is Steven going to be our new father?" Teddy asked.

"No, he is not!" Lulu answered, much sharper than she had intended.

Teddy was crestfallen, but his mother did not see the change in his demeanor. She was already walking out of the bedroom and wondering where Steven was.

"I love you, Mommy," Teddy said, as he went into the bathroom, but Lulu did not hear him. Lulu heard Steven coming down the stairs.

"Christopher, hurry," she said. "Do you need Mommy to help you on with your clothes?"

Before Christopher could answer, Steven came up behind her and said, "of course not. He's a big boy, aren't you, Christopher?"

Christopher stopped for a minute, and thought. "I can put on everything, but Mommy still has to help me with my shoes."

"Yes, shoes are difficult," Steven agreed. "I didn't learn to tie my shoes until I was about twelve," he exaggerated.

"Nah, that's not true!" Christopher giggled. "I'll learn to tie my shoes by next year. I'll be seven then, but not twelve."

"I'm telling you, it's true. Scout's honor, I was twelve when I learned to tie my shoes."

Lulu was consumed with anxiety. She had to get Steven out of her life.

"I'm going to grab the boys' coats. Teddy, please hurry!" Lulu said, as she walked to the coat closet in the hallway. She was rebuking herself as she went about gathering her coat and those of her children. What was she doing? She was trying to be a good mother; she was trying to learn what it meant to be a lawyer, and, damn it, after five years as a single mother and law school, she was bone weary. She needed a vacation from law school, from life, from her recent divorce, from her children. Yes, she was tired.

It was fortunate that the children would start Christmas break that day, at the end of the school day. She needed a break. The children would be with their father for six days, return on Christmas Eve, and then go back for Christmas break until school started in January.

She was still feeling guilty, angry, and self-pitying when Steven took her parka from her and helped her on with it. "Thanks," she mumbled. "Let's go, boys!" she said, handing each boy his coat.

"Where are our lunches?" Teddy asked.

"They are going to be catered," Steven answered.

"What does that mean?" Christopher asked.

"We're going to buy them from where we have breakfast, boys," Lulu answered.

"Mommy, you look sad," Teddy said. "Don't you want to have breakfast?"

"Sure she does," Steven said. "She just needs a little coffee, huh, Mommy?" Steven asked.

The boys laughed.

"That's right, boys," Lulu agreed. "I just need a little coffee."

"Okay, gentlemen, we are taking my car. Oops, my mom's car," Steven said.

Out of the door, the boys raced after Steven. Lulu watched the three of them, laughing and happy. She was miserable and scared. She did not even know how she felt about Steven. Did she even like him? Without his money, would he be the same person? Would she even go out with him? But how could she separate the man that Steven had become from his money? Was it not his money that gave him the freedom to wake when he wanted to, and drive the car that he wished, and to live where he wanted? And was this what was important to Lulu? She did not know, and the drugs did not help. She would tell Steven after breakfast that she needed a break from him, that she had to focus herself on her work and building her practice. All these thoughts ran through her head as Steven drove them to a local pancake house.

"Your children are gorgeous," Steven said to Lulu.

"Thank you," she said quietly. The boys chatted with Steven for the rest of the ride, and he made them laugh.

"Oh, shit," Lulu said. She clamped her hands over her mouth. "Sorry, boys," she said. "I forgot your suitcases. Your father is going to pick you up from school. We have to go back home."

The boys looked worried. Their mother always had their suitcases packed the night before they went to their father's house. Something was really wrong. It was the second time that their mother had forgotten something that day.

"Why don't you do it after breakfast, and after we take the children to school? You can come back to the apartment and pack their bags. I'll help," Steven offered. "And here's the pancake house, Mom!"

"Stop it, Steven," Lulu said, and Steven's face turned red.

"We can turn around now, but we're already here."

"You're right," Lulu acquiesced. "Come on, boys, Mommy does need some coffee, and you need some breakfast. Eggs and bacon with your pancakes. Not too much syrup!" Lulu continued speaking to them, but really to herself. The boys were already unbuckling their seatbelts and opening the car door.

It was almost eleven o'clock when Lulu walked the children into the principal's office, and got late notices for each of them. She kissed them both, and watched them walk down the hall to their classrooms. She could have cried as she watched their blue and red parkas disappearing around the corner.

Lulu brushed the tears from her eyes, and walked back to Steven's— or rather, his mother's—gleaming brown Jaguar. Lulu got in without a word. Steven did not look at her, but pulled out of the school parking lot and navigated down the quiet streets until he reached the exit to the freeway. When Lulu remained silent, Steven said, "a penny for your thought. Oh, I forgot—you're a lawyer. A dollar for your thoughts. Or, is it five, these days?"

"Actually, it's neither. You know, Steven, I've been thinking. You are lots of fun, and I really like you, but I think maybe this is all going so fast. I just don't know where I am. I can't have a repeat of the past couple of weeks, and certainly not this morning. You don't know my ex-husband. He's always looking for a reason to take these children away from me. He laid a lot of ground work in our divorce trial five years ago."

Steven was silent. "You are too hard on yourself. You wake up late once for the first time in, what? Five years? And you think you've committed a crime. You are human. You work like hell. You live on pennies, and it's not the way a woman like you should live."

Sitting in her old sweater and faded blue jeans, in a beautiful car with a handsome man, she was defending her life of scarcity. "That's all well and good, but right now, it's the life I have. The only one. It's a life in which I cannot afford mistakes of any kind. I'm afraid all the time. I really don't know what I'm doing as a lawyer. It was insane for someone like me to go out on my own. I don't even have a mentor, or someone I can turn to for advice. I'm afraid I'm going to get disbarred for making a gross error of the law. More than that, every day I worry about what and how I will feed the children. I worry if there's enough money for gas, or perhaps I shouldn't buy gas, and I should buy them valentine cards, or something that they want. It's not fair to them." Suddenly, Lulu began to cry. That's what she knew about, scarcity. The thought made her sob harder.

"Lilly, please don't cry..."

"I'm sorry. I guess I'm just tired."

"I guess you are. Can I get you anything?"

"Yes," Lulu replied petulantly. "A day at the spa! That's right," she smiled through her tears. "A day for a queen at the most luxurious spa in Seattle—or even Bellevue," she laughed.

"Now, isn't that coincidental? I just happen to have a close acquaintance that has a whole chain of beauty and health spas."

"I was only kidding, Steven."

"I wasn't. I'm going to use mother's contraption of a car phone and make a few calls."

"Oh, Steven, you don't have to."

But Steven was already punching buttons on the phone. "Delores, Steven Flaherty here. My mother is fine, thank you. No, I wasn't calling about either of my sisters, but I'm wondering if Jerry is in. He's in meetings? Well, tell him to get out of them. No, actually, you can probably handle this. Can you look in the main computer terminal—but preferably Bellevue and then Seattle, maybe Redmond—and see what's available for a manicure, facial, pedicure, massage, and make-up...sure, waxing?" He smiled as he thought about the sleekness he preferred in women, but which he rarely found. Lulu was that woman, hiding under her limited financial constraints. The whole works. "For whom? Lilly St. Blanc, my lawyer. Yes, she is a lucky woman, but she's a better attorney. Noon? Bellevue? Perfect. Tell Jerry I owe him one, and he can collect at any time."

"Was that Jerry Smyth's? That's impressive. You know Jerry Smyth? Did you meet him in London? Isn't that where his salons and day spas started?"

Steven laughed, "Everybody knows Jerry Smyth. He's actually a friend of my mother. He is in his late fifties, not my age bracket. My family invested a small amount of money in the London spa. It became profitable; Jerry really knows his stuff. Naturally, he wanted to bring it back to America, but you damn lawyers don't make it easy for anybody. He wanted to do the big cities—New York, Washington D.C., Miami—but the franchising was going to cost as much as the real-estate. This was where I came in. I suggested that he bring his ideas back home to Seattle. I told him to create a salon and day spa in Seattle, and then another one in Bellevue. Now, there's a dozen locations in the Puget Sound area. Complete spa experiences, right here in our little backyard. He's added hair and skin products. It's really worked out well, even though he's not a national chain. I think that's better, easier; there's more control."

"Were you a business major in college?" Lulu asked.

"How soon we forget... I thought I impressed you when I told you I had completed my graduate work back East. Surely you must have guessed one of the top business schools."

She had wanted a stupid manicure. She had sold out her life for a tiny bit of luxury.

She could see that Terry knew she was just talking to avoid what was really in her heart. "The bottom line, Terry, so to speak, is that I don't know why I was sexually attracted to Steven Flaherty. If I had to guess, I would say he was exciting, and a change of pace. The cocaine made me feel glamourous and sexy." Lulu stopped. She could see that Terry was not connecting with her. Lulu gave up, just like everyone here who had taken that first hit of cocaine, methamphetamine, alcohol, prescription drugs, or whatever had gotten them to this desolate place in Eastern Washington. "I don't know, Terry. I don't know. If I come up with an answer that seems to resonate, I'll share it with you. I'm like everybody else here." With that, she got up, and left the therapist's office.

TWENTY-ONE

Lulu went back to her room, and began to cry. She felt very alone. She had spoken to her older sister, and she had been judgmental, cold, angry, and disappointed. She had no one to turn to. The two friends she once had, her law school friend, Nancy, and Janine Zimmerman, her law school sponsor, had been alienated because of her drug use and her relationship with Steven—and because she had generally fucked up. Had she been so far gone that she had chosen, what? A fantasy? Yes, a drug induced temporary fantasy. Why had she not left with Janine and Nancy? Bitter tears stung her eyes. The blue Suburban. They had come in Janine's blue Suburban.

It was early evening, and the vehicle's beams cut through the darkness. The driver of the vehicle made no attempt to be discreet. The driver wanted to be seen and heard, and their tactics worked. Steven opened the sliding glass doors, and walked out onto Lulu's balcony.

"Lilly," Steven called. She had been darting about the kitchen, stocking tea in her cabinets.

"What is it?"

"Do you know somebody who drives a dark blue Suburban?"

"No," Lulu answered.

"That's interesting, because somebody in a blue Suburban wants our attention."

"What are you talking about?" Lulu asked. She left the tea, and walked to where Steven was standing.

"Look over there, right where the driveway turns towards your apartment. That car is hovering and waiting."

"Maybe they are looking for someone else's building. These units are so randomly placed," Lulu continued.

"I don't think so. I think that whoever it is checking the visitor's parking area."

"You're paranoid," Lulu laughed. "Besides, it's freezing out there. Come on inside. I'm going to make mulled red wine, or, at least, I think I am. By the way, what were we doing for dinner?" Lulu asked.

"Don't know," Steven said, as he continued to stand on the balcony. "Hey, Lilly," Steven said. "Were you expecting anyone?"

"No, I'm not. What are you doing? You're making me paranoid now!"

"Well, two people are coming out of that blue Suburban, and they look like they are headed here."

"Not possible," Lulu answered.

"Well, from what I can see, a redhead and a brunette are walking towards the steps to your apartment."

Lulu rushed to where Steven was standing, and she caught sight of her law partner, Nancy, and Janine Zimmerman. "Oh, shit!" Lulu exclaimed. "That's my law partner and my landlord! Oh, my god!"

"Calm down, Lilly. They can't do anything to you," Steven said.

"You don't know that!" Lulu said, as the doorbell rang.

"Lilly," Steven said. "Go upstairs. I'll tell them that you are getting ready for dinner."

"Do you think it will work?" Lulu asked.

"Get upstairs!' Steven hissed, as the doorbell pealed again. Steven walked to the door.

"Good evening," Steven said pleasantly, as he opened the door. Nancy Trujillo and Janine Zimmerman stood facing him.

"Is Lulu here?" Nancy asked.

"Why, yes, she is," Steven answered, without moving from the doorframe.

"We've come to see her," Janine Zimmerman announced.

"Was she expecting you?" Steven asked, the model of politeness. "I believe she is getting ready for dinner."

"Listen," Janine Zimmerman said. "I've gotten several calls from Nancy, and from Mr. Hughes, as well as from an acquaintance of mine. Nobody has seen or heard from Lulu in over a week. Now, where is she?"

"I've already said; she's here. She's getting ready for dinner. Would you like to come in?" Steven asked, as he moved away from the door and let the women through the foyer into the living room.

"Please have a seat." Steven gestured towards the sofa.

"Do you live here?" Janine asked. "If you do, I need you on the lease. If you're not on the lease, you can't stay here for more than three days without Lulu incurring fees."

"And you are?" Steven asked.

"I own the damn place. Lulu has not paid rent in six months. If you live here, I expect some rent, and some information about you."

Nancy Trujillo had, until this point, said nothing, but then said, "what's going on here?" Lulu's office phone has not been answered in days." Nancy would have continued, but Lulu walked into the room. She was wearing a gossamer yellow gown with a gold chain around her neck. On her feet, she wore delicate gold slippers. Her appearance was enough to silence both women.

"Lulu," they both said at once." Are you okay?" Both Nancy and Janine asked, as they pushed past Steven.

"I'm fine. I'm taking a break," Lulu said, with all the composure she could muster.

"A break?" Nancy said. "You have work to do. You can't take a break when the client is expecting an answer from you."

"You're so thin," Janine continued. "You look as if you haven't eaten or slept in days. What are you doing?" Before Lulu could venture an answer, Steven stepped in.

"Alright, that's enough, ladies. You have come uninvited. It's a few days before Christmas, and you have yet to say what you need so that Lilly and I can go to dinner."

"Let Lulu speak for herself," Nancy said. "She can speak for herself. What the hell are you doing, Lulu? Who is this man?"

"I'm her fiancée," Steven interjected. "Lilly won't be working with you anymore," Steven said to Nancy. "She's done with this little practice of yours. If she owes a client any money, let them send her a bill, and it will be paid. As for you," Steven said, addressing Janine, "how much back rent does she owe? I think I have a thousand dollars in my pocket," Steven said, as he took money out of his wallet. He counted out ten one hundred dollar bills. "Here, take it," he said, as he put the money in Janine Zimmerman's hand.

Janine took the money, and said, "you bet I will take it, it's probably all I will see of the thousands of dollars that Lulu owes me!"

"Send me a past due notice," Steven said to Janine. "Lilly probably won't be residing here much longer anyway."

Janine was caught off guard again. "What the hell is going on here?" Janine asked. "Lulu, you're engaged to him?" she said, as she came nose-to-nose with Lulu.

"Not officially," Lulu stammered. "We just...we just..."

"'We just' what?" Janine screamed in Lulu's face. "You just met him! Is that what you want to say? You just met him! Now you are acting the part of the desperate bar tramp? You meet some man for a month or two, and you marry him?"

Steven put his hand on Janine's shoulder to separate her from Lulu. "Back up!" Steven snarled at Janine.

"Take your goddamn hands off me," Janine said, as she pushed Steven's hands away and stepped in closer to Lulu. "You do this to me after all I have done for you and your two little brats? You marry the first man that bought you dinner in two years? What about me?" Janine screamed, with tears running down her face.

"Janine, Lulu," Nancy intervened. "This is getting out of hand. Lulu, get your purse. Come with us."

"No!" Lulu finally screamed. "Get the fuck away from me, you fat bitch," Lulu screamed at Janine Zimmerman. "You sick, fucking fat bitch! You don't think that I don't know all about your nasty secret dyke life? I know all about it. So don't come here pretending that you were concerned for me. You're not. You disgust me." Lulu turned away from Janine, who stood in shock.

"You called me fat." Janine began to blubber, and then Nancy began to yell at Lulu.

"So, Steven's to marry you?" Nancy sneered. "You can't manage to live without a man, can you, Lulu? You will find a man to pay the way, won't you? You disgust me, Lulu St. Blanc," Nancy spat, and then said to Janine, "come on Janine. Let's get the hell out of here."

Janine stood mumbling to herself as she clutched the money. "She called me fat."

"What do you think you are, dear?" Steven said, with a mean smile.

"You, you!" Janine sputtered, as she backed out of the hallway. "I'll evict you tomorrow," Janine screamed.

"Come on, Janine," Nancy urged. "Let's get out of here." The two women walked out of the apartment, Janine leaning on Nancy's shoulder. Their heads were bent together as they fiercely whispered.

When Steven shut the door and turned back to Lulu, she was huddled over in a corner. "Steven, those were my best friends, my only friends."

"Honey, those aren't your friends. Those are two fat women who want something from you."

"No, no. Nancy was my dearest friend all through law school. We studied together. And Janine, Janine has been so good to me. How did this happen? Janine's going to evict me!"

Steven walked over to Lulu and held her by the shoulders. "Lilly, Lilly, calm down. Nothing's going to happen, certainly not tonight, anyway, but we need to make some changes."

"What kind of changes?" Lulu asked.

"Well, for one thing, we're leaving these digs. Do you have a credit card?"

"No, I don't," Lulu answered.

"How about a debit card?" Steven asked.

"I do have one, but there's not a whole lot of money in there," Lulu said.

"How much is 'not a lot?'" Steven asked.

"I think I have about one hundred and fifty dollars," Lulu said.

"Well, that won't get us far tonight," Steven answered, "but it will get us a room at the Bellevue Western Plaza."

"The Bellevue Western Plaza?" Lulu asked.

"Yes, honey. Listen: tomorrow I will write you check for five thousand dollars. We will put it in your bank account, and use your debit card from now on. We'll only spend one night at the Western, then we'll check into the Four Seasons. But before we do all of that, we're going to go the court house and get a marriage license."

"What?" Lulu asked.

"We're going to get a marriage license. You know, one of those things that you fill out where you wait three days, and if you still want to, you can get married by a judge," Steven said.

"Steven, Steven, what are you doing to my life? Married? Why? I just met you."

"Lilly, tell me that you don't want to marry me," Steven said.

"It's not that, it's...I don't know."

"You do know," Steven said. "Now, take off that nightgown. Let's get out of here, get some food, and have some fun. Tomorrow we do banking and court and all other sorts of fun things."

"You are crazy, you know," Lulu said, getting up. "It's a merry-go-round, but the ride's still moving, so I might as well keep riding," Lulu said.

"That's the attitude," Steven said. "Bring only the essentials, honey." Steven continued, and Lulu went upstairs to pack.

As Lulu remembered the scene, tears rolled down her face. How stupid she had been. The two women had been her friends, had helped and supported her. And now they were angry with her, just like her sister was. She lowered her head and sobbed until she fell asleep on her bed.

TWENTY-TWO

It was morning when Lulu woke up. She looked over at her roommate's bed, and it was empty. According to the clock on her night table, it was barely six in the morning. She was still wearing the clothes that she had fallen asleep in. She began to panic. She had to get out of the rehab. She had to. Then she remembered what Anne had told the group just the day before. Never become too hungry, angry, lonely or tired. The acronym spelled "HALT." It was the signal to slow down, to eat if you were hungry. She wasn't tired. She was lonely and sad. She then remembered that the rehab had a sunrise AA meeting. She didn't change her clothes. She splashed water on her face, and went to find the meeting.

She found the group in a sunny room. Both men and women were in the group. There was no way for her to make a discreet entrance. The group was in a circle, and when she entered the room, everyone turned to look at her. There was a man in front of the group, and Lulu sat quietly and listened to what he had to say. The man was in tears, and was talking about how he had left his children and wife without food and money while he snorted cocaine with prostitutes. He told the group that he had lost his car, his house, his job, and finally ended up in jail. When he was done, the group clapped for him.

The next speaker was a young Native American woman. She began by saying that this was her sixth time in some form of rehab, and that she was nineteen years old. She had run away from home at fourteen, become a prostitute a year later, and now she was HIV positive and determined to beat her habit.

Then, a woman who was very jaundiced got up. She was connected to an oxygen tank. Her stomach was grossly bloated, and she could barely walk. Lulu was horrified that the woman was even in rehab, instead of a hospital. She began by saying that she knew that she was going to die, but that she wanted to die sober. When the woman was finished, she pushed her oxygen tank, and looked at Lulu.

The man in front of the room looked at Lulu and asked if she would like to share. She remembered what her group counselor, Anne, had said the day before: "You are as sick as your secrets. When you can completely admit to yourself your behavior—when you can own your behavior—you can start to heal, not from your drug or alcohol addiction, but from what drove you there." Lulu's heart was beating fast, but she got up and walked to the front of the room. She began by saying, "hello, my name is Lilly, and I am an alcoholic and drug addict." The room clapped. The man turned to her and asked how long she had been sober. Lulu said, "I think seven days." The room clapped again, and the man reached into a box. He gave Lulu a metal coin that had "Day One" written on it. Lulu touched the coin and cried.

"I didn't know that I was becoming addicted," Lulu began. "It all seemed so fun, so glamorous, so unlike me, and then Friday night eased into Saturday morning, and then into Saturday afternoon." Her face turned red as she remembered the early days with Steven.

When Lulu and Steven woke up the Saturday morning after her spa day, the sun was shining on Seattle and pouring into Lulu's bedroom. Her throat was dry, and she could not remember when she last ate.

"Steven, what time is it?"

"I don't know. Three, I think."

"Maybe I should ask, what day is it?"

"I think Saturday."

"Good, I guess," Lulu mumbled. She got up and rubbed her eyes. "I need water," she said.

"No, I need you," Steven answered, and pulled her to him.

"No, Steven, I can't."

"You can't what?"

"Make love to you again."

"What, you don't like me anymore?"

"No, it's just…"

"Coke is supposed to be a sexual stimulant. What's with you?"

"I don't know," Lulu said, as she looked at her newly lacquered nails.

"You remember when you were a little kid, and sex had that nasty feel to it?"

"I guess so," Lulu answered, feeling very uncomfortable.

"Well, think about it."

"Well," Lulu started, "I have never told anyone about this, not even my therapists, but I like the idea of domination." Lulu paused.

"Now you're talking," Steven said. He reached over for the Ziploc bag of cocaine, and put a rock in the pipe. "Here, honey, take a hit of this."

"I think I've had enough for the rest of my life," Lulu laughed ruefully.

"Darling, you haven't even started. Take one little hit for Daddy."

"Daddy?" Lulu asked.

"Yes, Daddy," Steven said. "I'm gonna be your daddy for a while. I'm gonna tell you what to wear, how to comb your hair and how to take care of Daddy."

As Lulu was about to protest, Steven handed her the pipe and said, "suck."

Lulu looked at Steven, and then pulled on the pipe. "Oh, my God, that was such a rush," Lulu said, as her head rolled back on the covers. Steven covered her mouth with his, and Lulu could barely suppress her moans.

"Are you ready to make love to Daddy now?" Steven asked. Lulu could only nod her head.

Later that evening, when Lulu awoke from her drug-induced sleep, Steven was on the phone. Steven blew Lulu a kiss, and then finished his conversation.

"Okay, baby, time to get dressed."

"Where are we going?"

"Shopping."

"It's seven o'clock."

"That's right! That gives us about two hours, if you get that fine ass of yours out of the bed."

"I can't."

"Yes, you can. Take a hit, put on the dress I bought you yesterday, and we're going to get you a new wardrobe."

"What kind of wardrobe?" Lulu asked.

"First of all, I am going to buy lingerie in every color of the rainbow. Dozens of pairs of thong panties. Ass like yours should never be covered. And those breasts? Who knew you had breasts like that?"

"You're funny," Lulu smiled. As Steven talked, he prepared the pipe for Lulu, and she inhaled. Once again, she lolled her head back. "If I keep feeling this way, you won't ever get me out of this bed," Lulu said, her eyes heavy-lidded and sensuous.

"That's the plan, baby," Steven said, as he took the pipe and inhaled from it.

"Now get up, in the shower, on with the dress, and, Lilly, no panties, please."

"Steven," Lulu was about to protest.

"I'm Daddy, and you're Baby, and I'm going to take really good care of you."

"Okay," Lulu said, and stumbled into the shower as Steven got back on the phone. Had she heard the conversation, she would have kicked Steven out of her home.

"Hey, Oz," Steven said into the phone.

"'Sup?" the man responded.

"Got the finest piece you've ever seen."

"She a blonde, man?" Oz asked.

"Naw, she a little bit of everything, and a lawyer, too."

"You lying, man."

"Word up!" Steven laughed into the phone.

"You say she a lawyer *and* she fine? Man, I got to see that."

"You will, we'll be riding over a little bit later tonight and you can take a peek at her."

"Just a peek?"

"Personal property, bro. She's mine."

"Damn Steven, why you tell me 'bout her, then?"

"You know I don't keep nothing for long, Oz."

"Yeah, you right, man." And both Steven and Buddy Oz laughed.

"Check you later," Steven said, and hung up.

Steven put the phone down, restocked the pipe, took a hit, and brought the pipe to Lulu in the bathroom. "You are one gorgeous woman," Steven said, as he watched Lulu wash herself in the shower.

"Come 'ere. Stick your head out of the shower and give Daddy a kiss."

"Hmm?" Lulu asked. "The water feels so good."

"It will feel a whole lot better once I give you a kiss."

Lulu opened the shower door and stuck her head out. "Kiss me," she said.

Steven complied, as water from the shower dripped onto the floor.

"We're making a mess," Lulu laughed.

"Here, honey," Steven said, and gave Lulu the pipe. Lulu tried to reach for the pipe, but Steven said, "I'll hold it for you."

"Oh, I like that." Lulu smiled and inhaled deeply. She moaned, and put her head back under the shower.

Steven took another hit from the pipe, and then closed the shower door. "Hurry up, darling. The stores are closing, and everybody will have bought up the thongs I plan for you."

"Mmhmm..." Lulu said, and Steven laughed.

"I'll be back for you in ten minutes. Be dressed. I'm going to get some wine and a little something else," Steven said, with a wicked laugh. "You hear me, Lilly?"

"Mmhmm," Lulu said from inside the shower. Steven laughed again, and then left the bathroom. He found his keys, which were lying next to the bed. He smiled again. He put on his loafers, and ran down the two flights of stairs. In the hall closet, he grabbed his cashmere coat.

He got into the brown jaguar. He looked at the gold watch on his wrist, and laughed quietly. He figured it would take him about a half an hour to make it to the sex shop in Bellevue. He knew that Lulu would not be straight enough to get dressed. He would order her a dozen sets of bras and thongs on his way to the sex store. He could pick them up on his way back. He would grab a case of wine, and then he would invite Buddy Oz over instead of driving into the city. Steven smiled to himself. It was going to be fun to turn the uptight Lilly Marie St. Blanc into a whore—*his* whore. She was enticing, and so sexually screwed. It would be lots of fun to turn her out. He picked up the phone, and pressed an automatic number.

"Ladies lingerie, please," he said into the phone. When a woman answered, he gave her a name and credit card number, and ordered the lingerie. "Gift wrap it all," he added. He then raced out of the driveway and down the freeway, heading east. He pushed the car's engine, and was at a store called "The Love Connection" within less than ten minutes. He pulled the car as close to the store's entrance as possible, and then hopped out. He walked quickly to the door and swung it open. The woman at the cash register recognized him, and she nodded. Steven nodded back in acknowledgement. A sales lady wearing a black leather outfit came up to him.

"May I help you?" She asked.

"Don't think anybody can help me, darling, but you can point me to your finest doggie leash."

"Doggie leash?"

"Yes, I want a pretty one. You know, something for a classy—" he paused, then laughed, and said, "bitch." He and the sales woman laughed, and they headed to a corner of the store. The woman handed Steven an elegant black leash that had studs around the collar. The chain attached to the collar was slinky. "That's just the kind I was looking for," Steven said. "Now for some fishnet stockings."

"Sure," the sales lady said. She sauntered over to a series of closed drawers. "Any particular color?"

"What have you got?" Steven asked, as her peered over the woman's shoulder.

"Pink, red, black, and white," The woman answered.

"I'll take one of each," Steven answered.

"What size?" The woman asked.

"I don't know," Steven said. "She's small. What sizes do you have?"

"Small, medium, large, extra-large, triple X...."

"Whoa!" Steven said. "Small. One of each color in small." The lady pulled four pairs of fishnet stockings from the drawer.

"Garter belt?" the woman asked.

"How could I forget?" Steven laughed. "Of course, garter belts. What kind are we talking about?"

"I got leather, vinyl....you name it," the sales woman said.

"Give me a leather and a vinyl," Steven said.

"She must be one really bad girl," The woman smiled.

"She will be, by the time I have her trained," Steven said. The woman looked up. This man was not kidding. He intended to train someone. She didn't say anything, but asked, "cash or charge?"

"Cash," Steven said, and walked towards the register. After he paid the woman, he hopped into the car and raced to the lingerie store. As he flew down the streets of the quiet community, he picked up the phone and connected with the lingerie store. The packages were not done being wrapped. "I'll be by in twenty minutes," Steven said to the woman who answered the phone. "I'm in a brown Jaguar, be waiting outside for me." He did not bother for the woman to answer. He put the phone down, and went to the liquor store before it closed.

Inside the store, he ordered a case of white wine, and charged it to his mother's account. The sales clerk put the wine in the car, and Steven tipped him five dollars. "Merry Christmas," the clerk said.

"It's been a merry Christmas, and it's been white as well."

The clerk looked at Steven, and said nothing.

Steven got into the car and headed towards the lingerie store. When he arrived, a woman stood shivering as she held several bags. Steven pulled to a stop.

"How much?" he asked the shivering woman.

"It's all La Perla," the woman said.

"I know what kind they are," Steven said impatiently. "How much?"

"Two thousand four hundred and seventy-eight dollars," the woman said, almost too afraid to speak the amount.

Steven reached into his wallet and started counting out hundreds. He gave the lady twenty six one hundred dollar bills. "Oops!" he said. "I forgot that I charged it all. Here's a hundred dollars."

"I don't have change," the woman said, as Steven handed her the money.

"Who asked for change?" Steven asked. "Merry Christmas," he said. He left the woman staring as he pulled the car from where she was standing and made a sharp U-turn. Before he headed back into the direction towards the woman, he took out the crack pipe, filled it with a rock, and deeply inhaled. The woman watched for a moment, and then hurriedly turned away and re-entered the store. As she opened the door and looked back, Steven had put the pipe down and picked up the phone.

"What's your favorite color, man?"

"For what?" Buddy Oz answered.

"For pussy, man," Steven laughed.

"Well, hell, you know the answer to that. It's pink!" Buddy and Steven laughed.

"Hey listen man, I got a favor to ask you."

"Naw, man, I ain't delivering to Bellevue. The police see a black man in Bellevue, they'll stop me."

"I'll make it worth your while," Steven said.

"What we talking about?" Buddy asked.

"Two large." Steven answered.

"Shit, man," Buddy exclaimed, "What, you having a party?"

"Yeah, a party for two weeks!" Steven laughed.

"For two, man, I will be there."

"Bonus round is that you get to see the pretty lady."

"Well, I got to see this," Buddy answered.

"Be there in an hour." Steven put the phone down and smiled. He picked up the phone, and dialed Lulu's number "Hey, darling girl," Steven said when Lulu answered. "You coming down, baby?" Steven asked.

"I don't feel good right now," Lulu said.

"Daddy will be home in a few minutes, and fix that all up for you."

"Good," was all that Lulu could manage.

"I have a surprise for you." Steven added.

"Really?"

"Yep," Steven said.

"What?" Lulu asked, but Steven had already hung up.

Lulu did not tell the group everything. She could not tell them that the crack had made her feel more sexually alive than ever in her life.

TWENTY-THREE

Later that afternoon, Lulu went into therapy with a new attitude. She wanted the events of her life to make sense. As she entered the therapy room, she said hello to Terry Berkquist, and began where she left off.

"I slept with Steven Flaherty because I was excited about his money, and the life that I thought it could give me. And, while I thought Catherine was tacky, I envied her and her money. I was competitive, and I wanted to take something away from her. Lastly, crack is a highly sexual drug. I think that's why so many people get addicted to it. In the beginning, it gave me an incredible orgasmic rush. I loved it. That rush got weaker and weaker, and harder and harder to get. I know that now."

"That's good work, Lilly. I'd like to go deeper. In one of our sessions, we talked about your childhood, and that your grandfather had died when you were five. What else happened? What we will try in the time you are here is to connect some of the incidents in your past with your current behavior."

Lulu nodded. "Okay," she said, with a sigh. She then began to tell Terry Berkquist about the years after her grandfather had died.

"I could never remember whether I had just turned seven, or was about to turn seven. It was still warm outside, but fall in Washington D.C. could be very warm. I had been playing with children from the neighborhood when my mother called to me to come into the house.

'The President has been shot,' my mother said, with tears in her eyes.

I did not know what this meant, but I went inside the house and sat in front of the television in the room where my sisters and I slept. My Aunt Verna was crying, and even my father and my Uncle Raymond, who was always happy, were sad.

'Why are they sad?' I asked my grandmother, when I went into the kitchen where she was cooking.

'Things will change, now,' Grandmother Celestine said.

'How will they change?' I asked.

'No one knows, darling,' my grandmother replied.

Because my grandmother said what was happening was important, I sat in front of the television and began to take notes. I remember writing that the Vice-President Lyndon Baines Johnson was sworn in on the steps of the capital. The newscaster said that he had chipped beef on toast. I thought that it was funny that the news anchor would mention what the new President ate for breakfast. I wrote a report about the new President, and I gave it to my teacher. She asked me to read it to the class. I remember the teacher asking me if I wanted to be a writer when I grew up, and I said no. I don't know why."

"But you became a journalist, didn't you?" Terry asked.

"I did, but I quit. I don't know why, but my then husband didn't want me on television. He wanted me to be a house wife, and to take care of the children. I didn't want to do just that. But we moved, and I moved with him, and I just gave up.

Anyway, I was never sure whether it was the President's death that had caused the change in my family, or if it was something else. At some point, after the man upstairs had started noticing me, so had my father. I was surprised, but happy about it. A few days after the President was shot, I remember sitting on my father's lap. I felt uncomfortable. I don't recall him ever touching me before. I don't remember him even noticing me, but he did that day, and I was surprised, happy, and scared. I only sat on his lap for a few minutes, and I remember the men in the room looking at me in a way that made me feel uncomfortable. Then, while I was sitting there, my mother came into the room, and she stopped mid-stride. She covered her mouth in surprise, as if she had seen something that shocked her. She was angry, and she walked across the room and pulled me off my father's lap. She said, 'you filthy little girl. Didn't I tell you to take a bath hours ago?'

I was scared. She was so angry at me. She had not told me to take a bath. She grabbed my arm, and I could feel her nails digging into my arm. She pulled me, and I almost fell, but she yanked me up by my arm. She dragged me up the stairs. She said, 'I'll teach you to disobey me.' She shoved me into the bathroom and turned on the water in the tub. She pulled off my dress and my panties. 'Get in!' she screamed.

'Mommy, I think it's too hot.' I cried.

'Get in,' she screamed again. I hesitated. She removed one of her high heels and began to beat me with it. The heel of the shoe cut my knee, and it started to bleed. I jumped into the hot water and danced around in circles as I tried to avoid my mother's shoe and keep my feet from being in the scalding water for too long."

Tears were streaming down Lulu's face. Terry handed her a tissue. "I thought my father would save me. He had me sit in his lap, but he didn't stop her from dragging me up the stairs and putting me in that hot water. I thought he would, but he didn't."

"Why not?" Terry asked.

"I don't think he cared. I think that they were both beaten as children, and they thought it was okay." Terry nodded, and Lulu continued.

"I really don't remember much about my mother, except for those two incidents, but my father began to take even more notice of me. When I turned nine, my breasts began to develop, and men begin to look at me. It seemed that whenever someone else paid attention to me, my father noticed. During the year I turned nine, a younger aunt had come to live with Aunt Verna. This aunt, Aunt Daphne, was unlike the rest of my family. She had dyed her hair red, and wore miniskirts and white lipstick. Aunt Daphne said she was 'mod,' which was something that I did not understand. What I did understand was that my mother did not like her, and my father liked her a lot.

It was Aunt Daphne who called me into her room and felt my breasts. Another time, Aunt Daphne called me into her room, and she was lying naked on her bed. I stared at her, and was stunned. I never knew why she did this. I had never seen a naked adult female. This first experience was startling. I backed out of my aunt's room and shut the door. My aunt laughed, and asked, 'you're leaving me?'

That summer, Aunt Daphne said, to no one in particular, 'that girl needs a bra.' All of the women within hearing distance pretended that they did not hear her. More than three years would go by before another aunt would buy me a much-needed brassiere."

"Where was your mother at this time?" Terry asked.

"I guess she was working. I never saw her. My grandmother made our meals. I rarely saw my father. I don't know where they were or what they were doing."

Lulu continued. "That summer, my father's attention increased. Many nights that summer, my father sat rubbing my back as we watched television alone together in the dining room, which was also the bedroom that I shared with my sisters. While the rubbing was comforting, it was also disconcerting. I somehow knew that it was wrong. As the nights of television-watching continued, my father became very interested in my nighttime ritual. He advised me that I should wash my face every night before I went to bed. 'Isn't brushing my teeth enough?' I asked. My father said, 'no, not anymore.' Every night afterwards, I washed my face with Palmolive soap. Some nights, after I washed my face, my father would brush my hair."

It was also during that time that my father began taking me for rides in his new black Cadillac. I felt privileged to ride with him in the front seat of his car. The rides varied, and we never really went anywhere. Sometimes, he would take me to see one of his medical school friends. On those occasions, I would sit on his knees, like I had done when my mother had grabbed me off his lap.

It was during one of those rides that a child darted across a busy street that intersected the street on which my family lived. My father slammed his feet on the car's brake pedal, but there was a dull thud. People in the neighborhood ran over to where a child was lying in the street. The sudden gathering of people scared me. I could not see what was happening, but I was very scared. My father was trying to tell me something: 'When the police come, tell them that she ran right in front of the car.'

I could not answer him.

'Listen to me, tell them that you saw the girl dash in front of the car.'

I stared at my father. I could not talk.

'I didn't see anything,' I stammered, and started to cry.

'Yes, you did, you saw that girl run across the street.'

'No, I didn't see anything, Daddy.'

He grabbed my hand and squeezed it hard, and I cried harder. 'You saw the girl dash across the street. Say it after me.'

'You saw the girl...'

'No!' He squeezed my hand harder. 'I saw the girl dash across the street.'

'I saw the girl dash across the street.'

'That's right, say it again,' my father ordered.

'I saw the girl dash across the street,' I said. My lips were trembling, and tears were streaming down my face.

Soon, two police cars and an ambulance arrived, and the crowd of people grew. I sat in the car, bit my hands, and looked away from my father. A few minutes later, a white police officer came to my father's side of the car. I turned my head as the police asked my father for his driver's license and registration. But, as I listened, I was startled to see another police officer tapping on my window, making gestures to roll it down. When I continued to stare at the officer, he spoke to me. 'Roll down the window.' I obeyed.

'How old are you, girl?'

'Nine,' I answered.

'Can you step out of the car?'

I looked to my father before I opened the car door, but he was preoccupied with the other policeman. On shaking legs, I opened the car door and stepped out. When I got out of the car, I saw the little girl lying in the street. She looked dead.

'Step away, girl,' the police ordered, as he steered me around to the back of my father's car and towards one of the police cars. I followed the police officer, but kept watching to see what was happening to my father, who was getting out of the car as well.

I kept watching my father, afraid for him. Our eyes met, and I could see the fear. The police opened the back door of his vehicle, and ordered me in. I got in the back seat, and could barely see above the glass of the window. We went to the police station, and we stayed there for hours. I don't know if the child was dead. I have been scared of driving ever since."

"That's a lot for a small child. Do you remember talking to your mother or anyone else about this accident?"

"No. Nothing. Something else happened that summer: my father beat me with an electrical cord until he broke the skin on the backs of my legs. My grandmother bandaged my legs and put sulphur on the wounds until they healed. Over the next few weeks, she would rub my legs, particularly the one that had a deep cut, and she gave me what would be considered physically therapy. It was painful, and I begged her to stop, but she said that if I didn't let her pull out my legs, then they would stay bunched up, and I would have a limp for the rest of my life."

The small room was silent. "Did the school authorities ever look into any of these incidents?"

"They did. My grandmother told me to lie, and I did. They went away, and I guess they closed the case."

"Your grandmother was very pivotal in your life," Terry remarked. "Let's talk about her some more next time."

"All right." And Lulu left the therapist's office feeling sad, but glad she had finally told someone about her childhood. If it was true, what they said at the rehab center, she had relieved herself of a number of ugly secrets. If telling someone about her childhood could help, she was ready to tell it all. Also, she had to find out what had happened to Pamela, her roommate. And where was Michie?

TWENTY-FOUR

The Friday after Lulu had failed to pack a suitcase for the children, phones across Lake Washington began to ring. David Hughes, Lulu's ex-husband, contacted Janine Zimmerman and Nancy Trujillo. Nancy recalled that Lulu had met a woman named Catherine Connors, and it was she who had introduced Lulu to Steven Flaherty. Janine Zimmerman gave David permission to go into Lulu's apartment, and she and Nancy Trujillo accompanied him. They searched through Lulu's desks and personal papers, and found Lulu's address book. Together, the three of them began to call anyone who might know where Lulu was.

They called Catherine Connors, who was so mad that she said that she would do everything in her power to help David Hughes protect his children from Steven Flaherty and Lulu. When they called Lulu's sister, Iris, she was stunned to hear that anyone would say that her sister was smoking crack in hotel rooms. Iris had never even seen her sister drunk. Crack was impossibility. "If she calls you for money, don't give it to her," David told Iris.

"I'll do whatever I damn well please," Iris shot back. She was not one to be intimidated. "If your ex-wife is smoking cocaine, don't you think that she needs help?" Iris asked.

"Yeah, but not from me," David said, and hung up the telephone. When Janine, Nancy, and David were done calling anyone who might know where Lulu was, they decided on a plan. A therapist should check out the children.

"Isn't Catherine Connors a therapist?" Janine asked.

"I think she said so," David replied.

"I think you should file a missing person's report," Nancy said. "She could be hurt."

"I think you should file temporary custody orders," Janine suggested.

"I believe you are right," David answered.

"Do you have a good attorney?" Janine asked, and then realized that Nancy was standing with them.

"I'm too close to the matter," Nancy said. "Besides, she was my friend and partner, so I couldn't accept your case, David."

"I have a great attorney, David," Janine said, as the three of them closed the door to Lulu's office. "You know what else? I have a camera in the car. We should take some pictures for both of us. I will use them to show how Lulu destroyed my property. You can use them to show the court what a mess this place was. Certainly not fit for children."

"You're right," David said. The three went outside to their respective cars.

David and Janine thanked Nancy for coming with them, and then got the camera and returned to the apartment. They each shot evidence of the disorder, dirt, or damage to Janine's apartment. When they had used two rolls of film, they felt that they had enough evidence to make Lulu look bad, and force her to be responsible to the damage to the apartment. As they parted, they promised to support each other for the sake of the children. That was their spoken mantra, but their hearts knew otherwise. David knew that this was his chance to gain custody of the children. Janine was going to get back at Lulu, because Lulu had spurned her and called her fat. "After all that I had done for that ungrateful bitch."

TWENTY-FIVE

When Lulu had been at the rehab center for almost two weeks, a new woman joined her therapy group. By that time, Lulu had learned that she was no different from anyone at the rehab center in terms of addiction. The new member of the group looked like she was fifteen, but she had to be over eighteen to be in the women's program. "Hi, I'm Kimberly, and I am an alcoholic and drug addict. This is my First Step. 'We admitted we were powerless over alcohol—that our lives had become unmanageable.'" Kimberly looked up from the Twelve-Step program book that she had read from, and then began telling her story.

"I started using drugs when I was fourteen. I lived in Port Orchard with my parents. They were older and strict, so I would sneak out of the house when they were sleeping and go to Seattle and go to rads."

Lulu's face showed her confusion. Kimberly picked this up, and explained that 'rads' were all-night parties that teens went to. "We get high and share drugs, listen to music, and dance. They are really a blast."

Ann interjected. "Your definition of 'rad' is what it's supposed to be like, fun. But from what I understand, young people get hurt at rads; they overdose, and they often become easy sexual prey to adults or older teenagers. Why don't you talk about the last 'rad' you attended? Isn't that why you're here?" Anne finished.

"I got arrested in Alaska where I was living with a group of friends.

The police raided the place where we were holding the rad, and I was arrested. I didn't have any identification, but I told the police my real name. They found me on a national missing person's data base, because my parents had reported me missing. The police called my parents, and now I am in treatment."

"How long were you missing?" Anne asked Kimberly.

"About two years."

"Where did you live when you were missing?"

"I lived on the streets, and sometimes in peoples' houses." Kimberly answered, and shrugged her shoulders.

"How did you make a living?" Anne asked.

"I panhandled."

"Anything else?"

"Sold drugs."

"Anything else?"

"Sometimes guys would give me money to have sex with them," Kimberly said quietly.

"Anything else that you would like to share with the group about your time on the street?"

"No," Kimberly said.

"Kimberly, part of accepting what happened is to tell the truth about what you really experienced. By saying it aloud, it will help you reinforce the true cost of your addiction. If you minimize your experiences out there on the streets, it won't seem so bad when you're frustrated and ready to give up, and perhaps escape by using."

"I was beat up, and I was raped," Kimberly blurted out in a sob.

"Was that a one-time occurrence?"

"No, it happened more than once. It happened a lot." Tears began to stream down Kimberly's face, and fell into her lap. Anne looked at Kimberly, considered closing out the dialogue, but chose to let Kimberly think about the cost of her addiction. She made a note of Kimberly's rapes, and would suggest continued therapy after she had finished her inpatient treatment. She also recommended that Kimberly be tested for HIV.

There was silence in the room, and Lulu wished she could hug Kimberly, but was sitting too far away from her. Anne picked up a folder, read something, and then said, "alright, let's hear from you, Cynthia." A heavyset blonde woman, who appeared to be in her early twenties, stopped playing with a small diamond ring on her finger. She had a sullen look on her face. It appeared as if she would rather be any other place than in the room with the other women.

"I didn't really have any consequences from my use of marijuana." The woman shot a look at Anne. "I'm not going say that I'm an alcoholic, because I'm not. I'm going to do my time in here, because that's what I have to do. I like smoking pot, and I'm going to continue using it when I get out." The woman looked at Anne again. "You can write that on my probation report if you want to. It won't make a difference. They don't care. All they care about is that I do my time here."

"So you don't think being arrested for selling crack cocaine is a consequence of your use?"

"No," Cynthia belligerently replied.

"How long were you in county jail? Thirty days?"

"Yeah," Cynthia replied.

"That's not a consequence?"

"County jail is no big deal. I don't *use* crack cocaine; I *sell* crack cocaine. I made a lot of money. If the people that buy from me did not buy from me, they'd find somebody else," Cynthia said.

"Doesn't it make you feel bad that you sold pregnant women crack cocaine? That you took money that people used to buy crack instead of food for their children? That people bought crack from you instead of paying their rent?"

"No," Cynthia lashed out. "No, that doesn't bother me one bit. People have a choice about what they do. I supply a need. That's not my problem."

"You wrote that those were something things that were ashamed of doing when you first entered treatment. Have you changed your mind?"

"I was told that I had to fill out each section of the paperwork I was given. I listed those things because I thought they were pretty bad, but, like I said, I filled a need. I didn't make the pregnant woman pregnant, or a crack addict. I sold her crack, which she would have purchased from someone else anyway." Cynthia stopped talking. She had said all that she was going to say. She did not trust anyone, and certainly not this treatment center.

"So, what happens when you get arrested the next time?" Anne asked.

"There won't be a next time," Cynthia said. Anne looked at her, and, with an expressionless face, wrote something in Cynthia's file, then put back on the stack from which she had pulled it. Lulu noticed that, despite Cynthia's belligerence, there was a worried look on her face. Anne looked up and called, "Nicole."

"I'm Nicole, and I'm a prescription drug addict. I don't have any experience with street drugs, and I have never been arrested. My fiancée suggested that I come here, so I'm here."

Anne looked at the pretty redhead dressed in a navy blue designer warm-up suit. The woman's hair was in a pert ponytail, and she crossed her legs at the ankles. She wore spotless white tennis shoes, and no socks. The woman looked as if she had come from a country club tennis court instead of being in a rehab clinic.

"Nicole, how long have you been in rehab?"

"Ten days."

"Did you admit yourself here?"

"Yes and no."

"What do you mean by that?" Nicole looked at her perfectly manicured hands, and said nothing.

"Well, you have another eleven days here; maybe you can begin to start telling the truth about your life sometime before you leave."

"I've haven't told any lies. I had a car accident. I took the Vicodin because I was in pain. It wasn't my fault." The woman's green eyes brimmed with tears.

"Whose fault is it, Nicole? Your doctor's? All the doctors that you went to see to get all those prescriptions for Vicodin? Did you tell any lies when you met with them to get your prescriptions? Did you lie to your insurance company? Did you lie to your seven-year-old son? Was he ever in the car when you took too many Vicodin? And how about when you couldn't get any more doctors to write you prescriptions? Did you try to buy some off the street? Where did you get the money to buy all that Vicodin?" Nicole continued to look as if Anne was talking to someone else.

Anne didn't sigh. She gave no indication of her personal feelings. Each member of the group would be a lesson to the rest. "When you can start telling the truth, at least to yourself, Nicole, you might have a chance out there in the real world. You might have a chance at marriage and being a mother. You keep up the pretense, and you'll just find another set of doctors to get another round of Vicodin. You got lucky. Maybe the next time you and your little boy might not be so lucky. Maybe you won't just run into a tree. Maybe the next time it will be a Mack truck. I am not wishing that on you, but your addiction has hurt your son already, in a physical way."

Nicole let out a loud sob, picked up her purse, and ran out of the room. The woman sitting next to Anne got up to go after her. "Stay where you are, Deborah," Anne said to the gray haired fifty-year-old woman. "Let her go."

Lulu watched the woman run out of the room. Lulu now knew that this rehab center was a last stop. Anything after rehab could only get worse. Either you worked it out here, or you'd be back to where you were, but the consequences were graver, and the road back steep and difficult. She had a little over a week to figure a lot of stuff out. She was beginning to understand herself, but she was becoming afraid of leaving the safe, structured, drug-free environment of rehab. All there was to do at the center was to get well. Someone cooked the meals. The staff washed her laundry and cleaned her bathroom and bedroom. The only thing that she was required to do was make her bed and show up for her group and individual therapy sessions—and, of course, the required gym time. When she got home, she would have a lot to clean up. And she would have to care for her children and work.

After the women stood and closed the meeting with the Lord's Prayer, Lulu looked at the clock, and planned what she would do between then and her next therapy session. In telling her tale to her therapist, she realized that her grandmother had both helped and harmed her, and that it was through Celestine that she had learned to dislike her mother, Octavia.

TWENTY-SIX

Celestine's parents were given the English names of Edgar and Elizabeth. Since both had been orphans, they were given the generic Indian last name of Singh. As a small child, even though he had been saved by the Catholic nuns, Edgar was brutally caned for the slightest infraction of any rule. Perhaps it was this strict upbringing in the orphanage that had opened the floodgates of Edgar's anger. He grew angry, and yet, there was little he could do. The orphanage had saved his life, and a beating was endurable compared to what his life on streets might have been. So he took his beatings, and buried his anger and resentment towards the Catholic nuns.

Edgar Singh was an untouchable, and, although a male, which East Indian culture venerated, he nevertheless was discarded by his parents. Had Edgar survived, which was unlikely, and lived in Bombay, as it was known at the time, he would be shunned and perhaps blinded, had his legs or arms amputated, or been disfigured in some way in order to become a more effective beggar. At his core he knew this,and therefore anything above that standard of living was tolerable. After he had moved to the island on the Sea of Cortez, Edgar became a money lender, a role which was hated by everyone. He took advantage of the poorest when they were the neediest, and people hated him for this. This exclusion and hatred towards him generated hatred and anger in Edgar. He distanced himself from the notions of grace, charity, and brotherly love, believing that it had all been a fraud perpetrated by the Catholic Church. The further away he got from the ideology of the Catholic Church, the more disdainful he became towards the practices of Catholicism. Finally, he became a Hindu.

Edgar's already violent and intolerant behavior began to manifest his culture's disdain for women. That and his anger led him to beat his wife and children in the way he had been beaten as a child. When Celestine returned to his home as a widow, her father considered her a burden, and wished that he could send her to an ashram for widows, like in India. Since that was not possible, his only hope was to remarry her. It did not matter to whom, since she had already been married.

To Edgar, the worst aspect of Celestine returning home was that her younger sisters did not compare favorably with her. When men saw Celestine, and later saw one of the sisters that they were expected to court, they were disappointed. The comparison was unfortunate, and Celestine had to go. Because she had no value as a widow or as a woman, he could marry Celestine to anyone who was willing to take her. If the man who wanted to marry Celestine did not want to keep Celestine's daughter, that could be accommodated as well. He could marry his granddaughter as soon as she was twelve, and promise her to a man when she was eight. So when a drunken, misogynistic man of mixed race agreed to marry Celestine, Edgar was agreeable.

Celestine was not. She begged her father to spare her from this unsuitable marriage. Because she had been married before, she believed she should not be marrying again. She also did not want to marry this particular man because he appeared to be cruel, harsh, and without regard for women, except as objects to gratify his base sexual desires. Celestine's pleas enraged her father, who beat her and told her that she should be happy that anybody would want to marry her and take on someone else's child. Celestine's mother could do nothing to help her daughter. Her mother was grateful that none of her husband's wrath had landed on her, since she had the misfortune to bear three female children.

Celestine wept and rocked her daughter, who was traumatized from seeing her mother beaten. Celestine would have killed herself, except she knew to do so would leave her daughter to a future that was worse than hers had been. Women's lives were scripted by their gender and culture. What choice had she as a widow in the 1920's, on an island with no commerce? Celestine had no choice; she would marry the man, but, as Celestine held her daughter to her chest, she vowed that her little girl and any other child that she would bear would never be bartered like an object to be sold off in marriage. Celestine vowed that she would rather enter her child as a novitiate in a Catholic nunnery than have her married to a man who could be her grandfather in age.

But even as Celestine comforted her daughter, she was grateful because she had gotten a chance to have a life—something many females of her father's caste had not been able to do. Many female Indian babies were aborted, or discarded at birth because they had been born females. Celestine shook her head to clear it, and saw that her child was finally breathing regularly.

Edgar Singh thought that he was very enlightened to allow his daughter to be married again. He lauded himself by arranging the marriage. In the world from which he had escaped, females were without much value—except for what they could bring in dowries. Personally, Edgar Singh did not like black people, but he would lend them money, and he would marry his daughter to one of them, if it meant survival for his other children.

He congratulated himself for coming so far in life. Celestine should be glad that she was not scrubbing toilets as a maid. And although the man his daughter was marrying was black, that culture did not seem to mind if women had children, and this was good. In his new country, things were not as rigid and defined. He felt he had done the right thing.

Celestine and her husband, who had seen her once, married within in a month. Edgar did not want the man to change his mind. There was no celebration. The groom drank no more or less whiskey than he would have consumed on an average day. The only thing that was different was that that night, he would not have to haggle with a prostitute for the price of sex.

Celestine's second husband could have easily accommodated his needs, if he had secured a hard-working maid, rather than a wife. With her second husband, Charles, Celestine's daily challenge was to avoid him. He was loud and obnoxious when he was intoxicated or when he was hung over. He was in one of those conditions most of his waking hours. The only thing that made the relationship tolerable to Celestine was that Charles drank in the dingy waterfront bars, with women seeking a shot of alcohol from any willing buyer. Oftentimes, her husband did not make it home.

Celestine dealt with her second marriage by spending as much time as possible out of the house. There was only one place to go, and that was to church. While her father had cast off his Catholic religion, Celestine had become a devout Catholic. Before her father had arranged her marriage, Celestine wanted to become a novitiate. That was now impossible, but Celestine went to mass every day at the Catholic Church. The first service was at five in the morning; the last at five in the evening. As she walked with her child to Mass in the darkness of the dawn hours, she dreamed of what her life could have been as nun. As she walked, her tiny daughter besides her, Celestine clicked the black beads, and silently mouthed her Hail Mary's. She prayed for God's forgiveness for her actions in her loveless marriage, and she prayed that she would not conceive another child. God had other plans. Soon, Celestine found herself pregnant again.

At twenty-two years of age, Celestine gave birth to another beautiful daughter—this one the color of burnt cinnamon. The child's father was disappointed, and did nothing to hide his displeasure. "You can keep her with the other one," he said. The remark was meant to imply that a female child had no value to Charles Douglas.

Her husband continued his drinking, and Celestine resumed her attendance at Mass, except now, she held one child by her hand and the other in her arms. This ritual would continue for the next several years, until one morning, as she and her daughters were walking to church, a policeman stopped her. The police officer was embarrassed as he addressed Celestine. "I am sorry to inform you, madame, that your husband is dead."

"Dead?" Celestine asked, with a look of disbelief on her face. The police officer took this expression for grief. It was not grief, but profound relief. Celestine had prayed hard to be free of her cruel husband. The police officer was embarrassed because it appeared that Celestine was a Christian wife, and her husband had been stabbed to death in a brothel. His body had been thrown into a ditch, where the police found him. The officer wanted to spare Celestine this information, and withheld from her the stabbing, and where it had occurred. He told her that her husband was probably hit by a car while walking home. The police added, for good measure, that he had probably died instantly.

Celestine became mute, and tears came to her eyes. "Is there anything I can do for you, madame?" The officer asked.

"No," she answered.

"You will have to identify the body."

"That is fine. My daughters and I need to pray first."

"Do you know where the morgue is?"

"No, but I will get there. I will only be a few minutes in prayer." With that, Celestine Dei Douglas was a widow again, at twenty-nine.

After the death of her second husband, Celestine did the unthinkable, and chose to live by herself with her two little girls rather than live with her parents. She legally fought off her second husband's family members, and she physically fought off her own father, who struck her about the head. When her father tried to scare her with the fact that her money would run out, Celestine told him that she would clean toilets. She smiled as the blood smeared her teeth. Beating her could no longer provoke fear or compliance. In time, her father gave up.

When her father stormed out of her house, Celestine called the frightened little girls into her arms. She set them down at the table, and began heating milk for cocoa. It was a treat, but she would not let her father's violence mar their lives. She would erase that memory as best as she could. Cocoa today, something else tomorrow, but she would teach her children that it was not all right to be beaten by anyone.

Celestine adopted the unspoken custom of women around the world who choose to shut out men from their lives, and allowed her facial hair to grow. Celestine and her children lived simple lives. As the months passed, Celestine grew lonely and wished for a friend, but no respectable married or single woman would come to visit her at her house, or allow her to visit them. She was off-limits, because widow custom required her to live with her in-laws, or her parents. Fortunately for Celestine, there were someone who was still willing to be her friend.

His name was Abhijit. He was courageous in his love for Celestine. He was the brother of Celestine's childhood friend who through her marriage was lost to Celestine, and vice-versa. He brought false greetings from his sister, but Celestine was too lonely to acknowledge his lack of sincerity. She was eager for adult conversation, even if it was from this young man who was impoverished, and who called himself a photographer. He knew that any kind of a respected relationship was impossible for them, but he had always loved her. Over time, he became Celestine's constant visitor. Despite the gossip, Celestine continued to meet him on her veranda to drink tea and eat biscuits.

Every time Abhijit came to visit, he tried to coax Celestine into allowing him to photograph her. It took several months, but Celestine finally agreed. There was a caveat: Abhijit would have to photograph her daughters, as well. He agreed, but he had a requirement: she would have to shave her facial hair. At first, Celestine refused. But even Celestine could not resist the prospect of being photographed. Photographs were still new, and only the prosperous were photographed.

Celestine and the photographer came to a compromise. Celestine agreed to shave her facial hair, but only if the photographer photographed her with her children. Abhijit agreed, but said he wanted a photo of Celestine by herself, and then one with her two children. He hung the photo in the window of his studio. It was that photograph that caught the eye of Cordell St. Blanc. Cordell went inside the photographer's studio. "Who is that woman?" he asked.

"Ah, she is twice widowed with two children," the photographer answered.

"I did not ask that," Cordell replied.

"But if you are taken with her, I should give you these facts."

"Where does she live?"

"That I cannot tell you," the photographer replied.

"What if I buy the photograph?"

"The photograph is not for sale, sir."

"Then why is it here?"

"It is an advertisement for other photographs."

"All right then, I want a portrait taken."

"Now that's more like it, sir. What did you have in mind?"

"A portrait of that woman and me."

"But, sir..." the photographer continued, and so it went for more than twenty minutes, until the two men came to an agreement. The photographer would bring Celestine to the studio. Cordell St. Blanc would have an opportunity to meet her. If it did not work out, Cordell would still have a portrait of himself taken. It seemed like a fair enough deal, but Celestine would not cooperate.

"Why do you really want me to go to your studio?" she asked, when the photographer would not leave her alone.

"To be truthful, a man wants a portrait with you."

"That is completely absurd," Celestine laughed. "No man in his right mind would ask a woman he did not know for a portrait. What kind of man is this, anyway?"

"Well, he seems rather educated. And he is unusual-looking."

"Unusual-looking?" Celestine asked. "What do you mean, unusual?"

"He's a quadroon."

"A quadroon? Did he see the right portrait? Did he see the color of my skin?"

"He did see the portrait."

"The answer is no, absolutely not. No, never. Never!' Celestine became shrill, and the photographer retreated back to his studio. The next day when Cordell returned to the studio, he was disappointed when Abhijit reported that Celestine was definitely not interested in taking a photograph with him. Abhijit added that the whole idea was preposterous. Cordell thought he would try one last thing. "Could you send her a note from me?" Cordell asked.

"Why, surely I can," the photographer replied. "But I don't think it will do any good. She's a fairly complex woman..."

"Alright, I'll come back in a day or two and give you the note."

"Suit yourself," the photographer answered. "Listen, I won't hold you to the portrait. They are expensive, and you look like a working chap."

Cordell said nothing. Then, "I'll see you in a day or two."

A couple of days later, Cordell returned with a heavy velum envelope, which was sealed with red wax. "Rather fancy," the photographer said.

"It's my one chance," Cordell replied.

"It won't work," the photographer said.

"We'll see," Cordell replied.

"I'll take it to her when I go by that way."

"When will that be?"

"In a day or two. Maybe on Friday, in the early afternoon. "

"Alright then, perhaps we will talk next Monday?" Cordell inquired.

"Sure, sure," the photographer answered.

Cordell left the photographer's studio, and, for the next two days, hid behind a building that was angled across from the studio. Every time the photographer left his studio, Cordell followed him. On Friday morning at ten o'clock, the photographer headed to a little house on a quiet lane. He knocked on the door, and the woman in the portrait answered it. He knew where she lived. He hurried back to the city, bought a bouquet of flowers, and had a florist deliver them to the woman's address.

On Monday, Cordell returned to the photographer's studio. "Well, did she send a note back?"

"Well, no," the photographer said.

"Did she say anything?"

"She liked the flowers."

"Good. Was there any hint of interest at all?"

"Well..." the photographer hesitated. From behind a curtain in the studio, Celestine appeared. "I wanted to see what kind of fool would send a woman widowed twice with two children, flowers."

"Me," Cordell answered.

"I see," Celestine said. "And you are of unusual coloring."

"You are laughing at me." Cordell was annoyed.

"Yes, I am laughing at you, but for the flowers, not how you look. You can no more help the color of your skin and eyes than I can help that I have been married twice and have two children. We can only bring unhappiness to each other. I understand you wanted a photograph with me. I will do it."

"No, I did not want a photograph of you. I wanted to meet you."

"Well, now you have."

"I did not just want to meet you. I want to know you."

"You are a foolish man," Celestine said, with a faint smile. "Please, Abhijit," she said addressing the photographer. "Could you find..." and she paused.

"Mr. St. Blanc," Cordell answered.

"Yes, Mr. St. Blanc and I some tea? That would be so lovely"

The photographer was as puzzled as Cordell, but he hurried to the hot plate in his studio to boil water. "So, tell me where you learned of Shakespeare's sonnets?"

"I learned them at school, at university," Cordell stammered.

"Where did you go to university?" Celestine inquired. "Please sit," she said, offering Cordell a chair. Cordell awkwardly sat, and began to tell Celestine about his education in Europe.

A life-changing trio was formed that day. This began the first of many meetings among the twice-widowed beauty, who had only a sixth-grade education, but who loved to read; the quadroon, who felt that he would never be understood; and the photographer, who had brought the two together. Celestine found Cordell St. Blanc odd-looking. He was a tall, caramel-colored man with the blue eyes of a white man. His hair was the color of sand and as hard as sand, but it didn't matter, because both Abhijit and Celestine were fascinated by Cordell's talk of Europe and London. Like the maiden with a thousand tales, Cordell St. Blanc lived to have another cup of tea with Celestine, because of his stories about Europe, and his love of the English language.

By the time rumors were rampant about the widow and her "high yellow man," Celestine had fallen in love with the mind of her highly-educated friend. When Cordell quietly suggested that they get married, Celestine laughed. "You must be a fool or a dreamer to want to marry a woman who has been married twice, with two children." Cordell St. Blanc looked steadily into the eyes of the beautiful woman before him, and said, "I am both. A fool for you, and a dreamer of big dreams."

They were quietly married a couple of months later. Abhijit memorialized the small wedding ceremony with his camera. Within a year, Celestine gave birth to Lulu's father, Cordell St. Blanc II.

TWENTY-SEVEN

It was another gray, overcast day. It was cold and uninviting, and the air at the high altitude stung. The mountains had lost their charm, and now they were like a wall that separated her from the rest of the world—a world where there was no one waiting for her to come home. The highlight of her day had become therapy. She was always on time so that she could give voice to the riot of images and memories that flooded her every waking moment. It was a painful place to be, and yet, Lulu realized that it was the safest place she could be right now. Even more depressing was that, in few days, she would have to leave the sparse blue room, where the twin bed now lay empty.

It wasn't that she had even really liked Pamela, but Pamela had been one of the very few people Lulu had spent any time with while at the rehab center. In the time that they had been roommates, Lulu had seen past the painted woman that Pamela had become, to the smart little girl she was who had to fight to protect herself and her childhood friend, Michie. Lulu had learned to respect Pamela. Pamela was a survivor. It was too bad that she had been so neglected; if that hadn't been so, then perhaps Pamela might have become the engineer that she had once dreamt about being.

Lulu bit back her tears. Pamela. She would probably never see her again, but she would be never forgotten. Lulu said a silent prayer for her, and made a mental note to search for Michie, who seemed to have disappeared when Pamela had. Lulu sighed. Her heart ached in a way she had never felt before. The riot of thoughts and memories flooding her brain, now that she had very few distractions, was emotionally painful. "Make the pain go away," had become her silent mantra. But wishing her pain away had not worked. Terry had told her experiencing and facing the pain she had buried so long ago was the only way to get rid of it. Lulu had told Terry that she felt that, if she let the pain out, it would break her into a million pieces, and that she would never put herself together again.

Terry's response had been, "from those thousand pieces you will re-create yourself anew." Lulu had no response.

She turned away from the black mountains, and walked down the blue hallway. She knew that she would miss these drab walls, and miss Terry, who had made the small therapy room into the safest place in the world for Lulu. Lulu's eyes burned with tears, but she held them back until she reached the door to Terry's office. She did not want any of her fellow patients to see her crying. She softly knocked on Terry's door, and placed her hand on the door knob so that she could enter as soon as she heard Terry's voice.

"Come in," Terry said, through the closed door that was already opening as she finished her statement. "We only have a few days left. I feel that you should at least begin voicing your feelings about your mother." Lulu did not respond. Terry was prepared to say nothing else for the next fifty minutes, and Lulu knew this.

Lulu looked to the ceiling. She wrung her hands as she began to relate her mother's story.

Her mother's name was Octavia Lei before she married Cordell St. Blanc. Octavia's father, Bennett Lei, was a well-known gambler. No one really knew what Bennett Lei's real name had been. When he had left Canton China, he renamed himself Bennett, so that he could become assimilated, and to better hide from the people he had owed money. He was a chef by trade, learning how to cook as a small boy to work in the homes of the rich in Shanghai. He also learned that he would never be more than a cook, unless he could earn more money. He didn't remember when he had started gambling, or why. It seemed that he had always gambled. He could not manage to find a way to America. Only the rich and connected Chinese at that time could manage to go to the land where movies were made, and everything was tall, and anyone could become rich. Instead, he had found his way to the island on the Sea of Cortez. It didn't matter. Bennett Lei knew that he could survive anywhere, and, so far, he had.

When he arrived on the island, he realized that it was small and poor. These were the cards he had be dealt, and he would use them. He began by doing what he already knew, and hired himself out as a cook. From there, he saved every penny that he had made, and, in a couple of years, he bought a shack, filled it with canned goods and whatever fresh food that he could procure, and began his first "restaurant." He eventually owned several grocery stores, restaurants, houses of prostitution and gambling, and he was nearly fifty when he married one of the young, attractive waitresses who worked for him. He was nearly twice the woman's age, but neither Bennett nor Sally, as she called herself, cared. She had become the wife of a "rich" man.

She made her home at the largest of the restaurants—or what the local people called "rum shops." Customers could eat at a table in the front of the store. In the backrooms, men played cards, dice, and mahjong, and smoked and drank. Sally Lei knew that the most important part of her husband's enterprise was the gambling. The men who gambled considered themselves professional, and, except for the click of dice or the slap of cards, or the cry or shout from a winner or loser, the rooms were quiet with the concentration of gambling.

Sally Lei now managed the waitresses who worked both the back and the front rooms. The waitresses did everything, from cooking and serving food, to making drinks, to sitting in the laps of men who were winning or losing big. Frequently, the girls would accompany a big winner or loser back to where the girl lived. The waitress' hours were never set. They knew they should come in early on Thursday morning to help Mama Lei buy meat and produce from the market. They knew they could sleep on little cots in the midday, but by early evening they were dressed in brightly-colored silk dresses that emphasized their small waists, and exposed as much of their breasts as Mama Lei thought was appropriate for the time of day. If by the end of their "shift" they were completely naked, or nearly so, and if the house had made money, Mama Lei would show her approval by serving that young woman a shot of whiskey, or tucking a coin equivalent to five dollars in a kerchief, and shoving it in whatever piece of clothing the girl was wearing.

Overall, Sally Lei had become an asset to Bennett Lei, except when she had too much to drink. Then, Sally became volatile. She would pull a knife on anyone, if she felt that she had been disrespected or cheated. She had a wicked sense of humor, and played jokes and pranks on anyone who she thought would not retaliate. When Sally drank, she could either be friendly and funny, bawdy, or murderously angry. It was in this environment that Bennett and Sally Lei's child, Octavia, had grown up.

For most of her life, Octavia Lei was often forgotten, or was the plaything of the waitresses, who Octavia related to as her friends or, when they got older, her aunties. One day, as Octavia sat and watched the waitresses apply their makeup, one of them asked her if she wanted to put some on as well. What started out as "putting a little powder on her face," turned into the child's face being fully painted. Her eyes were outlined in black, her face was heavily powdered and rouged, and her lips were painted a bright red. She looked like a tiny geisha. That evening, Octavia had run through the restaurant, showing off her painted face. It was during one of her forays through the gambling area that Bennett happened to see his daughter. He was shocked at how adult his daughter looked, and he became very angry. He grabbed Octavia's arm as she tried to hurry past him, but Bennett was too quick.

"Who put makeup on your face?" he asked her.

Octavia was too stunned to speak, but she spoke the truth when she said, "everybody." Her answer angered her father even more. He stopped the game he had just started, and pulled the child out of the room and into the kitchen.

"Who did this?" he asked. At this point, Octavia was crying, but the waitresses were afraid to admit what they had done.

When no one answered him, he took off the burgundy leather slipper that he had been wearing, and used it beat Octavia around her legs. When Octavia started to scream, her mother came to find out what was making her cry, and saw Bennett striking the child.

Sally had been drinking, and asked her husband, "what's wrong with you old man? What are you so angry about? That skinny long-face child of yours, a little powder can only help her." But before Sally could finish what she was saying, Bennett had backhanded her in her mouth. His big ruby and diamond snake-eye ring loosened one of Sally's front teeth. She rushed forward to strike back, but one of the gamblers grabbed her arm, and pushed her away from her husband. She could not strike out at her husband, so instead she screamed at the waitresses, pushed the man away, and yanked Octavia from the room to a bathroom, where Sally roughly washed the child's face with soap. She then sent her to bed without having eaten dinner.

Throughout the entire building, Octavia could hear her mother's screams, and as she put herself to bed, she hoped that her mother would be better by the next evening. The following morning, when Octavia awoke, she could not find her mother. The waitresses were crying, and two of them, who only worked at night, were still in the kitchen. Octavia knew that something was really wrong.

"Why are you crying?" she asked the women. One of the women pointed to a trunk that was sitting in the middle of the floor. Octavia still did not understand what was happening.

Finally, one of the women came over to her and hugged her. "Your mother and father are sending you away," she said.

"Where?" Octavia asked. The women shook their heads, and said she was going to the convent. Immediately, Octavia started to cry. All of her life, her mother had threatened to send her to the convent school. She could not believe that she was really going to be sent there. She only believed it when a car came to pick up her trunk, and she was put in the car. It would be almost ten years before Octavia Lei would come home.

While at the convent school, Octavia arose each morning when it was still dark outside. The first hour of each day was spent kneeling in prayer on cold slate floors. After prayer, she ate a meal of weak tea with milk, thin porridge, and perhaps a piece of fried fish. The rest of the day was devoted to work, and to study. At the end of the school day, the girls ate in the communal dining room. Dinner consisted of canned vegetables, salted fish or stringy meat, and rice or potatoes. The day ended with a reading from the King James Bible, then prayer and bed.

Sometimes the girls sewed, embroidered, or knitted. The sewing was performed for a fee, which was given to the convent, and not the girls. The knitting was for socks and sweaters for people living in England, whom the girls would never meet or see. The embroidery was just for the girls. From the time each girl entered the convent school, besides learning the manners of a middle-class English woman, each girl was also taught the talents of being a good wife. Those talents included embroidering enough napkins and ruffles for sheets and pillowcases, so that when the girl left the convent school, she took with her a tablecloth with embroidered lace, eight napkins, ruffles for at least two pillows, and a set of sheets.

The nuns were harsh. They enforced abstinence from alcohol, tobacco, men, makeup, sex, and loud laughter. The girls were taught to never look directly into a nun's eyes, to never talk back, or speak before they had been addressed. All orders were to be immediately obeyed, and without question. Disobedience of any kind was addressed with swift, harsh, and repetitive beatings with canes followed, with salt baths. Sexual improprieties, smoking, or leaving the convent grounds without written permission was remedied with inserting hot peppers into the girl's vagina while the others girls watched, or held down the perpetrator. As a result, Octavia became fearful of sex, and anything else that the nuns had told her was sinful. In their eyes, that was almost everything.

As Lulu finished speaking about her mother, she turned to Terry.

"My mother threatened to punish me with peppers," Lulu laughed. "She was always so surprised when I fought back, like I would willingly allow anyone to beat me."

"You say that with such venom," Terry said. "I would think you would feel sorry for her."

"Well, I don't. She was an uneducated, cowed woman. She never liked me, much less loved me. Why don't you ask me that question?"

"Well, Lilly, why do you believe that your mother doesn't like you?"

"Because she sees me as the other woman." Lulu said, abruptly rising from her chair and walking out of the room. Terry stared after her.

TWENTY-EIGHT

Terry Berquist always appeared unflappable. It came with the territory. After all, she was a therapist in a drug rehabilitation facility. She did not question Lulu about why she had left so abruptly from her last session. "Good afternoon, Lilly. How are you today?"

Lulu was apprehensive. She didn't want to talk about what had happened long ago. It didn't matter. However, she knew that Terry would continue to probe into the painful past.

She responded truthfully. "Anxious. Sad. Tired of being here. I wish I had a mother to go home to…actually, anyone who would take care of me. I'm exhausted by all of this."

"Would you like to continue our discussion about your mother?"

"Not really, but I will."

"I want to know how you feel about her," Terry added.

"I hate her. I'm angry at her. She did not protect me. She didn't like me. She always blamed me for her life going wrong." The words came out in a torrent of anger and sadness, and Terry once again wondered about what had happened to Lulu's mother.

Octavia Lei and Cordell St. Blanc II had met at a picnic. They did not know each other and Octavia was not going to introduce herself to him, especially since the convent school had done nothing to improve

Octavia's conversational skills. She was still very shy and very thin, weighing less than one hundred pounds.

Cordell St. Blanc II was shy as well, but masked his shyness and insecurity with false bravado. He knew he was a catch. All of the girls at the picnic flirted with him because his father was educated, and everyone knew that Cordell II was going to go to America to study to become a doctor. Octavia, who had been shut away at the convent, did not know this, but even if she had, she would not have flirted with him. She thought he was good-looking, but because he was, she felt insecure around him. She assumed that Cordell must be wild, because he rode a motorcycle.

From the beginning, Octavia and Cordell were an odd couple. She was Chinese; he was Indian, and was called a "Dougla," which was a mix of Indian and black. They were connected by an unusual circumstance, and, despite their racial differences, both had been raised as Catholics. Also, both of their families had money, and that put them on an equal level.

Cordell did not find Octavia attractive. She had a flat chest. She was very plain and pale. But what he was attracted to was that she was not interested in him. For that reason alone, Cordell began to pursue Octavia. The courtship of Octavia was a game, a challenge for him. He began by inviting Octavia to ride on his motorcycle. That ride turned into another picnic, and then Octavia introduced Cordell to her mother, who called him a "nigger." By then, Octavia was already in love with Cordell, simply because he was the only person who seemed to care about her. She knew that her father would also disapprove, so she hid her relationship with Cordell from them.

Octavia's life revolved around Cordell. When she was with him, she was no longer plain or pale. She saw herself as beautiful and interesting. She simply had to be, in order to attract such a desirable young man. For Octavia, Cordell would be her reason for life. It was a condition from which she would never recover. She snuck out whenever she could to be with him. She could do so because nothing had changed much after Octavia had returned home. No one noticed whether she came or went, making it possible to meet with Cordell at almost any time of the day. There came a day when Cordell whispered to Octavia that it was foolish for them to sit and hold hands. He was leaving for

Washington D.C. It was perfectly natural and reasonable that they should cement their relationship with sex. Besides, Cordell convinced Octavia that it was impossible to get pregnant the first time a girl engaged in sex. He reeled off five or six so-called scientific reasons to support his theory of the chances of getting pregnant during one's initial sexual act. In addition to all of this, Cordell told Octavia that they were going to get married. He would become a rich doctor, and he promised Octavia that he would buy her a big house and a fabulous car.

She was so lovely that she should have—and would have—the very best life, as the wife of a respected doctor. Octavia believed him. Of course he was going to be a doctor. He was so sincere and gentle. He was a wonderful young man, and they were both Catholics. It was in fact this last piece that persuaded Octavia to give herself to Cordell. "The bond," he had whispered into her ears, as he began to unbutton Octavia's cotton blouse. Her initial sexual experience was not the way that she had imagined it would be. Despite Cordell's promises of marriage, she cringed through the entire sex act. When it was over, she wanted to wash herself and run away. She was horrified at what she had done. She began to recall the nuns' words of shame. She would go to hell, and each time she would have unprotected sex that summer, she closed her eyes and held her breath until Cordell got off from being on top of her. She would feel this way about sex for the remainder of her life.

One morning, near the end of summer, Octavia woke up not feeling well. She thought that she must have caught the flu. She called downstairs for one of the waitresses to bring her some broth. She threw the broth up. The waitress brought her crackers. Octavia vomited those as well. She was supposed to meet Cordell that afternoon, and for a moment she thought that she should forgo meeting him. But even as the thought of how ill she felt crossed her mind, she knew that she would see Cordell. He drew her in a way that she was compelled to be with him; compelled to do whatever he asked of her. She was in love with Cordell. He would be leaving to go to college in a few weeks. She had to see him. She rushed to her closet to find a dress that Cordell had not seen before. She held the dress up to her face. It was a yellow dress, but it made her pale face look even paler. She pulled out another dress and held that one to her face. Better, she thought. Perhaps she should add a little rouge to her cheeks. Despite her best efforts, when Cordell arrived on his motorcycle, the mere smell of the exhaust made her feel nauseous.

"I feel terrible," she confessed to him.

"You look sick," he answered back, and her heart plummeted. "You should have stayed home," he added. She almost started to cry. He could see that he had made her sad. He relented.

"So, what are your symptoms?"

"Nothing," she said. "I think I'm getting my period," she lied. She started to cry. "Summer is almost over. You are going to go away and never come back! You are going to marry an American girl. I know you are. You will forget about me!" she sobbed. Cordell was taken back. Who had told Octavia the truth? Of course he was going to marry an American girl. Why in God's name had his parents worked so hard to send him to college in America? He was going to Howard University. He was going to Washington D.C. He was going to be a doctor. Why would he marry a flat-chested, un-educated Chinese girl whose mother was a waitress, and whose father was a cook?" He kept his thoughts to himself, and wondered if she really was so naive.

Instead, he said, "you are foolish to think that I will not return. I would marry you, but you are too young to do so without your parents' permission. I have something for you." He reached into his pocket and pulled out a small box. Octavia was still crying, but she took the box. "It's not a lot, but I wanted to give you something to remember me by." With shaking hands, Octavia opened the box. Inside was a little golden heart that opened, and where one could put two pictures. It was empty now, but Octavia knew that she would put his picture in it as soon as she could get one.

"That heart represents my heart," Cordell said. Octavia melted into Cordell's arms, and buried her face in his chest.

"Maybe I could go to America with you. Maybe I could go to Howard University as well," she said. For the second time that day, Cordell was shocked.

"It's not easy to get to America. It takes money. It takes money to go to college in America. It would take you years to apply for visas and to get into college." Everything that he said was true. Octavia knew it as well. "By the time I am in medical school, perhaps you can join me in America."

Octavia's face had withered. She turned away from him. "You should go now," she said.

"Why? What's wrong?"

"I'm sick. You are right. I should have stayed home." She held out the necklace to return it to him.

"No," Cordell said. "I bought it for you. My mother helped me pick it out. I can not take it back," Cordell said, as he stared at her outreached hand, where the heart and little gold chain lay curled. He backed away to his bike. She stood holding her hand out to him. He got on his bike. "Octavia?" he said. "Please don't do this." She turned from him and tossed the heart to ground. She ran blindly through the path she had come to meet him. She ran until she reached her home, and then ran up the stairs and threw herself into her bed. She wished she could die.

For days, Octavia languished in her bed. She had heard that Cordell had left. She was distraught, and yet relieved that she no longer had to live with the desire of always wanting to be with him when she could not do so. Through those first days, even her mother, Sally, left her alone, assuming that Octavia's illness was depression. Two weeks went by, and Octavia began to feel better. Color returned to her skin, and suddenly she was pleasing, and looked fuller and more adult. Octavia's mother was glad, and was happy that the arrogant young man with dark skin had left. He was probably going to jail or the military, Sally had figured. Either way, she was glad.

Octavia was brushing her hair when her mother came into her room. From her view in the mirror, she could see that her mother was angry. She put the brush on the dresser. Something was wrong. It was just ten o'clock in the morning, and her mother was usually asleep. Before Octavia could ask what was wrong, her mother had come behind her, and Octavia could smell the liquor on her breath.

"Why are there still pads in the bathroom?" Sally Lei asked. Octavia felt a wave of terror throughout her body. No pads, no menstrual period. Oh, my God! It could not be true!

"I don't know, Mama," Octavia stammered.

"Have you been with a boy?" Sally asked.

"No, no. I didn't do that! No Mama, I wouldn't do that."

Mama Lei step closer to her. "Take off that robe," she ordered.

"Why, Mama?" Octavia asked.

"Just take it off!" Sally Lei screamed. Octavia slowly removed her robe and laid it on her bed. Mama Lei put her hands on Octavia's breasts, and then on her stomach. She screamed in a way that was part howl, part screech. She ran out of the room, and before Octavia could put her robe back on, her mother ran back into the room. In her hand she held a broom from the kitchen, which she was swinging wildly. Octavia tried to run from her, but Sally slammed the door shut.

Octavia tried to hide in her closet, but her mother dragged her out and began beating her with the broom. Downstairs, the waitresses heard Octavia's cries, and the girls shook their heads. They had known for a month or so before that Octavia was pregnant. How pregnant she was, none of the girls knew. What they did know was that Mama Lei intended to beat the baby out of her daughter. The beating continued, but Octavia's cries stopped, and the waitresses' concern increased. Hopefully, Mama Lei would not kill her daughter. But when Mama came downstairs, her dress soaked with sweat, the waitresses were certain that Octavia was dead. Mama Lei was silent. The waitresses scattered, and waited to find out if she was dead. When lunchtime came, one of the waitresses offered to take tea and broth to Octavia, but Mama Lei forbade her to do it. Darkness fell, and still there were no sound from upstairs. At that point the waitresses feared that Sally Lei had killed her daughter. They believed that Mama Lei was must be waiting until nightfall so that she could dispose of Octavia's body. Throughout the night, the waitresses listened for movement or sound from Octavia's room. There was nothing. No footsteps, no sounds. The night came and went.

The next morning, Mama Lei awoke and was cheerful. Mama seemed not to have a care in the world. She drank, sang songs, and smoked her cigarettes. By mid-morning, Mama returned to her rooms. When she left, the girls drew straws to determine who would see whether Octavia was still alive. One girl would be the unfortunate one. If Octavia was dead, that girl would have to report the death to the police, or find another place of employment. If she reported the beating to the police, she could surely no longer work for the Lei's. So picking the short straw was a serious proposition. The unlucky girl crept up the stairs, and stole into Octavia's room.

Before she opened the door to Octavia's room, she could smell an awful stink. She opened the door and there was Octavia, lying in a pool of urine and feces. While her face had been left untouched, her body was a mass of welts and bruises. The waitress was sure that Octavia was dead. The girl held her nose and crept closer to Octavia's body. The girl touched Octavia's arm. It was still warm. Octavia was either unconscious or sleeping, but she was not dead. The girl turned to leave the room, and Octavia opened her eyes.

"Help," she whispered.

The girl froze. She could not help her. Mama Lei would beat her, as well.

"Help me, please," Octavia moaned. "Water."

The girl did not know what to do, so she ran downstairs to the other waitresses.

"She's almost dead," the girl said in rapid Cantonese. "She's awake. She wants water, but I am afraid."

"We cannot let her die," said one of the older waitresses, who had known Octavia since she was a child.

"What are you going to do?"

"We should at least clean her up."

"No, we should leave her alone," another said.

"Where is Papa Lei?" the older waitress asked.

"He is on the other side of the river. He is not expected back for days."

"We must get word to him somehow, or she will die."

The waitresses agreed that they had to do something, and the best thing was to alert Papa Lei that his daughter lay dying. The waitress knew that it would cost a lot of money to get a message to Papa Lei before the girl died. They pooled their money, and then sought help from one of their trusted clients. When a messenger was found and money was exchanged, all that the waitresses could do was hope that the message reached Papa Lei in time.

The morning crept by. The clock ticked past twelve o'clock and then one. The waitresses tried to busy themselves, but they knew that Mama Lei would soon come back to the kitchen area. At around one thirty, the women heard Mama Lei stirring, but they were fearful that Octavia would die. Mama Lei came into the kitchen. Her hair was oiled and held with an elegant hairpin. She poured herself a large glass of whiskey. She looked around the room at the waitress, who were quietly doing their work. "You all look like somebody died." She took out a pack of cigarettes, and began to smoke. She ordered one of the girls to bring her some food, and then she began tallying the previous night's receipts.

The girl had barely left to get the food when there was a knock on the door. When the door was opened, standing less than five feet tall and wearing her Sunday best, was Celestine St. Blanc. When the girl who answered the door went to tell Mama Lei that there was a woman to see her, Sally was surprised. Who would be coming to visit her? Still smoking her cigarette, she went to the door and stared at the impeccably-dressed woman before her. The two women stared at each other.

"Can I help you?" Mama Lei asked, and blew smoke out of her red lips.

"I hear that your daughter needs medical attention."

"My daughter does not need medical attention. She is upstairs in her room, sleeping," Mama Lei was about to shut the door in Celestine St. Blanc's face, but Celestine's slender hand stopped Mama Lei with such force that Mama Lei was taken by surprise. Celestine stepped in closer to where Mama Lei stood.

"My son has alerted the police. They will be here shortly. Your husband is being summoned. I think it is best that you get your daughter to the hospital. I have a taxi waiting. Any time you waste will be your time in jail. Now let me in." Celestine St. Blanc pushed her way past Mama Lei, and up the stairs to Octavia's room.

Celestine crossed herself, then entered the room and knelt down and to feel Octavia's pulse. Octavia's pulse was weak, but she was still alive.

Octavia opened her eyes and tried to speak. Celestine put her finger to Octavia's lips. "I'm going to lift you, as gently as I can." Octavia nodded. Celestine pulled the coverlet from off the bed, and wrapped Octavia's feces-covered body. She lifted up Octavia, who could barely hold her head up. "Lean on me. Put all your weight on me, and I'll help you out of here. With the grace of the Holy Virgin, we will walk out of here together." Inch by inch, Celestine walked, prayed, and lifted Octavia's almost lifeless body out of the room and down the stairs. When they reached the bottom of the stairs, the waitresses and Mama Lei had disappeared. Celestine laid Octavia's body at the bottom of the stairs. She stepped out to the veranda, and waived to the taxi driver. It was Abhijit, Celestine's old friend, who was still driving a taxi and taking the occasional photo. He ran from the car and into the house where Octavia's body was slumped. He had already been told of the nature of the taxi ride. He was still in love with Celestine, even though she had been married for almost 25 years. They had vowed always to love each other. Celestine and Abhijit lay Octavia in the back seat. The two old friends looked at each other. "As fast as it is safe." Celestine said, and Abhijit knew what she meant.

In the therapy room, Lulu was crying, and Terry handed her a box of tissues. "Your grandmother Celestine played a pivotal role in your life, as well as your mother's."

"She did," Lulu replied. "It was only after my grandmother had died that I heard my mother say that she had loved Celestine more than she had loved her own mother."

"At least the two of you have that in common," Terry said.

"It was puzzling," Lulu said, looking up at Terry. Lulu finally felt sadness towards her mother. "She really had a sad life," Lulu said, as she rose to leave Terry's office.

"Yes, she did," Terry agreed.

TWENTY-NINE

Back in her room, Lulu sat on her bed and looked at Pamela's empty bed. She had been sent back to prison to serve out the remaining time on her sentence. Lulu had mixed emotions about Pam's departure. She felt more at ease, bu, she missed the outspoken, jovial side of Pam, who she grew to think of as "Pamela." Beneath her tough exterior, Pamela's once optimistic, altruistic young self was present. Had the circumstances of her life not derailed her, she might have become an aeronautical engineer and airplane designer. For that lost little girl, Lulu was sad. She would miss the energy of the person Pam had been, and who she could have been. Lulu also admired Pam's unflinching loyalty to Michie. It was something Lulu could not emotionally comprehend. Pamela had essentially given up the life she had dreamed of to protect her childhood friend. Now, Pamela was gone, and since her departure, Michie continued to be absent from the rehabilitation center.

Michie and Pam had listened to Lulu's stories as a form of entertainment, and Lulu had used them to voice her emotional past. Lulu was aware that they ridiculed and made fun of her, even when she was in the same room with them. Pamela had committed murder as a teenager. Lulu knew that she could never really confront Pam, because Lulu was physically afraid of Pamela. While Lulu understood the childhood bond between Pamela and Michie, she did not understand why anyone would want to continue to support the person who Michie had become as an adult. There was little that Lulu had experienced with Michie which would cause Lulu to seek her friendship outside of the treatment center.

As Lulu sat on her bed, she reflected upon the people she had met while at the rehab center. She had little in common with most of her fellow patients. This was no place to meet long term friends. Friends, Lulu thought. What made a person a friend? Unwavering loyalty? Lulu didn't think so. And then, of course, there was her own relationship with Steven Flaherty. If it wasn't for the cocaine, what else had kept them together for the time they had known each other? The thought saddened Lulu, as she reflected on the first night that she and Steven had smoked crack in a hotel room.

She had been so sure that the hotel security would come up and arrest them, or call the police. Steven assured her that that was not about to happen. The following morning, without sleep, Lulu and Steven went to the bank, where Lulu deposited a check drawn from Steven's foreign account. The amount of the check was five thousand dollars. From the bank, Steven had driven Lulu to a boutique that sold expensive designer jeans. They bought several pairs, and tiny tank tops that exposed Lulu's breasts, something that Lulu would normally not do. From that store, Steven had taken her shoe shopping. Her loafers were discreetly put in a bag, and Lulu left the store in black stilettos with five inch heels. From the shoe store, they went to the makeup counter at the Nordstrom store in Bellevue, the wealthy bedroom community north of Seattle. When she left the store, she was almost unrecognizable, wearing the tight jeans, tank top, and black heels. Her lips were bright red, and her eyes were darkly outlined.

"Steven," Lulu said, as he opened the door to the Jaguar. "I feel like I'm wearing a costume. Do I look weird in these clothes and make up?"

"You look hot," Steven said, as he shut the car door. "I'm taking you to lunch at Mondrian's," he said. "I love the artichoke dip, and they have great single malt scotch. Then there's that view of the marina," he added.

"I know where it is." Lulu said.

"What, you don't like Mondrian's?"

"No, I like it a lot. My ex-husband, David. He used to live at the marina when I first met him."

"Oh," Steven said, as he veered the car into the exit of the shopping mall. "I guess then it's the Tower." Lulu remained silent.

"The court closes at four thirty, will we have enough time for lunch and the court house?"

"The marriage license. Of course we will. Give Daddy a smile while I fix you a hit. You look a little down. That's no way to feel as we plan our lives," Steven said. "I wanted to show you off. You are one good-looking woman."

"Thank you, babe." Lulu said, taking the pipe from Steven. He lit with the tiny gold lighter. The acrid smoke filled the car and her lungs. Lulu smiled. "I'm feeling better now. Let's go."

"Where?" Steven asked.

"Anywhere where I can have a salad and some protein," Lulu answered. "Then the court house."

"Yes, ma'am," Steven said, as he took a hit on the pipe and sped down the street to the freeway.

They'd made it to the court house just as it was closing. They paid the clerk the thirty dollar fee and, as Lulu signed her name to the license, the clerk turned to her and said, "you look just like an attorney that used to file documents from a Bellevue law firm."

Before Lulu could answer, Steven interjected, "nope, not her, but if I ever need a smart, good-looking lawyer, I will look her up."

The clerk looked at Lulu's name, and then at Lulu, but she said nothing. "If you still want to get married, return in three days with two witnesses, and a judge will marry you."

"Merry Christmas," Steven said to the clerk, and then slipped her a twenty-dollar bill as he ushered Lulu out of the clerk's office and into the hallway.

"Well, that was weird," Lulu said.

"What part?" Steven nonchalantly asked.

"Why did you want to hide the fact I was the attorney she was asking about?"

"No reason," Steven said. Lulu looked at him but said nothing, and walked with him to the car.

"Now that we are officially engaged, let's get the hell out of the Bellevue Western and into something more suitable, like the Madison Hotel."

"Wow. Fancy digs," Lulu said.

"It's a good intermediate hotel," Steven said. "In the car, and then back to the city."

"I'm ready." Lulu said.

It was the first of many days that would follow. In her drug-induced state, Lulu felt that she was having the time of her life. She was living a fantasy in hotels, where she dressed to go out shopping, and returned to her hotel suite to smoke crack. While in those hotel rooms, she and Steven ordered room service, and watched pornographic videos. They never stayed at any hotel for more than a few days. As it neared Christmas, they moved to the Four Seasons hotel, where Steven rented the Presidential suite. Roses were sent up to the suite, and Steven ordered two rings from a local jeweler. They smoked crack and planned their wedding. If not on the next legal day, then they'd have it sometime soon, like Valentine's Day. The rings would be sized by the day after Christmas.

On Christmas Day, Lulu called her boys and wished them a merry Christmas. Steven purchased shiny black and red electric cars, and other expensive presents for Teddy and Christopher. Steven's mother's housekeeper delivered the gifts to the children, who were with their father. They were told Lulu had contracted a horrible virus which she did not want to pass to the children. Lulu had felt guilty, but she had agreed to the plan.

It snowed the day after Christmas, and Lulu was excited, since it rarely snowed in Seattle. She felt that the snow was a good omen. As promised, Steven picked up the wedding and engagement rings. He returned to the suite with a bouquet of spring flowers dusted in snow, and dropped the boxes containing the rings on the bed. "Belated Merry Christmas, baby," Steven said.

Lulu could not contain her excitement. She ripped open the wrapping and opened the box. "Oh, my God, this is beautiful," Lulu gushed.

"Not as pretty as you, darling," Steven said. They admired the ring on her finger, and Steven called downstairs for a vase for the flowers.

"Oh, by the way, honey," Steven said, "I think that we're going to go to Canada for a while."

"Canada? My kids are coming back on the first of the year. I can't go to Canada. I have to be with my children."

"Darling, darling, calm down," Steven said.

"I won't calm down!" Lulu shouted. "Give me a hit on the pipe, please."

"We're a little low on that stuff. Sorry, Lilly."

"Low?" Lulu asked.

"Low, like, almost out."

"Well, call Buddy over here," Lulu said.

"He won't come over here. They will stop him in the lobby. Do you want to ride over there and pick up some stuff?"

"I don't think that I can drive," Lulu said.

"Okay, but I'm not so sure we should go over to Buddy's together."

"Why not?" Lulu asked.

"We're a little too high-profile, my darling. The car, you, and me."

"What can we do?" Lulu asked.

"We can take your car," Steven said.

"But then we have to go back to Bellevue and get it," Lulu pouted.

"Okay, how about this? I'll drive the Jaguar to Bellevue, and then I'll drive your car back."

"Can't you just keep driving over to Buddy's?" Lulu asked.

"I guess I could, but Buddy will give us a better deal if you are there."

"Oh, hell," Lulu said. "Alright, I'll come with you to get my car. I need some other shoes as well."

"Okay, then throw something on, honey, and I'll call downstairs for the car. Lulu, on second thought, sweetheart," Steven said, "why don't you pack your things up. Just in case. We're going to a beautiful hotel in Vancouver. You'll love it, and the dollar goes twice as far."

"I don't want to pack," Lulu moaned.

"Lilly, cut this shit out! Get your ass out of that bed, and get packed."

"You don't have to yell at me, Steven!" Lulu shouted back.

"Then don't piss and moan at everything I ask you to do!" Steven said, as he picked up the phone to request the valet service.

Lulu wobbled over to the dresser and began to pack her underwear and her jeans. She slipped into a pair of black jeans and black t-shirt.

"Isn't there anything left in the pipe?" Lulu asked.

"Bring it to me, and I can pull some scrapings from it."

"Okay," Lulu said, and brought the pipe to Steven, who took a small pen knife from out of his pocket and scraped the insides of the glass pipe. A few crumbs of resin came to the tip of the pipe, and Steven put them on a screen and handed the pipe to Lulu. He took his lighter out of his pocket and lit it for her. Lulu sucked deeply, and then shook her head.

"I guess it's dry." Lulu said.

"Yep, babe, it's dry. They are bringing the car around in a few minutes. Meet me downstairs in front of the hotel."

"But I'm ready now," Lulu insisted.

"Honey, I don't want you waiting while we get the car. Give me five minutes, and then meet me in front of the hotel."

"Okay," Lulu said. She waited for exactly five minutes, and then checked the hotel room to make sure that she did not forget anything. On a whim, Lulu grabbed the flowers that Steven had brought her, and took them with her. She walked out into the hall, balancing the suitcase and the flowers, and walked through the lobby of the hotel. As she approached the curved driveway, the hotel doorman opened the door, and asked if he could take her suitcase. Lulu was about to say no, when she remembered Steven telling her to always allow bellmen and doormen to help you, and never tip them less than five dollars. "Sure," Lulu said, as she handed the doorman her small suitcase.

"My fiancée is in the brown Jaguar," she said proudly.

Steven saw Lulu and the doorman coming, and he hopped out of the car, took the suitcase from the doorman, and handed him a ten-dollar bill. The doorman opened the door for Lulu, and she slid into the front seat.

"Why did you bring the flowers?" Steven asked.

"You'd just bought them!" Lulu protested.

"Do you know how tacky it looks to be walking out of a hotel with flowers?"

"I didn't think about tackiness, I thought about the fact that you had just bought them up for me."

"Well, don't do it again," Steven snapped.

"Don't worry, I won't!" Lulu snapped back.

Steven maneuvered the car out of the hotel driveway, and roared towards the freeway. In moments, they were heading out of the city and to Bellevue. The afternoon traffic snaked its way from West to East, and Lulu and Steven took the commuter lane. Steven weaved through the dense traffic, driving at speeds of over ninety miles per hour.

"Do you have a death wish?" Lulu asked.

"You're afraid?" Steven asked.

"No, it's just needless to speed in this kind of traffic."

"Don't back seat drive me, Lilly."

"I'm not. It's just that I don't intend to die in a crash," Lulu said dryly.

"I promise you, you won't die in a crash by my hands," Steven answered back.

"Can we stop this bickering?" Lulu asked.

"I'm not the one that's nit-picking," Steven said

"We're almost at my exit," Lulu said. "We can be nice to each other for another three minutes, okay?"

"Sure, anything you say," Steven answered, as he accelerated the car and swung off the exit onto the busy street that fronted Lulu's apartment. Steven raced the car up to the driveway to Lulu's apartment, and then stopped abruptly. There were two police cars in front of Lulu's apartment.

"Oh, shit," they both said simultaneously.

Steven put the car in reverse, and turned around. "Let's go over to that restaurant across the street and have a drink," Steven said.

"A drink?" Lulu shouted. "My hands are shaking, Steven. There are cops in front of my apartment. Oh, my God. What are we going to do?" Lulu wailed.

"Well, you're going to shut the fuck up and calm down," Steven shouted. "Do you have to do this panic crap at every moment?"

"You forget, I'm an officer of the court," Lulu screamed back.

"You've got to be kidding. An officer of the court? Give it a rest, Lilly!"

"How dare you yell at me?" Lulu shot back.

"I'll shout at you whenever you do this silly shit. Now shut up, and stop drawing attention to us. We'll get a drink. The cops aren't going to stay there forever. We've just had bad timing."

Lulu held on to the interior door handle. Steven pulled the car across the street and into the parking lot of the restaurant. Steven walked over to Lulu's side of the car, and opened the door. "Get out," he said. Lulu continued to sit.

"Come on, get out of the car and get into the restaurant."

"Okay, just stop shouting at me," Lulu said as she unbuckled her seat belt. She swung her legs out the car, and there were remnants of the snow that had fallen. "My shoes will get ruined," she said to Steven.

"Lilly," Steven warned.

"Okay, so I'll ruin my shoes," she said, as she gingerly stepped into the snow. Steven reached for her hand, and brushed her cheek with a kiss.

"The cops will leave. We'll sit at the bar and wait for them to leave. From the bar you can see the exit of your driveway."

"What if they leave somebody there to watch?"

"Lilly, whatever reason the cops are in front of your apartment, they can't afford to keep someone there for surveillance. They have real criminals to catch. It's probably your damn landlord trying to serve you, or something," Steven said.

"Oh, you're probably right," Lulu agreed, as she entered the bar. They picked a spot in the crowded bar and ordered margaritas with shots of tequila. Soon, Lilly was laughing, and had forgotten about the police. About fifteen minutes later, two sets of police cars exited Lulu's driveway.

"See?" Steven said. "They're gone. Let's finish up our drinks, get your car, and hit the road."

"Can I get some extra clothes to wear?" Lulu asked.

"No, we're getting in your car and leaving."

"Okay," Lulu said. "I was just asking."

"Come on," Steven said, as he got up from his bar stool. He took out two twenty-dollar bills, and dropped them on the bar.

"I'm not done," Lulu said.

"Oh, yes you are. You don't need any alcohol, anyway. We're picking up a big bag of rocks. Doesn't that sound good?"

"Actually, it does," Lulu said, and got up from her bar stool. Steven took Lulu's hand, and they walked out of the bar and to the car. They got into the car, pulled out of the restaurant, and into the driveway leading to Lulu's apartment. When they reached the apartment, as Steven predicted, there were no police cars. Steven pulled the Jaguar behind Lulu's car, and let her out of the car. As Lulu backed her car from the parking spot, Steven pulled the Jaguar into its space. Then he got out, and signaled for Lulu to get out of the driver's seat. "I can't drive my own car?" Lulu asked.

"Lilly, you are in no condition to drive, darling. Move over."

"Okay," Lulu said.

Steven got into Lulu's old BMW and gunned the engine. "Easy," Lulu urged.

"You, been babying this car for years, Lilly. It's a German car. It can go fast, and doesn't like to be driven as if it's been driven by an old lady."

"I'm an old lady now?" Lulu asked.

"Lilly, shush," Steven said. He swung Lulu's car onto the freeway and raced to the inner city. Before the last exist to where Buddy OZ lived, Steven pulled the car over at a gas station and made a call.

"Who'd you call?" Lulu asked.

"Buddy, "Steven said. "I want to just drive by, honk the horn, get the stuff, and go."

"Well, okay by me," Lulu said. Steven then sped to the next exit. He was headed towards the rundown part of Seattle known as the CD, standing for Central District. On Thirty-Third Avenue, Steven pulled up to a house that was next to an alley. He pulled into the alley and honked the horn. Buddy popped up from a door in the basement of the house, and he and Steven made an exchange. Steven was about to pull off, but Buddy put his hand on the door of the car.

"Hold up a minute," Buddy said to Steven. "Ain't enough, man, for what I give you."

"We're going to Canada. Leaving tonight. I'll check you when I get back," Steven said.

"Naw, man. I need a retainer."

"Shit, Buddy, what you goanna do? Embarrass me in front of my woman?"

"No, man, I just either need more money, or a retainer. That necklace your woman's wearing will do," Buddy said.

"My necklace?" Lulu asked.

"Jesus Christ, Buddy, how long have I been knowing you?"

"Give me back my shit then," Buddy said, as he tried to hand Steven back the money.

"Oh, hell," Lulu said, as she took the necklace off her neck. "Take it, but we're coming back to get it," Lulu said.

"I'll take good care of it, Ms. Lilly," Buddy said, as he weighed the heavy gold Italian chain in his hands. "Nice necklace, pretty lady," Buddy said, and smiled.

"Okay, man," Steven said, and drove the car out the other side of the alley. Steven handed the bag to Lulu.

"Thanks," Lulu said. She took the bag and the pipe. Her hands trembled violently as she put a big rock into the pipe, and held it for Steven to light it for her.

"Hold the pipe down," Steven hissed. "We're in the fucking ghetto. We stand out, even in your car."

"Okay," Lulu said.

Steven pulled over a block or two away from the house, and lit the pipe for Lulu. She inhaled deeply, and smiled for the first time in hours. Steven then took the pipe and took a big hit. They both looked at each other, and smiled.

"I'll get your necklace back," Steven said.

"You better," Lulu smiled, already high on the potent cocaine. Steven maneuvered the car out of the inner city and hit the freeway, heading for Vancouver, British Columbia.

THIRTY

Lulu sat in the brown plaid armchair, the shabbiness of which had been covered with crocheted doilies. She sat upright in her chair and played with the watch on her wrist. She was a few minutes early, and she was nervous. The Director of the rehab facility, Dr. Patricia Carmichael, had requested to meet her and another staff person that morning. This was surprising to her, because the meeting was scheduled during her group session. Group sessions were mandatory, unless one had a medical release, and those were not easy to come by. Lulu looked at the clock on the wall and saw that it was two minutes to ten. At the same time, she heard the muffled sounds of footsteps approaching the door of the office.

"I think it's extraordinary," a male voice said, as the door opened.

"Good morning," Dr. Carmichael said, as she entered the room behind the man. "This is David Osborne. Mr. Osborne, like you, is an attorney. He represents the facility, but, on occasion, he also represents individuals in treatment."

"Hi," Lulu said, and cast a nervous look at the man.

"David, would you like coffee?"

"Sure," David answered.

"Lilly, how about you?"

"Yes, thank you," Lulu answered.

"Why don't you both come into my inner office?" Dr. Carmichael offered. Lilly got up, and stood behind the man as Dr. Carmichael opened the door to her inner office.

"Take a seat," she said. Dr. Carmichael chose a key from the group she had been carrying, and opened her desk drawer. She pulled out a large manila envelope. She pulled out her chair and sat down.

"I've invited David here because you have been served by your ex-husband, David Hughes."

The words hit Lulu in her solar plexus. "What does he want?" Lulu asked, addressing her question to Dr. Carmichael.

Instead, David Osborne answered. "He wants custody of the children."

Lulu put her hands to her mouth and bit her lips. "Can he serve me here?"

"I think so," Osborne answered.

"I thought there was a privacy issue involved," Lulu said.

"There is, and there isn't." Osborne said. "We've researched it. Obviously, he knows you're here. Whether or not service had been adequate...that's another question. You can choose not to respond. You have a hearing two days after your scheduled release from here. You can challenge the service at the hearing, or you can respond, and we'll get the documents to his attorney and the court. It's up to you," Osborne said.

"I can't deal with this now," Lulu almost wailed. "I'm overwhelmed by all of this."

"Lilly, I know this is difficult. David has given you your choices. Obviously, this attorney hired by your ex-husband is not interested in your health or welfare. Let me call for the coffee," she said, reaching for the phone.

"Charles? Dr. Carmichael. Could you bring a pot of coffee and three cups to my office? Sure some cream and sugars?" She asked, turning to Osborne and Lulu. Both shook their heads. "No, black is fine," Dr. Carmichael said into the phone, and then said, "thanks, Charles," and hung up.

"Usually, David defends court orders for patient records. We assume that this attorney will seek your treatment records."

"What will happen then?" Lulu asked.

"David?" Dr. Carmichael said.

"We'll fight it as much as we can. Most likely they will file an order with the court suggesting that there are minors at risk, and that the safety of your children overrides your privacy."

"Will they get the records?" Lulu asked.

"Very likely they will," Osborne answered.

Lulu said nothing, and the air was pregnant with her fear and anger. There was a knock on the door, and Dr. Carmichael said, "come in." Charles, wearing his chef's uniform, came in with a tray on which there were three cups and a pot of coffee.

"You can set it right here, Charles," Dr. Carmichael said. The man set the tray on the table without making eye contact with either Osborne or Lulu. He backed out of the room.

"Thank you, Charles," Dr. Carmichael said. She picked up the pot and poured three cups of coffee. She gestured to a cup with the coffee pot. "Lilly why don't you have a cup of coffee?"

"I'd rather have a drink right about now," Lulu said.

"You're getting a first-hand example of one of your triggers, things that cause you to want to drink," Dr. Carmichael said.

"I'd rather not go into a lecture about drinking triggers right now," Lulu said.

"But, Lilly, didn't you expect something like this to happen?" Dr. Carmichael asked.

"Yes, and no."

"Oh, come on, Lilly, you had a week-long trial five years ago. What would make you think that you have entered into treatment wouldn't bring the custody issue up?"

"Please, don't go in to that now. I simply can't deal with this now."

"Lilly, this is what you do with everything that is painful for you. You bury it; you push it away. You don't deal with it. You take a drink, a puff of marijuana, a line of cocaine. You deaden yourself, and you hide. You can't hide from this. It's out in the open. I'm not saying that it's easy. I know that it's difficult, but you have got to stop burying your emotions and your fears."

"So, what should I do, cry? What good will that do?"

"It might make you feel better," Dr. Carmichael said softly.

David Osborne had been quietly sipping his coffee during the exchange. "Lilly, there's more."

"More? How could there be more?"

"There's a court order for you to take a drug test," Osborne said.

"A drug test?" Lulu asked, confused.

"Yes," Osborne said.

"Why?"

"I can see a couple of reasons. They have no proof that you've actually consumed any drugs. They have their suspicious, but no hard proof," Osborne answered.

"But I've been here for almost two weeks," Lulu said.

Osborne and Dr. Carmichael looked at each other. Dr. Carmichael responded, "Lilly, it would not be the first time a person who came to treatment had drugs brought to them. Obviously, either your attorney or your ex-husband thinks that your decision to go to treatment is a screen to cover future use. Or, as David has suggested, they're looking for residual drugs in your system. Marijuana can stay in your system for more than a month. They are looking for proof."

"Okay, "Lulu sighed. "So, what do we do?"

"We take you to the hospital in town. You give them a urine sample while someone watches, and then the results go to your ex-husband's attorney."

"Do I get a copy of the results?" Lulu asked.

"Only if you subpoenaed them when, and if, a trial date is set," Osborne answered.

"So I don't get a copy of my own urine test?" Lulu asked. "Trial date? You think that there will be a trial? A trial for what?"

"You're a practicing family law attorney," Osborne said. "Custody trials take a year."

"Look, Osborne, David, whatever your name is. I'm an attorney only in name. I got out of law school this past June. I've never had a trial before. I don't even know the rules of family law. I don't know how to defend myself. Don't you understand? I can't do this. He knows I can't do this." Lulu began to sob. Dr. Carmichael and Osborne looked at each other.

"This is the part about taking responsibility," Dr. Carmichael began, but was interrupted by Lulu.

"Don't give me an AA lecture now!"

"If not now, then when, Lilly? These are the consequences of your drug use. These very ones. You've got to take responsibility for what you have brought on yourself."

"Can't you at least be sympathetic?" Lulu cried back.

"I am sympathetic, but sympathy won't help you now. You need to face the truth. You need to be strong."

"How do I start to be strong? I've been afraid for my whole fucking life! Don't you understand? I live with fear every day. I don't even recognize it anymore! It's my constant companion. Now you tell me to be strong? I don't know how to be strong." Tears streamed down Lulu's face, and the mascara that she had put on that morning ran in black rivulets down her cheeks.

Dr. Carmichael handed Lulu a tissue. "Lilly, you have group therapy in a few minutes. Perhaps you had better wash your face, before you go to group."

"Group therapy?" Lulu lashed out. "I'm supposed to go tell a group of morons that my ex-husband wants to take my children away? What are they supposed to do? Figure out how to stop my ex-husband? Raise the money to get me a lawyer?" Lulu laughed bitterly.

Dr. Carmichael did not respond. "David, thank you for being here."

"Sure," Osborne replied.

"A lot of good you've done me!" Lulu spat out at Osborne. "You just rolled over like a dog! Your damn people stupidly accepted service. You should have better procedures in this place. When the server came here, your receptionist should have claimed that I was not here," Lulu continued.

"Alright, Lilly, that's enough. Stop blaming David for your problems. This is not his fault, or the facility's fault. It's not even yours; it's a consequence of your drug use. When you begin to see that, you'll stop being a victim."

"Victim, victim!" Lulu screamed. "What the hell do you know about being a victim?" Lulu's eyes were red from tears. "I'm a victim, a real fucking victim. Don't tell me about being a victim, I've been a victim," Lulu shouted at the top of her lungs.

David Osborne stepped back and Dr. Carmichael stood up. "Lilly, take a deep breath. Inhale," she urged.

"You told me to start feeling, to stop burying my emotions. So, I am. This is what I'm feeling. Isn't this better, Dr. Carmichael?"

"Thank you, David. Perhaps you'd better leave. I'll be in touch later. And thank you for everything."

"You're welcome," Osborne said, and quickly left the room.

Lilly had sunk back into the chair and was sobbing loudly into her hands. Dr. Carmichael picked up the phone and said, "do I have any meetings this morning? Okay, could you block out the next hour or so? No, that's alright. Will you please have Barbara handle that meeting? I have an emergency—and could you bring a glass of water? Thank you," Dr. Carmichael said, and hung up the phone. She turned to Lulu and said, "Lilly, why don't you tell me what's hurting you so much?"

"You won't believe me, even if I told you," Lulu sobbed.

"Why don't you think that I'll believe you?" Dr. Carmichael asked.

"Because my mother didn't. She still doesn't believe me," Lulu said, her chest heaving with emotion. There was a knock at the door, and a woman brought in a glass of water and set it on Dr. Carmichael's desk. The woman then left the room and shut the door behind her.

"What happened, Lilly?" Dr. Carmichael asked.

"I was twelve, almost thirteen," Lulu sobbed. "I was being punished by having to wash a sink full of dirty dishes," she continued. "It was Sunday, the Sunday before my thirteenth birthday. My aunt had come to give me the birthday present she had bought for me. She let me open my birthday gift early because she was going away that day, and she wanted to see me open my present before she left. It was beautiful, a red-and-white-checkered dress. It was the most beautiful thing that anyone had ever given me. And my aunt was so kind and wise. The dress had a built-in bra. I'd started developing breasts when I was nine or ten, but nobody seemed to notice. It was more than three years later, and finally someone was acknowledging that I had breasts. I put on that dress, and I looked beautiful. I looked at myself in the mirror, and there I was. What I kept looking at was how the bra inside the dress made my breasts look huge. I didn't recognize myself." Lulu's sobs had quieted down, and she picked up the glass of water. She stole a look at Dr. Carmichael, and then took a sip. She lowered her head, and continued with her story.

"My aunt was going to take all of us to McDonald's. It was a treat for us to eat out anywhere. My aunt was single, but she had a good job so she could buy us clothes and things. She didn't have any children, and my mother had five. Then, just as we were about to get in the car, my father, who had been sleeping, looked out of the upstairs bedroom window and asked if we had finished all of our housework. Of course, I had not finished all of my housework. There was a pile of breakfast dishes still left in the sink. Neither my aunt nor my mother said anything. I guess it was not my aunt's place to say anything, and my mother, well, she never protected me from him. I hate her just as much," Lulu said, spit coming out of her mouth and tears streaming from her eyes. "She didn't do a goddamn thing," Lulu sobbed.

"Go on, Lilly," Dr. Carmichael said.

"He said I couldn't go. My aunt said she'd bring me back something, and they all got into her car and drove away. My father was watching, and he told me to come upstairs. I still had the dress on. I walked upstairs, and I was afraid. He was always doing mean things to me. He was always beating me. I have scars on my body from where he beat me with an electrical cord," Lulu sobbed. Dr. Carmichael was silent.

"Anyway, I walked up the stairs. He was standing in the doorway of his bedroom. He was wearing one of those t-shirts, you know, the ones without arms, and he was in his under shorts. 'Get in here,' he said, and shut the bedroom door behind him. I did not know what to expect. If anything, I thought that he would beat me for not having done the dishes. Instead, he told me to take off the dress. I was so used to taking orders from him, I started to take the dress off, but it zipped in the back, and I couldn't unzip it myself. He saw that, and he came behind me and pulled down the zipper.

I could feel him breathing heavily behind me. I pulled the dress over my head and I used it to cover my breasts. I had on big white cotton panties, and I was ashamed. He told me to turn around, and I did. He pulled the dress from my hands and threw it on the floor. I almost started to tell him to stop, but I didn't. I stood there and stared at the dress on the floor. He put his hand on my breast, and I froze. He lowered his mouth to it, and I pushed him away. He slapped my face, pushed me on the bed, and held his hand over my mouth. He got on top of me. I was still trying to prevent him from taking off my panties, and he pushed my hands away. I fought with him, but he was stronger, and pulled them to the bottom of my legs. He then kneeled down on the floor and put his head between my legs. I was looking down at him, and all that I could see was his pink tongue against the blackness of his face. I tried to push his head away, but he was huffing and puffing. I guess he was pulling his underwear off. He held me down with one hand, and as he got up his underwear was off and his penis was hard.

He kept saying over and over, 'you've done this before, you've done this before.' He put spit on his hand, and then he crouched his body over me and stuck his penis in." Lulu sobbed and shook her head.

"When he was done, he told me to go wash myself. I got up, and there was greenish-looking come and blood on his penis. I raised myself from the bed and bent over to pull up my panties. They were torn around the waistband, and I held them up around me. I covered my breasts and tried not to look at him as I left the room. The dress was still in a ball on the floor. I picked it up and ran out of the room. I went into my room, held the dress to my chest, and wept—as if it could comfort me." Lulu continued to cry softly, and Dr. Carmichael looked at her.

"Was that the only time, Lilly?" She asked.

"No," Lulu croaked. "It happened a lot over the next two years." Dr. Carmichael was silent. She waited until Lulu's tears had subsided.

Lulu looked up at her and tried to holds back her tears. "I'm not well, am I, Dr. Carmichael?"

"Lilly, there is so much to say. Yes, you were victimized at that time, but you don't have to remain a victim. You will need a lot of help. You're very brave. You've been holding a lot inside and hiding for a long time. It's time to let Lilly come out from wherever she went all those years ago. You will find the help that you need; we can only help with the symptoms, Lilly. The symptoms are your drug use. They are only the tip of the iceberg. I'm sorry for what has happened to you. I'm sorry that your ex-husband has chosen this time to seek custody of the children. We'll help you as much as we can."

There was silence in the room, and neither woman said anything for some time. Finally, Lulu broke the silence. "I have ten minutes before group is over and lunch starts. What should I do?"

"You may sit here until lunch is served, or you may join your group for the last ten minutes, whatever it is you need to do. What do you need to do?"

Lulu turned confused eyes to Dr. Carmichael. "You're actually asking me what I need to do. Not what I think I should do, but what I need to do. Where do I look to find the answer?" Lulu asked.

"Look inside yourself," Dr. Carmichael said.

Lulu was silent for a minute. "I think I will go back to my room and wash my face. Then I will have lunch. I'm so tired; maybe I will lay down for a while." Lulu looked at Dr. Carmichael.

"Yes, it's that easy. Not always, but more often than not, you simply have to look inside. You've been looking everywhere else but inside."

"Dr. Carmichael, will I ever get well?" Lulu asked.

"I believe that you can get well, Lilly. It will take a lot of work. First, we must take away all of the things that you use right now to stop you from looking inside. The alcohol and the drugs are the first steps."

"But there's more, isn't there?"

"Yes, there is more, Lilly. You use a lot of things to hide away from yourself. You've done good work here, but it's just the beginning. It's safe in here; use it as much as you are able to. The real world awaits you out there. All the things that you left are still waiting for you. My hope is that you will have the information and the strength to help you to not to pick up that first drink, or that first joint, or that glass pipe. It will be up to you."

"What will I do with all of the people that I know who use drugs?"

"That will be up to you to decide," Dr. Carmichael said.

There was silence for another minute or two, and then Lulu rose.

"Thank you, Dr. Carmichael. Will you tell me when I need to take my urine test?"

"You're welcome, Lilly. Yes, I, or someone else, will come to fetch you."

Lulu turned and left. She sighed, and began the walk down the hall to her room.

THIRTY-ONE

After meeting with Dr. Carmichael and having lunch, Lulu went to meet with Terry Berkquist. She was emotionally tired.

"Lilly, I have checked the records, and you've had no visitors."

"That's true," Lulu admitted.

"Why has Steven not visited?"

"I don't know," Lulu said.

"No ideas? Have you spoken to him since you been in treatment?" Lulu shook her head. "All right," Terry said. "How did it end?"

"What do you mean?" Lulu asked.

"Why did you choose to seek rehab? How did your drug spree end?"

"I guess we ran out of money. And coke. And options," Lulu answered. "Somewhere in the middle of the second week of January, I put my debit card in a debit machine, and the machine took my card." Lulu started to laugh. "The scene seems so ridiculous now."

Lulu was wearing a full-length mink coat and shoes with four-inch heels. She ran down the street to the hotel, to the elevator, and down the hall to the hotel room

"Steven," she said, as she burst through the room. "The card doesn't work anymore!"

"What?" Steven replied, not really caring what she said, as he concentrated on the video that was on the television screen.

"Will you stop looking at that shit for a minute, and talk to me?" Lulu shouted.

"Shut the fuck up!" Steven said.

"You shut the fuck up!" She shouted back. "We don't have any money, and our hotel bill has got to be thousands of dollars."

"Look, we're broke. My family probably cut off the funds to my bank account. You know I failed to make my appearance at the family Christmas affair."

"What are we going to do?" Lulu asked.

"Leave," Steven said

"And go where?"

"I don't know yet," Steven said, still engrossed in the pornographic video on the television screen.

"I knew that I was not going to get his attention," Lulu continued, looking at Terry. "Steven is addicted to pornography and prostitutes. I am embarrassed now as I recall our sexual acts with prostitutes. They were all tall and blonde, which didn't help my self-worth. I'm brown and five feet, five inches. At first I had wept, and asked Steven if I was not enough for him. When Steven did not answer, I had gotten into a terrible funk. Steven continued to invite the prostitutes to the hotel suite, where we smoked coke with them. These women would do anything he asked. It didn't matter how humiliating or unhygienic it might be. They were addicted, and high on crack cocaine.

Steven paid these women thousands of dollars to perform lewd, unthinkable acts with him, as I jealously watched. Sometimes, he asked me to wear leather corsets and shoes with six-inch heels and dog collars, and to participate in sexual acts with some of these women. I felt worthless, cheap, and debased, but drank straight vodka and worried how I could recapture Steven's attention.

We actually went to strip clubs, and I had tried to learn to strip as the girls there had. But Steven was no longer interested in me. That day, as I stood trying to get his attention about the debit card, I realized that I had just been a temporary interest in a game, a game he had played for a long time."

Lulu stood and watched as Steven was mesmerized by the two women on the video. He turned and saw her watching him watch the video.

"Will you stop staring at me?" Steven grumbled. "Go do something. Go pack."

"So we're going to walk out of the hotel?"

"As soon as you put your lovely things in your suitcase."

"Do you have any plans after we skip out on our hotel bill?"

"Yeah, I'll get the car."

"Did we not pay at the Four Seasons?" She asked.

Steven laughed. "What, are you a detective now?"

"No, it's just that these hotels have been put on my debit card."

"And my money has been put in your account," Steven snapped.

"Well, something is wrong!" Lulu yelled back.

"Get packed!" Steven snarled, and grabbed a red blowtorch that one of the prostitutes had brought over as a present. Steven picked up the torch and the pipe. He inhaled deeply, and put the pipe on the table.

"Aren't you going to pass me the pipe?" Lulu asked.

"Come get it, it's here," Steven grumbled.

"Do I have to light it with that torch?" She asked.

"Does your cute little gold lighter work anymore?" Steven asked.

"You know it doesn't," she said.

"Okay, come get the pipe and the blow torch." She walked in front of the television screen and picked up the pipe. She took a rock from the almost-empty baggie on the coffee table and put it in the pipe. She inhaled, and then sat down next to Steven. Together, they watched the video. Neither said anything to the other. They passed the pipe between them, and kept the blowtorch lit. They were so exhausted that they both fell asleep.

Sometime later that evening, Steven and Lulu awoke. They were exhausted from staying up for days, and were shocked that so much of the day had slipped by. They had to sneak out of the hotel, so they quickly packed their suitcases. Steven went to get the car, and a few minutes later, Lulu followed with the luggage. Fortunately, they had kept the keys to Lulu's car, and would not need the valet to bring it around. When Lulu got to the floor where the car was parked, Steven started the engine. She opened the passenger side of the car and hoisted the suitcases into the back seat.

Steven said, "no, put them in the trunk."

"You put them in the trunk!" Lulu snapped back.

"Oh, shit," Steven said. "I forgot you are a fucking princess wannabe." He opened the car door, pulled out the suitcases, and put them in the trunk.

"Did you leave the torch in the hotel room?" Steven asked.

"No, it's in your suitcase," Lulu said.

"Oh, fuck, are you dumb!" Steven said.

"What? What did I do?"

"The torch. We have to cross the border."

"I didn't think about it," she said.

Steven opened the suitcase and took the torch out. He walked over to a trashcan and threw the torch away. He got back inside the car. "We have enough gas to get to Everett. We'll spend the night there."

"Everett?"

"What, Everett not good enough for you?"

"No, it's just that we were so close, why not go to Bellevue?"

"Because we're going to regroup in Everett where no one knows us. Tomorrow, I'll see what I can do about some money, but for now, we're in Everett, unless you have some money."

"I might have a child support check," she said.

"How much was that for?" Steven asked.

"A few hundred dollars."

"Good. That will give us enough coke for about a half a day."

"A half a day?" Lulu asked.

"Honey, we were smoking about a grand a day."

"Oh, my God," she said.

"If we don't get some cash, we'll have to take stuff to the pawn shops."

"Pawn shops?" she asked.

"Yes. They take everything from CD's and televisions, to computers and gold. You're going to have to ante something up to this party," Steven said, as he pulled the car out of the underground parking lot. Fortunately, the guest-parking card still worked. Steven drove the car at the speed limit, hoping not to attract attention.

When they were on a main street, he sped to the freeway, and to the U.S. border.

Before they got to the U.S.-Canadian border, Steven pulled the car over at a gas station. "Comb your hair and re-do your lipstick."

"Why?"

"We're crossing the border late at night. We have enough crack to put us in jail for a long time. We're going to take a hit before we get to the border, and then throw the pipe away. I want you to take the rest of the stuff in the baggie and stick it down your pants."

"What?"

"You heard me. Stick the rest of the stuff as flat as you can in your panties." When Lulu continued not to comprehend what Steven was saying, he said, "the choices are, we dump the crack, or we keep it in the suitcase, or you hide it."

"But, why me?"

"Because the border guard is likely to be a man, and if you look nice enough, he will buy the fact that we have been on a vacation. But if you look high and messed up, he might question us."

"All right," Lulu said. "Give me a hit, and then I'll go and clean up."

"Sure," Steven said, and got the pipe. He put a large rock in the pipe, and lit it with a book of matches. He handed the pipe over to Lulu, who sucked as if her life depended on it.

Steven took the pipe back, took a hit, and handed it back to her. She inhaled until the rock had disintegrated, and then handed it back to Steven. He took a last hit, and dumped the pipe in a trashcan. He walked back to the car, and handed her the remains of the drug. She took it from him, and put it in her purse. She got out of the car and went to the lady's restroom. When she returned, her hair was slicked back in a ponytail, and her makeup was freshly applied. She got back into the car, and smiled at Steven.

"You look good," he said.

"Thanks," she smiled.

"Now, when we cross the border, the guard will ask you your country of origin; just say the United States. Don't say anything crazy, like the Sea of Cortez."

"Okay," she nodded.

"The guard will then ask the purpose of our visit. Answer vacation."

"Got that," she said.

"Finally, he will ask you if you bought any gifts, or things for yourself. Answer no. He will ask you how long we have been in Canada. Just say a few days."

"All right, got it," she said.

Steve pulled the car out from the gas station, and drove the speed limit to the border. The border guard asked all the questions that Steven had said he would. They managed to cross the border without arousing suspicion. A few miles south of the Canadian border, Steven pulled the car over, and Lulu took the baggie from her underwear. They both laughed, relieved to have crossed the border. Steven even made a joke when she took the crack from out of her underwear.

"Now you know why they call it crack," he laughed. It took Lulu a second, but then she laughed as well. They were only sad that they did not have a pipe so that they could celebrate the border crossing.

They drove an hour to the city of Everett, Washington, which was an hour north of Bellevue. They pulled into a Harmony Inn, and Steven went into register them while Lulu waited in the car. When Steven returned, he told her to get out of the car, but not to take the suitcases. "We won't need them," Steven said.

The following morning, Steven gave Lulu another check to cash, and she wobbled into a Bank of America. When she got to the window, the teller refused to accept the check. "Ms. St. Blanc," the teller said. "I think you should see the manager." Before the woman could say more, Lulu took the check and rushed out of the bank.

She was relieved to see that Steven had the car waiting for her. She got into the car and said to Steven, "They won't take the check. The teller told me to see the manager." She was shaking all over.

"Okay," Steven sighed.

"Steven," Lulu said. "I really need a hit. I feel awful."

"I know. We'll drive into the CD to get a new pipe."

"All the way to the CD to get a pipe?"

"They don't sell them just anywhere."

"Alright, let's go," she said.

After they bought a pipe, they headed to a Motel Six in Kirkland. Steven got on the phone and made a few calls.

"I called in a favor," Steven said. "I'll be back."

"How long will you be gone?" Lulu asked.

"Just for a few hours. Don't worry, I'll be back, and I'll leave you the pipe, honey."

"Thanks," she said, relieved.

Steven left, and, unbeknownst to Lulu, went to her apartment. He made sure that there was no one lurking about, and then went inside. He got a few bags and boxes and began to put things inside. He took jewelry, her computer, and other expensive items. When he was finished, he got into the car and drove to downtown Bellevue to pawn them. He got about seven hundred dollars. He put gas in the car, and, while at the gas station, he called Buddy Oz. After the call, he headed towards the Central District.

By the time Steven returned, it was dark. Lulu sat staring at the television. She had smoked most of the crack that Steven had left. Steven took the baggie of rocks out of his pocket, and dropped it on the hotel dresser.

"Thank god!" she said. "I'm glad you're back."

"Me too," Steven said.

"I'm starving," she told him.

"Take another hit," he replied, opening the baggie of crack. "Where's the pipe?"

"Here," she said, sliding the pipe and an ashtray from beneath the bed.

"You're hiding the pipe?" Steven asked.

"You never know who will walk by," she said.

Steven laughed, and took the pipe.

Lulu sighed. "That scenario repeated itself over and over, with Steven selling my things when we ran out of crack. Even more embarrassing was that he started to take back clothes that he had purchased for me, and getting Nordstrom to take it all back for cash. The store is known to take almost anything back, worn or otherwise.

I knew, once there was nothing left for me to sell, that Steven would do whatever he had done before. There were probably lots of other women before me that he had wined and dined and gotten high, and left when there was nothing else to give or take.

One night, he brought a woman named Amber to my apartment. We couldn't pay for hotel rooms anymore; I guess we never could, or did. He left with Amber, and I panicked, cried, and screamed. Finally, I sat on a chair in my bedroom and pondered whether I should kill myself. I took some pills to sleep, and then fell into my bed, not knowing whether I would wake up or not. I did awake, early in the morning. I got down on my knees, and prayed to God to save me, and to free me from the addiction of cocaine. I bargained that I would always be faithful to Him, if I could just get better. I called my sister, Iris. She set up and paid for my rehab here."

Tears streamed down Lulu's face. "We sold more of my things. I was so sick, so thin and malnourished. I knew that I was going to die. I think he realized how really ill I was. We borrowed some money from a woman he knew. She also gave us some candy bars. We bought gas, and we drove here."

"Why didn't Steven check himself in as well?"

"No money. I don't know. Maybe he thought he didn't need it. Didn't want to, I'm not sure." Lulu was silent. Then, she said, "my roommate is gone. She didn't say goodbye. Did something happen?" Lulu asked.

"Pamela is being transported to Purdy women's prison to serve a four-year sentence for assault with a deadly weapon."

"You are kidding, right?"

"No," Terry answered.

"And Michie?" Lulu asked.

"Also taken to the women's correctional facility."

"It's all so sad," she continued.

"Lilly, you go home in a couple of days. Are you ready?"

"I don't know. I'm afraid."

"Of what?" Terry asked.

"Of everything," Lulu answered.

THIRTY-TWO

It was the last day of February, and the morning was bright, cold, and crisp. Lulu had gained ten pounds in the three weeks of rehab, so she was wearing a pair of jeans for which she had traded another patient, a larger size that would fit her body. She stood in the lobby of the rehab facility and waited for her former client, Fiona Winters, to arrive. It had been a complete surprise to Lulu when Ms. Winters had called her at the rehab facility. She was even more surprised when Fiona offered to drive Lulu back to Seattle from Yakima. Fiona had explained to Lulu that her father had been killed at the hands of a drunk driver, and that she had dedicated her life to combating addiction, and to helping others who were afflicted by it. More than this, Fiona felt that it was her Christian duty to help Lulu, especially since it appeared that many of her former friends had turned against her.

At eleven o' clock, Fiona's Black Mercedes turned into the center's driveway, and pulled to a stop in front of the entryway. The elegant blonde woman turned the car's engine off, and got out of the car. For a few moments, the women looked at each other, each uncomfortable and not knowing what to say. Lulu broke the awkward silence by stepping forward, and saying, "thank you, Fiona, I am so grateful that you have come to take me home."

"You're welcome," Fiona said. "Do you need help with your suitcase?"

"No," Lulu said. "I'll get it and put it in the back seat."

"That will be fine," Fiona said, and she watched Lulu walk back into the lobby where patients were already milling around, waiting for lunch to be served. When the suitcase was in the car, the two women drove in silence through the gates of the center. They drove through the mountainous area, which was still covered in snow. Slowly the car twisted downwards through the mountains, and past the farms on either side of the road.

"Why did you want to help me?" Lulu finally asked.

"I hope that if I were in your situation, someone would help me," Fiona answered.

"Was that it?"

"Does there need to be more?" Fiona asked.

"I guess not," Lulu answered.

"Look, Lulu, you will find that people who have been in recovery for a while are willing to help people newly in recovery. Most people have been where you are. We got to wherever we are currently with the help of other alcoholics. I'm not in recovery, if that's what you want to ask. More than all of that, I believe in you, and I know that you are, and will continue to be, a fine lawyer. You did a good job with my case before you got really ill. You need help. Things are not going to be easy for you. The first thing I guess I should tell you is that you have been evicted from your apartment."

"Oh no, how could Janine do that to me?"

"I don't mean to burst your bubble any further, but I know Janine Zimmerman. In my opinion she is not what she appears to be. I believe she can be calculating and cruel if she feels she has been crossed."

"But she's been so nice to me!"

"I'll cut to the chase. She's a closet lesbian. She's been interested in you. She's been trying to groom you all of these years."

"I don't believe that," Lulu argued.

"Believe what you will; it's not important. You will find an eviction notice on your apartment door when you get there. Your apartment is a complete wreck. There are burns on the carpet, but that's just for starters. I think you'll find some of your items missing."

"What are you talking about?" Lulu asked her anxiety level rising.

"You know Steven's in jail?"

"Yes, I talked to his aunt and to his sister."

"Did they give you any details?"

"Not really."

"Steven has a history of domestic violence, as well as an arrest record. He's been in and out of trouble since he was in his teens. He is a drug fiend. He cleans up well, but he'll never have a good chance of recovery. He tells too many lies to himself and other people. He doesn't even know what the truth is anymore. The Bellevue police arrested him as he was trying to leave the apartment complex in your car. In the back seat, they found your stereo equipment and other items. They charged him with theft, and violation of his probation."

"How do you know all of this?"

"Your ex-husband approached me, and asked me to write an affidavit regarding your handling of my case. I told him that you had done a good job for me, and that anything that I would write would be positive. He suggested that I take a look at what some of the other people had written about you. The police report and Steven's police record are a part of the information which he was submitting to the court at the temporary hearing in two days."

"What other people wrote affidavits against me?"

"Well, Janine Zimmerman, for one."

"Janine?"

"Yes, I have a copy of the paperwork. You can read it for yourself."

"Where is it?"

"Back at my house."

"Who else wrote about me?"

"Your ex-boyfriend, Lorenzo, and Catherine Connors."

"Lorenzo and Catherine? What do either of them know about me?"

"Lorenzo wrote about his drug experiences with you, and Catherine provided the court with her professional opinion of the mental state of the children."

"That's ridiculous. Catherine has lost her license to practice as a social worker. And Lorenzo, that woman-hating bum!"

"The 'woman-hating bum' that you went out with."

Lulu wrung her hands. "I can't believe this."

"You better start believing what I'm telling you. You've made a lot of people angry, especially your ex-husband. You have a court appearance in two days. I think you know that, don't you?"

"Yes, I know," Lulu answered.

"I will try to help you as much as I can. You can stay at my place. I don't think you should stay at your apartment right now. For one thing, it is filthy beyond belief. For another thing, I think that you will be depressed. You can fight the eviction, if you're up to it, but right now, I think you should concentrate on your court appearance. Do you have a suit to wear to court?"

"I think that I can find something to wear to court, but I don't feel as if I'm capable of even pulling the covers over my head and going to back to bed," Lulu said.

"That's better than taking a drink," Fiona said.

"Thanks, but both are forms of denial. At least sleeping won't kill me."

"That's right," Fiona said. They laughed, then Lulu asked Fiona, "What else do you know about Steven Flaherty?"

"Besides the fact that he is bad news?"

"Yes, like, what happened after I left?"

"He ran your place as if it were a party den. Lulu, there were reports of women coming and going. I know you think that you care for him, but he does not care for you. The police were called in because of complaints about noise, and people coming and going all hours of the night and morning. Lulu, you need to stay away from Steven."

"He's in jail. I can't exactly see him, now can I?"

"He'll get out of jail. His family is rich and powerful. He'll be out of jail as soon as he completes his mandatory thirty days for violation of his last probation."

"What exactly does his family do?"

"He's one of heirs to Allied Canadian Lumber Company."

"Jeez, and he's a drug addict."

"What do you mean by that?"

"I don't know. It seems that someone who has everything would choose something else besides drugs."

"It's funny that you would say that, because there's a lot people who think you have or had it all, and look at you."

"I guess you're right," Lulu said.

"Are you hungry?" Fiona asked.

"These days? Always," Lulu laughed.

"You still look pretty thin to me," Fiona said. "There's a little town up ahead. Let's pull off the highway, and see what's down there."

THIRTY-THREE

In Seattle, David Hughes and his girlfriend, Verna, were having a heated argument about Lulu. David had just received the letter from her, and was wondering whether he should call off the hearing until Lulu had more time out of rehab.

"What are you trying to do?" Verna shrieked. "Give her a chance to get on her feet?"

Verna could not forget meeting Lulu two years ago, when Lulu, wearing a lush fur coat, had come to pick up the children from David's house. Lulu had thought that Verna was a maid David had hired to help him with the children. Lulu had offered her a twenty-dollar bill as a tip for coming in on a holiday to help David. At the time, Verna had been too stunned to make it clear that she was not hired help, but David's new girlfriend. Verna had never forgotten that incident, and now that she had an opportunity to get back at Lulu, she was going to take it.

"No, it's just that I think the court may think the timing of this is ugly and unfair. After all, I served her at a rehab facility. There's a lot of people on the bench who are recovering alcoholics. I just don't want this to look so unfair. She's kind of a tragic figure with her history."

"Tragic, my ass! She's beautiful, smart, and had a wealthy husband and two children. She threw it all away. No one but you, David, feels sorry for her. She's got you under some kind of spell."

"I'm under no spell; I just want the appearance of fairness, that's all. I think it will serve me better in the long run."

"Let the judges decide whether it's fair or not. This is war. The children are at stake."

"But the children love her," David said.

"No, they don't. They don't know any better. They think they have to take care of her. They feel responsible for her. They don't love her."

"Verna, she is their mother."

"So what? That's just biology! Has she been a mother to them? I don't think so. She's a nasty, self-centered, egotistical woman who thinks a lot more of herself than is warranted."

"She's still their mother."

"And just what does that mean? That she gets to damage the children while we stand by? She lives with a drug addict that she's going to expose them to, that she *has* exposed them to. These are the rights that she had as a mother? I don't think so, David. She writes a silly letter from her treatment facility, and all of a sudden you go soft. Where's your head? You go soft now, and she will get those children back. Is that what you want?"

"No," David said. "No."

"Then you should call your lawyer and tell him that you want to go ahead with the hearing in the next two days. Let the judge decide what's fair and what's not fair. "

"All right," David said, and walked to the phone.

In downtown Seattle, in the tallest building in the city, Steven Riesman was writing a legal brief. Attached to the legal brief was a series of subpoenas issued to every physician, mental health worker, or therapist that Lulu had been treated by within the past six years. On Riesman's desk was another stack of subpoenas; these were issued to the various banks that Lulu had had financial transactions with within the past several years.

Riesman was hunched over his computer. He was a thin, rat-like man who dressed as if he wished to fade into the dun-colored wallpaper of his office. The lawyer's hair was the same dusty brown of a field mouse. His skin was mottled, and hinted at ancestors who were once dark. He wore a brown suit and a white shirt, and a brown and cream tie.

But if this man's dress and appearance were dull, his mind certainly was not. Riesman had a brilliant mind, and had done exceedingly well in law school. Because he was so non-descript and completely without a personality, no law firm had offered him a job. He had started out on his own, and had made himself a reputation of being a lawyer that performed meticulous work. With every case he took on, there was no issue left unaddressed. He was also known to be a man who was so committed to whoever had hired him, that he was completely focused on that person's issue without regard to fairness to the other side. He, like David Hughes, was a man who was able to carry out unpleasant tasks without blinking an eye, as long as he had agreed to do the work. It was this man, Steven Riesman, who David was going to call to tell him to go ahead with the hearing in the next two days.

In still another part of Seattle, a heavy-set, red-haired woman with large green eyes was pacing the floor in front of a fireplace. It was Janine Zimmerman. She was in the living room of her Lake Washington home. She was dressed in a dark green wool dress. Wrapped around her shoulders was a shawl with large purple designs that picked up the same green color as her dress. On her small feet, she wore moss-colored suede shoes with delicate suede flowers at the top. On her short, stubby fingers, she twisted a large ring, whose yellowish stone sparkled in the mid-morning sun.

As the woman paced the floor, which was covered with rich red carpets, she talked to herself. Janine was also waiting for a phone call from David Hughes. She was scheduled to fly to Idaho the next morning and would not be returning for a few days, but she would cancel her trip if necessary in order to testify against Lulu.

Janine had learned that Lulu would be released from the treatment facility that morning. She needed to find out if David knew whether Lulu would return to her apartment. Janine needed to serve Lulu the eviction notice. She had had the sheriff's department put yellow police tape across the front door and attach an eviction notice, but that was not going to be enough. She had to personally serve Lulu.

Janine shook her head, as if to clear it. Lulu was such a stupid woman when it came to people. It was almost paradoxical how someone could be so book-smart, but people-stupid. Lulu was so unaware that she had missed all of her overtures towards her, some of which were so blatant that even Lulu's children had sensed that there was an unusual affection between Janine and their mother. The youngest child, Christopher, had even suggested that Janine was a man. Even then, Lulu had not understood what her six-year-old son had figured out.

Janine felt that her generosity towards Lulu and her children had been betrayed. How could Lulu think that her generosity was not to be paid back in some form? Damn it, if she were a man who had displayed such kindness towards Lulu, Lulu would have gotten the picture. Why had Lulu not realized that Janine was wooing her when she lavished her with gifts, and dinners in nice restaurants? Did Lulu think that Janine took every law student out to dinner to fine restaurants because they were law students? And what about the trips that Janine had invited Lulu on? Janine stopped her pacing to make a written note on a tablet on her desk, reminding herself that the blue silk blouse that she had bought as a Christmas present for Lulu this year needed to be returned to the store. How could Lulu be so blind? Had she not made it clear that she desired her? For a few minutes, Janine stopped her pacing. What was it that Lulu had told her a few weeks ago? That she would look a lot younger if she lost a few pounds? The comment had incensed Janine. Didn't the foolish young woman know that she ate because she could not get what she really yearned for? She would punish the little airhead.

"How dare she call me fat?" Janine fumed. "Silly little piece of—"

The phone rang, and Janine grabbed the receiver with claw-like hands.

THIRTY-FOUR

In downtown Seattle, almost directly across the street from the courthouse, was the county jail. In a non-cell area, Steven Flaherty sat wearing an orange prison jumpsuit, signifying that he was a violent offender. He was waiting in line to use the public telephone. On his feet were blue flip-flops. His normally well-trimmed red hair was curling at the ends. His fingernails were dirty, and his eyes were wide open and staring. Steven had learned that Lulu was being released from treatment that day, and he wanted his sister to send her flowers. Steven impatiently jiggled his legs. He almost laughed out loud. The jail was a joke. He could get almost anything inside the jail that he could outside. The inmates knew he had money, and were willing to trust him until he got out—and he would get out.

In his own way, Steven felt that he cared for Lulu. She was pretty and smart. She was also a lawyer, and he felt that would always be handy. He was not sure how much Lulu knew about what had happened after she had entered treatment. Whatever she had heard, Steven would simply deny it, and attribute the information to the jealousy of the teller of the tale. He had found that this strategy always worked on women, especially if they wanted to believe something other than the truth.

The real question he had to ask himself was whether Lulu was worth cultivating. It really came down to a matter of dollars. He had screwed up Lulu's life. Her car was not working. He had pawned a lot of her valuable art and jewelry when his family caught on to the fact that he was using again. Maybe all he owed her was a few thousand dollars, but he still felt bad about how quickly Lulu had crashed and burned. She was certainly not cut out to be a hardcore user. She was a nice person; naive, but nice. He owed her something. How much, and what, would depend on what he could extract from his mother's large checkbook.

The inmate in front of him had gotten off the phone. Steven grabbed it and placed a collect call to his sister's phone. He waited a few moments while the operator got approval for the call, and then, in what would have been an award-winning performance, he began to cry into the receiver. Real tears streamed down his face, and his voice caught in his throat. By the time the call was automatically disconnected within ten minutes, Steven's mother, who had happened to be with his sister, said, "get him out of there. I don't care what it takes." An hour later, a bouquet of white lillies was sent to Lulu's apartment. The flowers would be waiting for her when she arrived later that afternoon.

THIRTY-FIVE

The smell of urine and feces permeated the morning air. Lulu's hands shook as she pulled the car into a parking space on the street. Her heart was beating rapidly, and she could feel sweat forming under her armpits. Her shaking hands searched for the keys to the car, and her legs shook as she stepped onto the street. "Dear Lord, help me," she prayed. She fumbled in her purse, and found four quarters. It was probably not going to be enough for the time she would be in court, but that was all that she had. She put the quarters into the meter. She smoothed her hair, and began the two-block walk to the courthouse.

Lulu averted her eyes as she walked past people wearing dirty, ragged clothes. Some were still sleeping, wrapped in old sheets on cardboard boxes. Bleary-eyed men and women with alcohol-swollen lips and faces swayed down the street, held up only by some miraculous form of balance. Girls whose faces were heavily made-up, with thick, black lines contouring their eyes, and purplish-red lipstick accentuating battered lips, sashayed past the drunks laying on the grassy area next to the courthouse. Finally, at the Fourth Street entrance of the courthouse, Lulu sighed with relief, and silently thanked God that her drug experience had not taken her to the same depths as the people she had just passed.

She pushed her way through the revolving door to the courthouse. She put her purse on the belt to be x-rayed, and she walked through the metal detector. The Fourth Street entrance to the courthouse was actually the second floor. The King County courthouse had two entrances. One on Third and James, and the other on Fourth and James. The Third Street entrance was on the first floor, but, since the building was built on a hill, the Fourth Street entrance was on the second floor. The Family Law Calendar, where Lulu's case was scheduled to be heard that morning, was on the third floor of the courthouse.

Four small courtrooms surrounded a large central seating area. About twenty people could comfortably sit in each of the four small courtrooms. In years to come, when the volume of family law cases grew too great for the small court rooms on the third floor, it was transferred to the second floor, where there were three large court rooms which could easily hold at least one hundred people. There, the family law cases were heard for many years, until a major earthquake damaged the building, forcing the need for enhanced structural support. Then, the family law cases were moved to the eighth floor.

By the time Lulu reached the third floor, her mouth was dry, and she desperately needed a drink of water. She looked for a water fountain, but could not find one. Instead, she stopped in front of a large easel where the legal participants' names were written. Lulu scanned the board for her name, and saw that her case was to be heard towards the end of the calendar. There were thirteen cases to be heard before hers. She also noted that the Commissioner hearing her case was Susan Rothman. Lulu had been introduced to Commissioner Rothman when Lulu was in her third year of law school, and had voiced her interest in practicing family law. Commissioner Rothman would be sure to remember Lulu. Lulu was ashamed, because, at one time, Rothman had expressed her admiration. Lulu felt a sting of embarrassment; now the Commissioner would see her, not as a lawyer, but as a drug user in recovery. Now, Rothman would think that her admiration might have been misplaced. Rothman was also a mother, and would have to determine whether Lulu should be granted a continuance, so that she could prepare a response to her ex-husband, who was asking Rothman to remove the children from Lulu's care.

Lulu also knew that, despite the fact that Rothman had met her, it would not be enough of a reason for Rothman to recuse herself from hearing Lulu's case. Rothman's one-time meeting with Lulu would not affect Rothman's ruling in the matter. In fact, Rothman would bend over backwards to appear to be fair to both parties, even if that meant a ruling against Lulu. But Lulu was determined that no substantive ruling, meaning no ruling on the facts of the case, would be made that day. Instead, only a procedural ruling would be made; Rothman would only rule on whether service to Lulu in a treatment facility was proper. If Rothman ruled that it was proper, then the second part of the question would be whether or not Lulu had been unduly prejudiced by that service: did where and how she was served allow her the means to effectively respond to her ex-husband's desire to remove the children from her custody?

As Lulu entered the central seating area, she saw her former husband, his girlfriend, Janine Zimmerman, and what appeared to be her attorney and David's attorney, Steven Riesman. Lulu stopped for a moment. She saw Janine confer with her attorney, and then the man got up, and walked towards Lulu. "Miss St. Blanc?" the man asked.

"Yes," Lulu answered.

"I have some papers from Ms. Zimmerman." Lulu said nothing as the man reached inside his brief case and pulled out a sheaf of documents. He handed them to Lulu. "I'm sorry to do this, but you are hereby served with a notice of eviction."

"Thank you," Lulu said, and accepted the papers. She turned around, crossed a narrow aisle, and sat on a bench in the first row. She wanted to tear at her hair and scream. Instead, she pretended to read the documents, but the words on the paper swam before her eyes as they filled with tears. As she lowered her head, tears fell from her eyes and smeared the ink on the heavy stationary. The reality of her eviction hit her. She would have no home in which she could live with her children. The court would take this information into consideration. Janine had almost insured that the court would award David temporary custody of the children, since Lulu had no home in which to house them. She would have to get a place where she and the children could live before the next hearing, but, for the moment, she had to pull herself together to face Rothman and Riesman. She could not cry before the Commissioner, and the gallery of other attorneys who would be in the courtroom. The only way for her to regain any semblance of her career was to make a strong appearance. The continuation of her ability to practice law was her fastest way to make money, so that she could find an apartment for herself and her children. She breathed slowly and deeply to calm her rapidly-beating heart, and to diminish the truth of the precarious position in which she had placed herself. She pushed this reality from the center of her thoughts, but it still gnawed at the edges of her consciousness.

Minutes later, the court's bailiff opened the doors to each courtroom, and Lulu watched while David and Verna, accompanied by Riesman, walked into the courtroom. Janine and her attorney had risen, but Lulu could hear that Janine was dismissing her attorney, for he had already done his work. Janine then entered the courtroom, and sat next to Verna. Lulu watched while Janine's red head turned conspiratorially towards Verna's curly, reddish-brown head. The two exchanged brief words, and then both quietly laughed. The light, happy laughter of the two women frightened Lulu even further. If Lulu could have run away, she would have, but she could not. The bailiff was already announcing the arrival of the Commissioner, and Lulu got up from the bench on power that must have been extraterrestrial, and walked to the courtroom to sit in the last row, while Commissioner Rothman ordered the gallery to be seated.

"This is first call of the court calendar. Will each party please state if both parties are present, and if we are ready to proceed? The first case is Christian v. Conway."

Rothman continued calling the names of the litigants. Finally, she said, "St. Blanc v. Hughes."

"The Petitioner in the matter is present, Your Honor, with counsel," Riesman said.

"The Respondent is present," Lulu stood, and managed to croak.

Rothman continued with the list of the names of the parties scheduled to be heard that morning. The first few cases were domestic violence cases. Many of the parties were unrepresented, and the victims were accompanied by a facilitator from the Domestic Violence Prevention Unit. These cases, unless there were children involved, were usually dispatched quickly. Rothman granted a restraining order, if she felt there was enough evidence that the person requesting the order could be in danger from the person being asked to be restrained. If the Commissioner felt that there was not enough evidence, or that one party was using the court system to keep a parent away from a child, the restraining order was usually denied, and the matter was sent to Family Court Services. Family Court Services would investigate the matter, and report to the court.

At the conclusion of the domestic violence portion of the calendar, Rothman held a second calling of the calendar. Any party who was not present at the second calling was stricken from the calendar. Those litigants would have to re-file their petitions to the court, and reschedule their hearings.

One by one, Rothman heard each of the petitions before her. She began each proceeding by saying, "Counselors, I have read your paperwork. Please proceed. You each have five minutes, and I will hold you to five minutes. You may reserve a portion of that time for rebuttal."

Each litigant, if not represented by an attorney, would state their case before the Commissioner. Litigants were limited as to what they could tell the Commissioner by what they had written in their paperwork. Therefore, no new information could be brought before the court. A litigant, or his or her attorney, could clarify or expound on certain issues of what had been presented in the written documents, but that was all.

It was after eleven o' clock when Commissioner Rothman would finally hear St. Blanc v. Hughes. Normally, the person requesting an action from the court was called the Petitioner. The person who respondeed to the Petitioner, and informed the court on why he or she should not be granted what they were asking for, was called the Respondent. Since Lulu had been the Petitioner in the divorce case between herself and David, she remained the Petitioner, and David the Respondent, although now David was the Petitioner in a motion to modify the parenting plan that had been in place for five years.

Normally, it was very difficult to modify a parenting plan and especially difficult to change the custodial parent. However, Lulu had damaged her chances of retaining custody of the children by her drug use and increased the chances of her losing custody by being evicted from her apartment. For now, Lulu could not even argue the concept of stability. She could say that the children had been living in their home with her for four years, and that a change of residences would be difficult for them, but she also would be moving the children to a new residence. If the court had to choose between a two-bedroom apartment and David's luxurious home, it would not be difficult to see which new home would be better for the children. But these issues would come later; today, all Lulu wanted was a continuance, and an opportunity to see her children.

Rothman began the preceding by noting that the court had not received a response to the petition filed by Riesman. Lulu spoke up. "Your Honor, I was just released from a drug and alcohol facility two days ago. I was served with this matter while I was in treatment. I am here to ask for a continuance."

Commissioner Rothman took off her glasses, and looked over to where Riesman and his client were standing. "Counsel, is this true, what the Respondent is contending?"

"Yes, Your Honor, it is true, but Ms. St. Blanc..."

But before Riesman could finish whatever he was going to say, Rothman struck her gavel sharply against the wood of her dais. "Mr. Riesman, please answer the question. Was Ms. St. Blanc served while she was in a treatment facility?"

"Yes, Your Honor," Riesman said.

"Ms. St. Blanc, how much of a continuance would you like?"

"A month, Your Honor."

"Counsel?" Rothman turned to Riesman.

"There are grave matters before the court, Your Honor. The well-being of two children is at stake. A month is simply too long to hold over this matter. We would ask that Ms. St. Blanc be given a week. Your honor, may I advise the court that Ms. St. Blanc is a licensed attorney in the state of Washington?"

"The court acknowledges the information, and, Mr. Riesman, the court also acknowledges that Ms. St. Blanc's bar number is so new, that it is of little value. All right, here is the court's ruling. Mr. Riesman, you may re-submit your documents to Ms. St. Blanc, and I'll see everybody back here in two weeks."

"But, Your Honor, I can't prepare a response in two weeks. And what about my children? I haven't seen my children in over a month," Lulu said.

"Counselor, you cannot have it both ways." Rothman turned her glare on Lulu. "Either we are granting a continuance, or we hear this matter on its merits. And since you have submitted no paperwork, I suggest that you accept a continuance, and find yourself an attorney." At Rothman's words, Lulu deflated.

"Please appear back in two weeks. Mr. Riesman, would you please draft the order and bring it to me before Ms. St. Blanc signs it?"

"Yes, Your Honor." With those words, Rothman picked up her papers, and called the next case.

The parties left the courtroom, and Lulu once again forced herself not to moan out loud. Over and over in her mind, all that she could say to herself was, "Jesus, what have I done? What have I done?"

Riesman, his client, and Zimmerman had formed a semi-circle with their backs towards Lulu. When Lulu walked up to the group, Riesman barked at her, "Ms. St. Blanc if you don't mind, I'm conferring with my clients." Lulu jumped at the iciness of his words, and Verna tittered behind David, who towered over her.

Lulu backed off, but said nothing. She walked to the other side of the room, sat numbly on the bench, and waited while Riesman finished talking to his client. Through the glass doors, Lulu watched as the four people bent their heads close together, and Riesman appeared to be lecturing them. After a few moments, Janine kissed Verna and left the group. David reached for Verna's hand, and the two of them sat down. Moments later, Lulu could see Riesman bending over his yellow legal tablet, scratching the Commissioner's order onto a court supplied document. He arose when he was done, and re-entered the seating area, heading back into Rothman's courtroom.

"Hey," Lulu said, and Riesman halted at the sound of her voice. "Commissioner Rothman said to bring it to her before I sign it, not to bring it to her before I read it. I would like to read it, if you don't mind." Riesman stared at her.

"Sure, you can read it." Riesman handed the document to Lulu. As he did so, he smiled. Lulu managed to hold his stare for a moment, and then she began to read the document. She was keenly aware of Riesman's dislike and disrespect of her. It was true that she was a new attorney, but she was still an attorney, and Riesman owed her at least that much respect.

"So the hearing date is the fourteenth of March?"

"That's what it says, two weeks from today."

"Well, I didn't know whether you counted today or not."

"Shall we ask the judge?" Riesman asked.

"No, it's okay," Lulu answered.

Riesman walked to the front of the courtroom and stood towards the side, waiting for Rothman to conclude the hearing that was being conducted. When Rothman had finished issuing her order, Riesman handed the document to the bailiff, who handed it up to the Commissioner. Commissioner Rothman signed the document, and handed it down to her bailiff. "Mr. Riesman, make a copy of the order for Ms. St. Blanc." And with that, the Commissioner watched the young woman and the attorney walk out of the courtroom. Rothman paused a minute, took off her glasses, cleaned them, and then called the next case.

"Do you want to wait for a copy?" Riesman asked Lulu, when they were outside in the seating area.

"No, just fax it to me."

"Fax it to where?" Riesman asked.

"Here's my address, and phone and fax number," Lulu said.

"Is this your business address?" Riesman asked.

"No, it's the home of a friend, where I'm staying until I settle my affairs." Once more, Lulu heard Verna snicker, and this time Lulu looked over at the woman and gave her a contemptuous stare. Then Lulu turned and walked away from Riesman and his client.

THIRTY-SIX

Outside of the courthouse, Lulu breathed deeply. Across the street from the courthouse was the jail. Steven's sister had told Lulu that she could use her bar card to gain entrance to see Steven. Lulu stood on the steps of the courthouse, not sure of what she wanted to do. Everything that she had heard about Steven's behavior since she had left to go into treatment suggested that he was not who he purported to be. Or, perhaps it was who he said he was. She could not decide. But she was right in front of the jail. She had to talk to Steven at some point. It had best be now, while she was in the vicinity of the jail. Reluctantly, she pushed open the big green doors. Behind a screened cage sat a prison guard. He pressed a button, and his voice came over an intercom. "May I help you?"

"Yes, I am here to see Steven Flaherty."

"Are you an attorney?" the guard asked.

"Yes," Lulu answered, and pulled out her bar card. The guard pushed another button, and a tray came out from the cage. She placed her card into it, and he drew the card into his cage. He looked at it, and then asked Lulu for another piece of identification. She gave him her driver's license.

"All right," the guard said, and the tray came out one more time so that Lulu could retrieve her license and her bar card. "I'm going to press a button, and the door will open. You will pass through the metal detectors, and then take that elevator behind you to the third floor. I will alert the guards that the prisoner is to be brought down."

"Thank you," Lulu said, and went through the metal detectors. Behind her, the big green door slammed shut, and Lulu jumped at the sound. She had never been inside a jail, and there was something about the permanence of the door closing that scared her. She entered the large elevator. She waited while the oversized doors slowly slid closed, and then she pressed the button for the third floor. Slowly, the steel elevator rose, and banged to a stop on the third floor. The doors opened from behind her, and Lulu turned around to see a guard in a brown uniform, sitting behind a door with thick glass, the insides of which were crisscrossed with wire. The man's voice eerily sounded from an overhead intercom. "You are here to see...?"

"Steven Flaherty."

"Wait one moment." The guard spoke into a microphone, and said, "send prisoner 33402 down to the third floor." The guard looked at Lulu, and said, "you may sit in the waiting area." The metal doors slid open, and Lulu saw a row of bluish-green chairs lined up against a wall. Lulu nodded to the guard, and sat down.

She had only to wait a few minutes when, from an interior elevator, Steven Flaherty was escorted in by another guard. The guard stood a few inches from Steven. Steven's hands and ankles were shackled. The guard led him to a blue door with a narrow window. Steven hobbled the three or four steps to the room, which the guard opened with a key. Steven went into the room, and the guard followed. In the meantime, Lulu had risen from her seat, but neither Steven nor the guard appeared to notice her. A few minutes later, the guard exited the room. He avoided eye contact with Lulu, but said, "you have twenty minutes."

"Thank you," Lulu managed to mumble, and she walked to the room and opened the door. Steven was sitting at a little table, in one of the two chairs.

Lulu stood with her back against the door, and simply looked at Steven. His normally clean-shaven face was thick with copper-colored stubble. His hair was badly in need of a trim, and his face was puffy and red. "Aren't we a pair?" she asked, bitterly.

"Is that all that you have to say?" Steven looked up at her.

"I think you should be the one doing the talking," Lulu said.

"I'll leave right now," Steven said, and rose slightly from his chair.

"Go," Lulu said, calmly. Steven sat back down.

"What do you want me to say?"

"For starters, how about sorry?" Lulu hissed.

"About what?" Steven hurled back at her.

"For using my apartment as a party pad, for one; two, getting me evicted; three, my ex-husband seeking custody of my children. Shall I go on, Steven Flaherty?"

"You brought that on yourself," Steven sullenly replied.

"Yes, I brought on the custody issue; you simply sealed the deal by having the police called for noise, and getting me evicted."

"That place was a dump anyway," Steven said.

"But it was my dump, damn it," Lulu shot back at him. "You have a whole lot of fucking nerve to be sitting here, in your red pajamas and blue flip-flops, and tell me I used to live in a dump. Fuck you, you arrogant son of a bitch!" With this, Lulu turned to leave the room.

"Don't!" Steven cried. "Please don't go. I'm sorry. I am embarrassed for you to see me this way. Please don't go. I love you, Lilly, I really do."

Lulu looked at him. "Please don't call me Lilly. I prefer to be called Lulu. Perhaps we can start on the right foot, by you calling me what I prefer, rather than what you prefer."

"Okay. Okay," Steven said. "Didn't you just hear me tell you that I love you? Doesn't that mean anything thing to you, Li—?" Steven hesitated. Lulu could hear that he had stumbled over her name. He was going to call her Lilly, but caught himself.

"Good," she thought. She was silent for a minute. "I have learned one thing—no, let me correct myself. I have learned many things in treatment, but one thing that I did learn was that words and promises from other addicts are meaningless. We—and notice I said we—would say anything in order to get what we need at the moment. So, no, you saying that you love me means nothing. It is acts that count. So far, I consider your actions to be far from love."

They were both silent for a minute, then Steven said, "did you get the flowers?"

"Yes, I did," Lulu said, and she softened for a moment. "They were very lovely. Not what I need right now, but lovely."

"What do you need right now, Li—Lulu?" Steven asked, once again stumbling on her name.

"I need money, a place to live, a car, food. You know the basic essentials. I'd like my stuff out of the pawn shop." The anger rose in Lulu again.

"All right, I'll get those things for you. Will that make a difference, Lulu? Will that begin to show you that I care?"

"It will be a start, Steven, but only a start. I have a long way to go. I'm in deep shit. Every day that I am out here, I realize just how deep the shit is." Lulu stopped.

"I see you learned how to curse in treatment."

"I guess you could say that," Lulu said, "but I prefer to say that I am learning to express my anger. I've been angry for a real long time. I've chosen to be 'good' instead of being pissed off at all the assholes that I have come across my path in the last twenty years."

"Does that include me?" Steven asked.

"Yes," Lulu said.

"My mother wants to meet you," Steven said.

"That's just great. What did you tell her about me? That I was the lawyer that was going to help you break your trust, but instead I became a crack addict?"

"No, I told her that you are an alcoholic."

"Oh, I see. A respectable alcoholic. Steven, don't you see that it's just another camouflage, another set of lies?"

"You want her to help us, don't you?"

"Help us? What do you mean, help us?"

"I told her that I wanted to marry you when I got out."

"Steven, stop. I don't want to marry you—or anybody else, for that matter.

"Lilly, Lulu," Steven said, as he reached for her hand. "I cannot tell you how much I regret placing you in this situation. It was wrong. Please, please forgive me? Can you forgive? I swear to you, Lulu that I will spend the rest of my life making this up to you. I want to be sober, be sober for you. I'm tired of this life. I want out. I want a family, and a home and a job, and life, Lulu, a life with you." The tears streamed down Steven's face.

"Oh, Steven, please don't. Please don't."

"Please don't what? Cry? Tell you that I'm sorry? Tell you that I love you? What is it that I should 'please don't', Lulu?

"Oh, God. I'm not supposed to have any relationships for one year.

They told me that in treatment. I'm supposed to give up all the people that I used drugs with. That's damn near everybody that I know, and it's especially you, Steven. Don't you know that I will have everybody looking at me? Every lawyer, every judge who knows me, who knows I went to treatment, will be looking for signs of my drug use. Don't you think that I know that the very best thing for me is to cut you loose? Don't you know that my ex-husband will be far more lenient with me if you're out of the picture? I can't choose you over my children. Not this time, Steven. Not this time."

"Don't leave me, Lulu. Give me some hope. Everybody leaves me, Lulu. Everybody. Please don't be everybody. We can kick this together. Please let me help you. Please. You need me more than you know right now. Please, don't go off on this by yourself. You will need my help. I love you. Please, please believe me. You are my one hope, Lulu. It's you."

"Steven, you have to get sober for yourself, not me. I've going to go. Otherwise, I'm going to get a parking ticket that I can't afford right now. I've got to go."

"Don't leave without telling me where I can reach you."

"I can't accept collect calls on my friend's phone, Steven. Please, you go your way, and I'll go mine. Haven't we caused each other enough hurt?"

"Won't you please, at least, call my mother?"

"Steven, for what?"

"To get the money to get your things out of the pawn shop," Steven said, as he slipped Lulu a piece of paper with his mother's phone number.

"It's almost time for me to go."

"Please meet with my mother and my sister."

"We don't have the time to discuss this right now."

"Promise me that you will call my mother?"

"Steven, I am not making any promises to you."

"No, you have to promise me that you will call my mother. Lulu, she won't blame you. I promise you, my mother is more knowledgeable than that. Please call her. Won't you?"

Steven rose. He moved towards the door until he was only inches from Lulu. He reached over and kissed her.

"Steven, please don't," Lulu said.

"I love you," Steven said. "And I am going to make you believe that."

The guard knocked on the door. "I've got to go," Lulu said.

"Remember, I love you," Steven said. "And you look great in that blue suit."

"Thanks," Lulu said, but the guard was already opening the door and ushering her out.

As Lulu walked out of the jail and away from Steven Flaherty, she felt free. She took a deep breath, walked towards a city trashcan, and threw Steven's mother's number away. She could take care of herself. She would regain her legal career, and her children. Today was the first day of a new future.